LIONS AT
LAMB HOUSE

Edwin M. Yoder Jr.

LIONS AT LAMB HOUSE

Freud's 'Lost' Analysis of Henry James

Europa
editions

Europa Editions
116 East 16th Street
New York, N.Y. 10003
www.europaeditions.com
info@europaeditions.com

Library of Congress Cataloging in Publication Data is available
ISBN 978-1-933372-34-1

Yoder Jr., Edwin M.
Lions at Lamb House

Book design by Emanuele Ragnisco
www.mekkanografici.com

Printed in Italy
Arti Grafiche La Moderna – Rome

CONTENTS

For Theron Raines and Jonathan Yardley
and in affectionate memory of Peter Taylor

LIONS AT
LAMB HOUSE

"... The 'historic' novel is, for me, condemned, even in cases of labour as delicate as yours, to a fatal cheapness ... you have to simplify back by an amazing tour de force—and even then it's all humbug ..."

—HENRY JAMES TO SARAH ORNE JEWETT,
OCTOBER 5, 1901

"... I delight in a palpable, imaginable, visitable past—in the nearer distances and the clearer mysteries, the marks and signs of a world we may reach over to as by making a long arm we grasp an object at the other end of our own table ... That, to my imagination, is the past fragment of all, or almost all, the poetry of the thing outlived and lost and gone, and yet in which the precious element of closeness, telling so of connexions but tasting so of differences, remains appreciable ..."

—HENRY JAMES, PREFACE TO "THE ASPERN PAPERS"

Rye, Sussex, England, Late Summer 1908

"Hold on," Horace Briscoe said. He placed a restraining hand on Noakes's shoulder. "*Just a moment!* Let's get a good look at the great man before he spots us."

Henry James's young house guest from Boston and the writer's valet and man Friday, Burgess Noakes, were watching as the 3:15 from London, via Ashford, puffed and screeched into the handsome Palladian station and came to a halt. Their small reception party of two had hidden itself behind an ice wagon that someone had conveniently parked across the street. They watched a trim figure in a tailored salt-and-pepper suit step down from a rear carriage and glance up and down the platform. Horace blushed to be spying. James had sent him and Noakes to welcome James's distinguished visitor to Rye and to Horace it seemed a violation of Lamb House hospitality to delay their greeting. But then, it wasn't often that a literary junior, an apprentice on the Olympian heights, could steal a glimpse of a celebrated alienist—none other than Dr. Sigmund Freud of Vienna—without making his scrutiny obvious.

Freud was surely wondering why no greeting party had appeared. Having now taken his bearings—the place was Rye, Sussex, England, the year 1908, the season late summer—Freud stepped briskly through the station exit, tapping the platform with a slender cane. As he crossed the circular driveway, Noakes and Horace stepped with an air of innocence from their place of concealment.

"Dr. Freud!" Noakes called out. "Dr. Sigmund Freud?"

Freud stopped as the expected greeting party of two crossed the street, pulling a small luggage cart.

"Ja, I am Freud," the visitor said.

"May I present myself, sir, I am Noakes, Mr. Henry James's manservant. And this"—he said, indicating Horace—"is Mr. Horace Briscoe, Mr. James's house guest from America."

Freud bowed in acknowledgment, as did Horace. Noakes, moving sturdily on his short legs, deposited Freud's bag with a practiced motion in the wooden wagon.

"Mr. James," he said, "sends his compliments and regrets that he is not here to greet Dr. Freud. Mrs. Wharton was here to luncheon and has only just now departed. You may have noticed her huge old motor moving along the High Street as the train drew into town. It is a spectacular sight around here, and a fright, too. Takes the horses hours to recover from the shock." Noakes laughed at his exaggeration, a habit of speech he had picked up from his employer.

"Ja, I see," Freud mused. He knew Edith Wharton by name, the distinguished American novelist, but not her motor car, which was of no interest to him, and wondered in passing why she had not asked to stay for his visit. "Shall we be ein cab taking to Lamb House?" he inquired, then silently scolded himself for getting the verb in Germanic order.

"Oh, no sir, saving your health. 'Tis but a short walk up the hill to Lamb House. For a fit gentleman like yourself, Dr. Freud, no bother at all." Freud, who looked to weigh no more than a trim 130 pounds, nodded his assent. He sniffed the air again, perhaps suspecting that Noakes and Horace had called at what the English called a public house on their way to the station.

"Lead on, *mein freund*," Freud smiled. "These legs could use a stretching."

The trio marched out of the station and, crossing the street, began to ascend Market Lane, a cobbled street which after a short dogleg to the right along the High would place them on the stretch of West Street leading up to the front door of Lamb House, a hilltop house whose freehold Henry James had enjoyed for a decade. Freud tapped his cane rhythmically along the cobblestones as Noakes, leading the way, pulled the bouncing wagon. Freud's suitcase, its only burden, jumped up and down with a faintly audible rattling within. Freud stretched out an anxious hand.

"Please, Mr. Noakes! There are fragile vessels in my bag." Noakes, wondering what "fragile vessels" the good doctor might be carrying, stopped and, with an accommodating glance at the visitor, threaded a small leather strap through the handle of the valise, securing it to the wagon. The three resumed their climb. Horace was relieved to see that Freud was smiling. Their visitor obviously savored the ambiance of the old town, with its mossy garden walls, settling houses and overarching trees, just now beginning to take on feathery tints of yellow and red.

"This is a jolly walk, Mr. Noakes. Does Mr. James also himself exercise?" Freud asked as they puffed along. It was a pleasantry, but Horace reflected that since Freud had never met Henry James he could have no idea how plump he was, how he almost waddled when he walked. And yet, paradoxically, Henry James did take exercise—as Noakes was quick to say, ever loyal to his master.

"Oh my, yes, Doctor," he said. "Mr. James is quite the exerciser, he is. Rides 'is cycle far and wide over the countryside, and often walks his little dog clear round the golf links when none of the other members is striking the ball. He is quite the athlete, is Mr. James. I know athletes when I see them, sir, for you see I box quite a lot."

Noakes, though an accomplished boxer of the feather-weight class, was stretching a point, and Freud was smiling skeptically. The word *athlete,* applied to a sedentary storyteller now well into his sixties and, from all William James had said, of settled habits, was clearly an amusing conceit. But Freud would soon discover that Noakes's inventive chatter, with its cheerful exaggerations, was one of the many pleasant diversions of Lamb House.

Freud's visit had been inspired by an exchange of correspondence with Henry James's brother, and Dr. James had spoken at length in a letter of unusual candor that the visitor had tucked carefully into the passport pocket of his jacket. As Freud followed Noakes, Horace and the bouncing baggage cart up the cobbled lane in the dappling afternoon sun, he was seen to pat the pocket as if to assure himself that the letter was still there, along with the formal note of introduction in the same hand.

My dear Freud,

All of us here look forward to your visit to Clark next year, when we shall hear of the dawning science of psychoanalysis from the horse's mouth, as it were. Meanwhile, you may recall our exchange of letters about the work of my brother Henry (whom we fondly call Harry), the writer. You had written to me with some astute speculations and queries about his story entitled "The Turn of the Screw," which had deeply engaged you. You expressed a yearning to meet him but said you were reluctant to intrude upon his privacy. I now understand that you plan to visit England this summer and autumn. I have this from Dr. Stanley Hall, your prospective host in Worcester. It occurred to me that your approaching journey to England might afford an opportunity to meet my brother. Harry has long made his residence there, finding it more congenial to his work than Paris, where he first stationed himself when he left Boston.

He has also expressed a lively interest in you and your work and is conversant in some depth with the main psychoanalytic doctrines—unusually so for a layman. Harry, I may say, is inter-

ested in everything. He has mentioned to me that he recently read your The Interpretation of Dreams, with profit, though I think you will find him genially skeptical of the more systematic interpretations of the human personality. Should you have time and inclination during your sojourn in England, he would be happy to welcome you to the old mayoral manse, Lamb House, where he has lived now for the better part of a decade. It is at Rye, Sussex, on the south coast, one of the two "ancient towns" associated with the so-called Cinque-Ports and the defense of the realm. (As a student of history, you will recall the matter of the ship money assessments, and their connection with the troubles of King Charles I.)

I shall not conceal from you that I write with something of a double purpose. Not only to promote a meeting between two far-ranging minds, allied as they are in the quest for the deep secrets of human consciousness; but also because I do worry a good bit about Harry's more eccentric preoccupations. They seem to me to exhibit what you and I might call a certain fetishism. Perhaps your term would be "obsessional," although without clinical study I would be slow to speak of "neurosis" in Harry's case. He is in fact very balanced and healthy-minded. But as you might imagine in the case of a literary lion, his eccentricities take literary forms. In recent years he has begun to write his novels and tales in what he calls his "third manner," to my plodding and plebeian taste a labored style of exquisite Mandarin elaboration which at times reaches a fabulous impenetrability. It is as if the purpose were more concealment than revelation. There is no doubt of his genius, even in this autumnal floridity. But I often remonstrate with him about it, so far to no avail. "Say it out, for God's sake," I tell him; but he remains heedless. Indeed, he has said to me rather sharply that he would rather (as he puts it) "descend to a dishonored grave" than write what would satisfy my own plain taste in storytelling. So much for that, although I worry about it all the same. He has more recently embarked, and *is very much at sea, on the project of "translating" or "revising" his limpid early works into the new manner for uniform publication in an edition being brought out by Scribner's at New York. I simply fail to fathom this project. It seems a bizarre investment, even dissipation, of creative energy, with the single qualification that he is writing so-called "prefaces" to accompany each volume; and so far, if one can survive the ethereal reach of them, they promise to be monuments of criticism. With your own extraordinary insight into the mysteries of artistic craftsmanship—I think for instance of your monograph on the great Leonardo—I wonder if you might not also discreetly probe this enigma. And along with all of this literary Lucullanism (as one might term it) Harry is now much taken with the digestive theories of a certain Dr. Fletcher, whose idea it is that masticating each mouthful of food several dozen times is a sovereign cure for all digestive difficulties. Harry did not like it when I laughed aloud at this "Fletcherisation," saying that if he had ever dissected a human stomach, he would not underrate its powers of reducing food to the needed consistency. This, so far as it may be a fetish or obsession, might bear looking into, should you have opportunity to broach the subject tactfully.*

I do not mean, my dear herr doctor, to overload this letter with sleuthing duties. It is a happy thought that two masters of the human spirit might meet and commune; and it would be my pleasure to arrange it. Shall I write to Harry in your behalf?

· Freud patted the pocket containing the letter once more, as if reviewing its contents. The note from the novelist's brother had closed with elaborate pleasantries, but Freud detected its intent. *When the wind is southerly I know a hawk from a handsaw,* he told himself, echoing one of his favorites among Hamlet's gnomic sayings. Yes, he knew and admired Henry James's work, or much of it, and had been especially intrigued by the ambivalence of "The Turn of the Screw," a masterly horror tale, with its curious but ingenious hints at the sexual precocity of the two small children, Miles and Flora. That "ghost story," Freud believed, offered yet another intimidating instance in which a supreme artist had anticipated, and even trumped, his own clinical findings—an angelic vaulting into the realms of the high imagination into which a poor clinical investigator could only toil step by tedious step.

"We are nearly there, Dr. Freud," Horace said, pointing up the steep street to the mellowed brick wall and bow window that seemed to enclose it at the summit. The party of three had now executed the last slight dogleg at the corner of Mermaid Street and begun their final ascent to the old Georgian structure. Freud was visibly excited, exhilarated to be meeting a man he placed in the pantheon of supreme storytellers. As for the problems William James had cited in his letter—assuming that they really were problems for anyone other than a rivalrous older brother—they would make fine fare for talk should the subjects arise naturally. Between William James's urbane lines, as powerful as subtle, Freud sensed an intense competitiveness. What, after all, could be more natural than an ongoing struggle between two such brilliant and accomplished brothers?

Less than an hour earlier, at Lamb House, once the home of Rye's mayors, two stately figures had enacted, for perhaps the twentieth time over the years of their friendship, a practiced ritual of leave-taking.

"Are you entirely sure, dear girl, that you can't linger for the reception of the Viennese sage?" Henry James said to Edith Wharton. "You could lodge at the Mermaid down the way and enjoy Mrs. Paddington's choicest roast."

"No Henry, and again no. I have guests coming. It will be all my good driver can do to get me back in time. Mr. Kipling and his lady may even now be hovering ungreeted at my doorstep, and you know how punctual he is. Curious as I am about what Sigmund Freud is like in person, I must deprive myself of your guest's company and flee."

Her portly host bent at the waist and extended both arms in a gesture of resignation. He stood beneath a high canopy at the imposing dark green door of Lamb House, which was slightly ajar. James's broad pink forehead gleamed in the afternoon sunlight, and his careful dress seemed to complement his ornate speech. He wore a figured waistcoat of green silk and a frock coat that hung loose at his hips over the worsted trousers, which were adorned with a faint pin stripe. His departing guest was a stylishly dressed woman, some twenty years younger, in a long violet dress and matching petticoats. As she moved in her graceful and almost ceremonial way to the open door of her car she adjusted a large-brimmed hat over dark upswept hair. Her driver, Charles Cook, stood patiently waiting and trying to suppress a sigh. Cook had often witnessed the ritual leavetaking and knew that it usually lasted about five minutes but, fortunately, no longer.

"Very well," James said. "I resign myself to bereavement. All the same you, my dear, must blush with shame to retreat in the hour of impending siege, to flit away to safety on your motorized wings. To leave your poor friend open to the assault of scientific scrutiny. Only an inspired sculpture by our young friend Andersen could capture the poignancy of it—something no less tragic than the doomed burghers of Calais in their chains. And yes, ever spreading her silvered wings to fly away . . ." He gestured skyward, but as he did so a rumble of laughter slowly made its way to his throat.

"Please, Henry," Edith Wharton said, joining his laughter. "This is a bit thick, even for you. To feign fright of Sigmund Freud! I'm sure you will cope with every threat of the Viennese sage as you call him. What is there to fear? I thought you told me that it was William who had, as you put it, 'arranged this collision of art and science.' You seem to survive the family psychologist. Why not the one from Vienna?"

"*Touché*, my dear. Ah, the ever-officious William! This is his wicked and unsolicited doing. I have already disclosed my suspicions regarding this visit. But I do look for a visit more medical than social, if William has anything to do with it. Why, he even mocks at the infallible Dr. Fletcher and the chewing remedy!"

Edith Wharton opened her parasol. "If I am to stand here for an eternity, Henry, I must shade myself. But brace yourself and be manly. You have a whole army behind you—Smith, Mrs. Paddington and dear Burgess Noakes, with Mr. Horace Briscoe as the *masse de manoeuvre.*"

"Yes, Briscoe, the dear and reinforcing boy. But what can that *naïf* know of the serpentine subtleties of Viennese neurology? A meager shelter, he, from the storm, a flimsy refuge."

A stranger reading a bare transcript of the exchange would miss its tone and key, which soared into high registers of verbal teasing, self-mockery and exaggeration—a near imitation of the jaunty letter-writing style they had devised for their frequent communications. Edith Wharton's chauffeur, Cook, still waited patiently at the door of the huge automobile, pretending to ignore what was being said. He could have composed the exchange from previous encounters, nearly identical, except that the anticipation of Freud's visit to Lamb House seemed to add a dimension of anxiety. Usually, any parting between James and Mrs. Wharton, whatever the setting, passed through predictable stages before it ended with her leaving and James's mock-crestfallen surrender to it. Often as not he would remove a large polka-dotted handkerchief from his sleeve and stand waving it in salute as the motor crept away. Now, the exchange finally subsided and Mrs. Wharton seated herself, with a rustle of silks and taffetas, in the back of the Chariot of Fire. Down the hill in the distance, less than a mile away, a whistle announced the approach of the 3:15 train from Ashford and London. Henry James consulted his watch and cast a mournful glance down the hill.

"Oh dear, oh dear," he said. "Freud will be on that train, so I must at last suffer the angel of devastation to fly. Goodbye, Edith, and do remember, please, to ask your gardener about my borders. They sigh for his counsel."

"I will, Henry, and you shall hear of it soon. But your herbaceous borders will thrive, as will you. You always do. There is rain in the air . . ."

Cook, with an air of relief, slammed the door and with much coughing and rasping of gears the machine began to jolt slowly down the cobblestones of West Street. Henry James waved quickly, abbreviating his usual farewell, and stepped into the house.

"Smith!" he called. A somberly dressed man, James's butler, appeared at the rear of the entrance hall, seeming to prop himself with one hand against the staircase.

"Would you do me the kindness of asking Mrs. Paddington to lay out a small collation in the dining room for our guest's arrival? No doubt he will find our scones and mild tea a scant substitute for the pastries and creamy coffee the Viennese consume the livelong day in their public houses. But in Rome, he must eat as the Romans eat. He must cope."

"Very good, Mr. James," Smith said, and lurched away in the direction of the kitchen. Henry James shook his head sadly. "Poor old fellow," he murmured. In the more than sixteen years he had employed Smith he had plied the man with temperance tracts and alarming bulletins on the perils of dipsomania, but to no avail. Many a time over those years he had asked himself, angrily, why he tolerated the hulking, red-nosed man whose habit of waving serving dishes in menacing circles over the heads of his dinner guests he despised and had long tried to stop. This patient toleration of Smith was the stranger, he felt, in that Mrs. Smith (the two came as an ensemble) was so mediocre a cook. It had been a relief to hire the excellent Mrs. Paddington in her place when he had finally fired Smith, some years past. But then, only two months earlier, Smith had knocked, desolate and penitent, at the Lamb House door, whimpering like a disfavored dog. Against all better judgment, James's resolution had wilted and he had not had the heart to turn Smith away. So here he was again, on probation. But still bibulous! James shook his head again.

Horace Briscoe, Dr. Freud's escort from the train station, had often confessed to his diary, as well as in the letters he sent back from Rye to his mother and sister in Newport, that he was greedy—that was the word, the *mot juste*—for the Lamb House scene and its cascades of brilliant talk. As such a gourmet of chatter, he had been asked to lunch with Mrs. Wharton before joining Noakes in the walk down to the station. He had sat in silence, hardly touching his food, amid the feast of repartee. But as Smith removed the dessert dishes, Uncle Henry—as, by special invitation, Horace had been asked to call the great writer, uncle in fact to his best friend and college roommate Billy James—had asked him to go with Noakes and the luggage cart as one of the small greeting party for Dr. Freud. First Edith Wharton, now Sigmund Freud! He was dazzled.

Horace was one of the Newport Briscoes; and apart from his Harvard friendship with Billy James, the family connection went far back. A century earlier, as Horace understood the tribal links, a distant cousin of the Albany Jameses had married a distant kinsman of the Rhode Island Briscoes. It followed that when Horace's mentors in the English department at the Johns Hopkins University (where he was now pursuing one of the new doctor of philosophy degrees) learned of this connection with Henry James, they urged him

to exploit the entree and write his thesis about James's stories—parables—of art and artists, with emphasis on his comic
sense, an unusual exception to the rule against writing about
living writers.

"Uncle Henry will resist, you can be sure of that," Billy
James had replied to his letter. Thus with flattery, he thought
artful, citations of such stories as "The Figure in the Carpet"
and "The Death of the Lion," Horace had outlined his doctoral project in a letter to Lamb House. An unpromising
silence had followed and he had not been surprised when the
delayed reply brought a cool response. Uncle Henry seemed
firmly discouraging to Horace's project, though he wrapped
the discouragement in fragrant strands of persiflage. The note
from Rye could be called inconclusive:

> *My dear Horace Briscoe* [it read],
> *It gives me unimaginable pain, you may be sure, to direct so
> much as a syllable of discouragement to the grandson of one of
> my oldest and fondest friends; and on that consideration I shall
> not stamp a rude obstat on your idea. But speaking, as you so
> flatteringly do, of "The Figure in the Carpet," with its mad imag-
> ined chase after an author's innermost thematic secrets, you cer-
> tainly will be aware of the distance I strive to keep from the crit-
> ical enterprise. All the more, when critics aspire to stretch my
> slight and modest butterflies of fancy upon the rack of earnest-
> ness! You will perhaps cry "hypocrite" in view of the many, many
> pages of literary criticism of which I have been the perpetrator—
> not least* [the letter was dated in early April 1907] *the "pref-
> aces" which I am now affixing to my New York Edition. What
> can I say, then, but that your scrutiny of these pale leaves of my
> slighter foliage could wither them? Please, my dear young sire,
> indulge with second thoughts of mercy your most obedient and
> humble servant, Henry James.*

But Henry James hadn't said no, and Briscoes weren't easily discouraged. Horace showed the letter to Billy James. "It doesn't say yes and it doesn't say no. How do you read it?"

"It's Uncle Henry's way of saying it all depends," Billy James pronounced, and with that encouragement Horace continued to press his case. The result was that one day he had been summoned to Washington and escorted into the huge drawing room of Mr. Henry Adams's town house at 1603 H Street for an audience. The big room stood empty when he was shown into it, though a fire was blazing on the distant hearth. He had cautiously sunk into an easy chair near one of the windows overlooking Lafayette Park and the White House and had fallen into a reverie when Henry James swept majestically into the room, not so much appearing as materializing. Horace jumped to his feet as the idol approached. As he wrote in his diary later, Horace found himself confronting "an animated Sargent portrait," a lofty expanse of forehead and dark, penetrating, merry eyes, a man dressed with English understatement, an expanse over the ample stomach of red silk spangled with discreet emblems of the golden fleece. Uncle Henry sped across the room and greeted Horace with a cordial handshake, as he arose, feeling awkward and rawboned.

"Ah," James exclaimed merrily, "my would-be Boswell, it seems."

Horace shook his head vigorously. "No, no, sir," he sputtered, "nothing like that! No such presumption, sir. Mere plodding scholarship." (He silently cursed himself for the stilted words.)

"Please, Mr. Briscoe, don't take this old trouper's jest so seriously. If you really must descend on our small domestic scene, our menagerie as it were, you will find that I am far less formidable than the sage of Lichfield. I usually find myself entirely at a loss for those thunderous pronouncements for which we fondly remember Boswell's subject."

Horace was overwhelmed by Henry James's friendliness, and stunned by the sudden, if implied, invitation to visit the great lion in his den. He edged a toe cautiously into the warming waters. "Do you actually mean, sir . . . that is, that I might call on you at your house, at Lamb House? In England?"

"By all means, Horace Briscoe," James said. "Why not?" As if the arrangement had never been questioned and as a matter, somehow, of natural right. "By all means! You shall lodge for as long as you like this summer in the attic with Noakes and the other servants. The low ceilings will threaten your noggin, tall as you are, but there will be compensations. The view over the marshes toward Winchelsea is fine on clear days. We shall walk the golf links, we shall haunt my garden, we shall talk of the great literary issues!"

Great literary issues? Horace wondered uneasily, fearing for a moment that James had confused him with someone else he had been scheduled to meet through the good offices of Henry Adams. He was relieved when James continued.

"Briscoe! A great name in my book of memory. I vividly recall those lovely summers of my youth visiting your family cottage at Newport—Sea Beacon, was it?—when your grandfather and his jolly brood overflowed the wide porches and ramparts. Does the house still stand, or has it been destroyed in the pitiless tide of nouveau richesse? If I recall, your grandfather was the first to pipe the waters of the sea into a heated swimming bath?"

"He was, Mr. James," Horace said, but continued with sadness. "Sea Beacon went the way of all our properties in the Panic of '93—at any rate, it is no longer ours. Some New York millionaire owns it."

Henry James shook his head. "*Sic transit . . .*" he said, then looked at his watch.

"Oh dear," he said, "I must flee to Mrs. Codrington's for tea and after that to the White House with Mr. Adams. I am collecting gossip and impressions, you see. But I shall look forward to your visit. Come and stay as long as your project requires. You shall meet some of our choice young friends, Horace Walpole and Jocelyn Persse of the luminous Irish Persses—and others. We shall light the calm horizons of Sussex . . ."

And that was how Horace found himself in the greeting party for Sigmund Freud. By early summer Horace was so happily installed at Lamb House that he had begun to dread ever leaving. He grew giddy with delight when he found one day that Uncle Henry depended on him to help entertain the "Viennese sage." He was to stay on for the duration of the "Freud emergency," at least, if not longer. Horace knew almost nothing about Freud. He had heard or read or vaguely recalled from the usual academic chatter in which he had bathed daily back in Baltimore that Freud had shocked the world a few years earlier by bringing sex to the fore as the cause of female "neurosis." It seemed that the Freudian system presumed that human psyches were cauldrons of hidden appetite, from the moment of birth. And there was something else, dimly recalled, about "polymorphous perversity," whatever that was. There, Horace's fragile grasp of Viennese thought abruptly ended. He was otherwise in the dark and merely echoed Uncle Henry's conversational leads when the subject of the impending visit arose. With one exception—Horace had adopted a policy of discretion, avoiding the scandalous aspects of Freudian theory in the certainty that Uncle Henry regarded him as a mere boy, too young for any talk of birds and bees. And oddly, in some ways he was precisely that innocent, though that was beginning to change, and sharply so . . . He had recorded the transition, now some weeks old, in the private journal he kept well hidden under the mattress in his attic room. By old habit he sometimes found it useful to address himself in a tone of reprimand. He blushed at the melodramatic tone, but it served:

Come now, Briscoe! Doesn't it embarrass you to carry this threadbare Boswell act so far? Playing the faux-naïf bumpkin— maybe not so bumpkinish as the original but taking it pretty far! After all, you are now well into your twenties, with six years of "higher" education behind you. You have learned a lot from and about Uncle Henry in these weeks, so that you ought to disgust yourself when you pretend that you were born yesterday. Isn't that why you slipped Uncle Henry's copy of The Interpretation of Dreams *from the library shelves when he was busy dictating in the Garden Room and read it so eagerly? And Dr. Fletcher's magnum opus on the mastication of food as well? Aren't you now pretty well equipped to hear and judge the feast of conversation, wherever it may lead?*

Uncle Henry had first mentioned Freud at the breakfast table one foggy morning, not long after Horace had settled in. Nothing could be seen from the windows of Lamb House; and from the attic dormer that morning when he arose, the small space seemed to float above the clouds. At the table Uncle Henry was as usual practicing the techniques of "Fletcherization," chewing each mouthful of eggs and bangers several dozen times. As he perused the morning mail, Uncle Henry glared as only he could glare at a letter, just opened, from his brother Dr. James, Billy's father. He pushed his pinchers down on the bridge of his nose and the silent rotation of the jaws accelerated. Horace tried not to stare, but Henry James was uttering strange little visceral grunts of displeasure and surprise. Ummmmm. Ummmm. Ummmp! Horace usually did not consider it his business to speak unless spoken to and kept his silence.

"Damnation!" James suddenly cried, having at last swallowed the well Fletcherized mouthful. He slapped the letter with the back of his hand. "Damn, damn, damn!" He glared at Horace across the table.

"William is up to his tricks, Horace. He has suggested to Dr. Sigmund Freud of Vienna that he call on me here during his forthcoming trip to England. Here, at Lamb House! Out of the blue! Without consultation! Just like that."

"Freud?" Horace asked with an air of innocence. "Isn't he the fellow who thinks baby boys want to sleep with their mothers, like Oedipus?" He knew that it was a smart-alec thing to say, one of the few he had ventured; and it exhausted his hearsay notion of Freud's views. But he sensed that it suited Uncle Henry's mood.

He was right. "For shame, Horace," Uncle Henry scolded, his mock rage subsiding. He wagged his finger and his twinkling eyes belied the reprimand. "You dare to mock the latest advance into the largest latitudes of human science." With their musical inflections, rich in irony, the words seemed to dance and glimmer. Henry James again adjusted his pinchers and, spooning a generous mouthful up, he went on reading the letter, occasionally reacting with small groans and grunts: a muted *obligado* of pretended annoyance.

"William is so confoundedly patronizing," he said, looking up. "He is always trying to fix either my writing or my digestion. Listen to this, Horace." He read aloud:

"'. . . I have taken the liberty of telling my Viennese colleague how fearful I am that your late style—that high confection of light, air and mirrored illusions—will at last lead you into total incoherence. It is my prayerful hope, Harry, that the good doctor may render a useful diagnosis and cure you of this obsessiveness . . .'"

"That, you see, my boy, is his idea of brotherly teasing. William is being witty in his clumsy way. I have had to beg him to stop reading my tales. I live in terror that he may like one of them. And I had rather descend to a dishonored grave than appease his philistine admonitions. I have told him that, too."

Horace nodded. He was trying to avoid being dragged into a brotherly quarrel.

"Of course, Horace, you do see that such outbursts of temperament as this, such confidences, are under the seal of secrecy. You must breathe not a s-s-s-syllable of this to your chum, Billy James, who might then tell his father. I fear that all of this might plunge us to the verge of a C-C-Cain and Abel showdown." Horace had noticed that when Uncle Henry was formulating his half-serious, often florid reactions to some minor provocation he seemed to stutter—deliberately.

"Naturally, sir. My lips are sealed. But will you in fact invite Dr. Freud to visit?" Horace already suspected that Uncle Henry relished the idea, but for amusement was pretending otherwise. How could a writer of such catholic observation resist a new specimen?

"I fear, dear boy, that the die is cast. How can I be disobliging to William or to his colleague? I shall write to Vienna this day, then go to ground and wait." His eyes shone again. "No doubt, the Viennese sage will wish to inspect your poor old host as a sort of, as one might say, s-s-specimen." (It was, uncannily, the very word Horace had thought of.) "But perchance the experiment will prove to be . . ." Uncle Henry paused, raising a finger and seeking the exact word in a way that reminded Horace of a bloodhound snuffling for a trail— "will prove to be . . . ah, of reciprocal benefit!"

Having asked Smith to see that tea would be ready for his guest, Henry James mounted the stairs to his paneled bedroom for a moment of rest. He stood before the tall window overlooking the fishhook bend of West Street as it ascended along the brick façade of the Garden Room. A hundred paces away the cobblestones yielded to a grassy churchyard and, just beyond, the handsome west façade of Saint Mary the Virgin. The old church crowned the ridge on which the town itself perched and the early-eighteenth-century builder of Lamb House, old Thomas Lamb, had situated his Georgian manse in a respectful filial relation just below the church where the people of Rye had worshipped for five centuries. With the nearby Ypres watchtower, where lookouts had once guarded against French raiders, the two edifices had companioned one another ever since.

Of course, the ecclesiastical fashions and usages had varied. Rye had not escaped the sectarian tremors rippling out over the years from London or Canterbury and other centers of theological agitation—the upheaval over benefit of clergy, Thomas Becket's assassination; the revolutionary convulsion wrought by the second Tudor; the iconoclastic fury of the Roundheads during the civil war; and within the memory of the older residents of the town, the subtle vibrations across the realm when Pusey, Newman and the Tractarians, in Oxford, had recalled the English church to its apostolic roots.

The repercussions of that more recent controversy had been felt, however faintly, in Rye and even in the neighborhood of Lamb House: aftershocks of a minor theological earthquake. Henry James delighted in the unreliable tales he heard from fellow townsmen around their evening fires of the far-off battles over communion tables and altars, priestly vestments and positions and other liturgical quirks. He had devoured the ironies of Froude, the Oxford historian defrocked for heresy, on the Oxford counter-reformation; and read his Trollope on the subtle politics of the country clergy. Not least, he relished the gentle, meditative pages of Cardinal Newman's *Apologia.*

From time to time, musing in the privacy of his notebooks, Henry James had glimpsed a fleeting *donnée,* a seedling, that might someday yield a tale of ecclesiastical agitation. As felt and observed, it might be, by a fine consciousness like the Guy Domville of his failed drama: a sensitive "reflector," attuned to the issues but somehow standing above them. But the idea would no sooner dance before him like a grain of dust, just out of hand, than it would dart away. He understood its fugitive nature. The challenge would lie, as always, in the writing, in the demands of specificity, of real people, of names to be named, of convincing narratives of creed and zeal. There was an old story, as improbable as it was colorful, that half a century earlier, young zealots of the high-church party, in the name of some bygone *furor theologicus*, had hidden among the tilted, tottering, mossy old tombstones in the St. Mary's churchyard (towards which he was looking just now) and fired bird shot at the top hats of some evangelical churchmen on their way to evening prayer. Fact or legend? On its face, such a raucous disturbance seemed improbable and in any case, it was unlikely that such battles would have failed to leave a deeper dent on the town's folk memory. At St. Mary's, bathed as it was now in mid-afternoon sunlight, the Catholic and apostolic party had ultimately prevailed in such latter-day controversies as penetrated this far corner of Sussex, setting the uses of the church as firmly as its old buttresses. The votive candles in the south aisle (which had inspired one of his recent stories, "The Altar of the Dead") attested to that.

Suddenly, Henry James's musing eye was drawn to a familiar figure who stood alone in the churchyard, a hundred yards up the hill. His hands clasped behind him, he seemed to be studying some small feature of the architecture. He wore one of those broad-brimmed black hats that had been familiar clerical regalia in the Oxford of fifty years before, together with a long coat, breeches and gaiters. James raised a small opera monocular for a closer look. As he had supposed, it was none other than Archdeacon Fengallon, the scourge of high churchmen in Rye and, he had good reason to know, not a welcome figure at St. Mary's. There was the laughable episode of the purloined chasuble, for instance. Fengallon had snatched that eucharistic garment from the altar rail one day and made off with it as, he said, "a popish frippery," defying anyone to stop him. The rector, Father Morris, had threatened the archdeacon with excommunication and, soon enough, the embroidered item was meekly returned. But it had been a symptomatic episode in the archdeacon's war against the terrible Tractarians, even though most warriors in that campaign had reached a truce fully half a century earlier.

Fengallon persisted, a tireless holdout against the accepted return of the ancient forms—a fiery, restless, faintly louche ecclesiastic who had set his florid face against the Catholic party. He had tilted with no less than Mr. Gladstone over church matters in the *English Review,* and was a throwback to an earlier age when "priests" (he disdained the word) had been gentlemen and had ridden to hounds with the gospel in one hand and a hunting horn in the other. And there was a rumor that his departure from the "living" at Wells, where he had been a prebendary and then archdeacon of the diocese, had not been altogether friendly nor free of some faint wisp of scandal . . .

Fengallon had insisted on befriending the master of Lamb House, and seemed to think of Henry James as an implicit ally in the church wars. James had often been treated to the archdeacon's vigorous but entertaining dinner-table tirades at his half-timbered Tudor house, the Old Hotel, just down Mermaid street. Fengallon kept a fine table, decorated by the beauty of his handsome niece and ward, Agnes. Henry James pictured him as an amusing and harmless, if combative, eccentric, a fugitive out of time from the pages of Fielding's *Tom Jones.* But he avoided him when he could.

For Henry James, such certainties as Fengallon entertained were merely amusing, friendly or not to religion. He and brother William were bred to appreciate theological eccentricity; for the memory of their own father's faith was engraved on their spirits, an enduring imprint of Swedenborgian fantasies of interstellar messaging. In the elder Henry James religion had been a gentle concoction, a sort of love potion, distilled from stronger brews. But for all his filial piety, Henry James the younger was of a far lower theological temperature than his father—or even than William who had, after all, dallied with the Society for Psychical Research for want of other metaphysical certainties.

Indeed, in idle hours when he was not writing or thinking about his writing, Henry James would fall to musing, not without envy, on his father's strange romance with mystical imaginations. He felt that he himself had no aptitude for them at all; in his case the spiritually rich and strange had been perversely dissolved back into mere flesh. No angels had come down from on high to whisper to him about the ultimate structure of the cosmos, as they had to Emanuel Swedenborg. And the wonder of it all was augmented, to Henry James's way of thinking, by the fact that Swedenborg (and for that matter, his own brother William) had come to their spiritualist speculations from backgrounds in science—mine engineering in Swedenborg's case, medicine and physiology in William's. But in his resolute openness to the astonishing wideness of human sensibility, Henry James's thoughts on these aberrations (if such they were) were ever benevolent, more quizzical than censorious. He was certain that many charlatans lurked at the outer edges and margins of these exotic spiritualist feasts; but he was prepared in all charity to acquit his father and William—and even Swedenborg—of imposture or fraud. Indeed, in their case it was unimaginable; they were transparently earnest in these interests and had to be to entertain their high fantasies. But as for him, Henry James told himself with relief, he was quite happy to be a spectator only.

It was over related matters that Henry James often found himself musing as he gazed up West Street toward the old church and, now, at the eccentric parson walking in the churchyard. Why these reveries, and why just now? Might they have to do with Dr. Freud's arrival? Hadn't William assured him that Freud was a resolute foe of religion? That he regarded divinity as an intoxicant not far removed from delusion? That he viewed the Author of Peace and Lover of Concord as a mere *projection*—was that the term William had used?—of earthly fathers?

Below stairs, the huge knocker on the front door banged and Henry James started from his reverie. Freud was on the doorstep, and suddenly Henry James shuddered at the thought that Freud and Fengallon, returning from the church, might cross paths there. The thought chilled him. Freud and Fengallon! Now *that* would be a poisonously explosive brew, and he silently vowed that at all costs those two gentlemen must be kept far apart during Freud's visit. The chance of such a bizarre collision seemed safely remote; and indeed Fengallon seemed to have left the churchyard in another direction and now, as the great visitor arrived, was nowhere to be seen. James paused, frowning, at the pier glass by the door, straightened his collar and cravat, and hurried toward the staircase as the door knocker resounded again. No doubt Smith was dozing somewhere in the back of the house, but why the deuce didn't Noakes simply open the door with his key?

Horace, witnessing the scene from outside, was astonished at the force with which Noakes swung the door-knocker, metal clanging upon metal as if to wake the dead. But Noakes was physically deceptive, destined to become a regional boxing champion in the featherweight class and, later, a valiant soldier in the Great War. Uncle Henry had hired him in the modest capacity of what the English called "knife boy," but he had proved so winning and reliable that he was now, apart from Miss Bosanquet, the dictationist, the star of the domestic scene.

Horace stood to one side awaiting the ceremonial opening

of the door by Smith, if that groggy personage had bestirred himself. Uncle Henry would be waiting just inside, in the spacious entrance hall, peering cordially over Smith's shoulder. When the door at last swung open, the ceremony unfolded exactly as he had expected. The two great men, the Stanley and Livingstone of the human psyche, greeted each other as if it were the meeting both had been waiting for all their lives. Horace was amused, and a bit embarrassed, when a mischievous comparison popped into his mind. Who has not watched two high-bred and nervous dogs sniffing and trembling, tiptoeing around and around one another? Dogs relied on the sense of smell (they were said not to see very well), a power now denied to human beings as they had evolved. Even so, Horace had the feeling that this "historic" meeting involved a nearly audible sniffing. There was, in any case, elaborate bowing and exclamation, with small cries of pleasure and unworthiness from Uncle Henry, attended by repeated exchanges of "my dear herr doctor" and "my dear Mr. James."

The scene to Horace's skeptical eye derived from the most exquisite manuals of courtliness; but beneath the rituals, a close observer might have picked up distinct signals of wariness. Horace had an advantage, of course. He had been a sounding board for the expressions of chagrin, real and pretended, with which Uncle Henry had reacted to Dr. James's letter proclaiming Freud's visit and, as Uncle Henry pretended to believe, some sly medical or neurological inspection.

After following Freud and Noakes in, Horace excused himself and climbed the stairs to his attic room with every intention of study. He could hear the stir on the floor just below as Dr. Freud was shown by Noakes and Smith to the large guest bedroom, just across from the Green Room, and informed of the location of the house's single water closet.

"Tea, doctor, at 4:30," Smith said dryly, having been assured that Freud would do his own unpacking and arrang-

ing. Horace spied from the bannister just above as Smith wob-
bled down the spiral stair. It was a rare mid-afternoon, as
Uncle Henry pretended not to know, that found Smith unfor-
tified by strong drink.

When he had closed his door and stared blankly at a book
for some minutes, Horace crossed the room and bent to the
small window. He peered out over the marshes. He had not
been invited to tea and knew that he needed some stimulus,
some diversion. He plucked the small notebook from the shelf
over his desk and opened it to a special series of entries marked
"Uncle Henry & the Viennese sage." He might be witnessing
an epochal conjunction of destinies—those were the inflated
words that sprang to mind—and this was one way to make the
most of it. He had no doubt that Henry James was the greatest
living writer of fiction, possibly excepting the doddering
Tolstoy and Joseph Conrad, the Polish émigré and sea captain,
who was a special case.

"Today," he wrote, after dating the page, "Noakes and I
met Freud's train. He was awkwardly dressed for the country.
He looks a bit like Conrad . . ."

He paused and put his pen down, trying to remember the
funny, and as always original, things Uncle Henry had said
about Conrad.

"For one thing, Horace," James said, when Horace reported that he had been reading *Almayer's Folly,* "I met him
through the good offices of our common agent Pinker and, I
might add, through the mediation of the unctuous and assuming young Ford Hueffer. But don't bother trying to meet
Conrad, you couldn't understand him; his English is impene-
trable"—Uncle Henry gave the word a French sound.
"*Impénétrable!*" he said again, with emphasis. "Why, a Chinese
laundryman in the East End speaks clearer English.
Nonetheless, his writing has genius; he is a marvel."

As he stared at his journal, Horace tried to recall some of Uncle Henry's choice words on Freud. Yes, he had said, Freud had now assumed the mantle of Joseph, the Biblical interpreter of dreams. He also claimed to trace the so-called "neuroses" to a mysterious sexual force that in childhood drew children toward the parent of the opposite sex. Uncle Henry had no sooner uttered the forbidden word, sex, than he blushed and eyed Horace as if he might have been ten years old. "But we shall talk of other features of his science." Uncle Henry's gentle mockery had not discouraged the idea that Freud might be a sort of charlatan with what the English called strange notions. He had gathered about him in Vienna certain acolytes committed to defending the purity of his doctrine, as if he were more a cult figure than a neurologist. So Uncle Henry said, perhaps repeating what he had been told by Dr. James, although he too had read *The Interpretation of Dreams*. Indeed, "psychoanalysis" had the look of a faith. But no doubt this picture was incomplete. Horace resolved to approach the sage with deference and an open mind. He had quickly sensed that Uncle Henry and his guest liked one another rather more than either had expected. He dipped his pen and resumed. "Dr. Freud has come for the weekend, but I gather that neither he nor Uncle Henry would mind very much if the visit stretched out beyond Monday morning . . ."

In this, Horace's intuition was far more accurate than he knew.

As instructed, Freud, his hair and beard freshly brushed, descended the staircase at exactly 4:30. He found his host waiting in the dining room, to the right of the staircase. James gestured towards the double glass doors, which stood open to the mild afternoon.

"My garden, herr doctor. As you can see it is quite large for a modest house."

Freud stared obligingly out at the expanse of grass and shubbery, feigning interest. The English, and some Americans, he knew, attached quite extraordinary importance to private gardens and lavished upon them what from a Viennese standpoint seemed an extravagant care and attention. They were full of flowers and trees and ponds and the more expansive ones called parks were meticulously designed by the man Capability Brown and his successors to look as if nature had arranged them with a casual hand.

"Ja," good manners obliged him to say, despite his lack of interest. "It is so very pretty."

James turned to the table, where a tea service, a toast rack and a silver plate of scones had been laid out a few moments earlier by Mrs. Paddington. A tiny swirl of steam drifted up from the spout of the waiting teapot. James indicated a chair facing the doorway. "Will you sit there, Dr. Freud, so that you may enjoy a full view of the garden?" Freud sat. He watched as James poured two cups and added cubes of sugar and a splash of cream. Then, as if to plunge unceremoniously into a lengthy agenda, Freud cleared his throat. "I must repeat, sir, how delighted I am at Lamb House to be. But now, Herr James, I must pay you the compliment I have at times paid Sophocles and other great writers. I have been waiting long to say this . . ."

"Merciful heavens!" James said. "You place me in exalted company."

"Not too exalted, however. I have read many of your novels and stories—more, I confess, since your distinguished brother suggested that I might visit. But none with more surprise or profit than 'The Turn of the Screw.'"

"Oh, my dear herr doctor! That you should fix upon that cunning and, as one might say, irresponsible little tale: a fairy tale pure and simple!"

"Fairy tale?" Freud said, astonished. "You do slight justice to its penetration."

James smiled benignly, slowly munching a scone and waiting to see where the tribute would lead. He assumed a look of professorial solemnity, though the hint of a smile played at his lips. Having chewed twenty times he swallowed. "To be sure, fairy tales are sometimes penetrating. But pray go on," he said.

"Happily with your permission. You know, Mr. James, that I scandalized the medical world a few years ago when I announced what I am now calling my theory of the neuroses . . ."

"So I have heard, herr doctor."

"Imagine my astonishment, then, when I turned to your little tale of the haunted house—Bly, is it?—and found that what I had discovered, you, sir, had imagined."

"Indeed?"

"Indeed, sir, you imagined what my critics scorned—the universality of infantile sexuality. Your Miss Jessel, the disgraced former governess, has allied herself with the butler, Quint, to pervert the children. Hence you ingeniously endowed them with precocious sexuality, even though the young lad Miles has entered what I call the latency period, when sexual interest temporarily subsides. But of course! It all fits together. Miles has carried Quint's smutty talk back to school with him—'said things' to his schoolfellows—and has been rusticated by the priggish headmaster. No doubt the headmaster himself is repressed, for that matter."

"Extraordinary!" James cried, with a delight that Freud may have misread. "I do wish I had had your insight to consider while I was writing that little tale. Or at least when I was recently writing a 'preface' for the New York Edition. You open artless eyes, herr doctor. And yet, knowing too much of the deeps might well have proved f-f-fatal to such a confection, such a piece of . . . such a piece of *f-f-fluff* . . ."

Freud waved aside James's dismissive noun. "Assuredly not fluff, Herr James. The proof is there, the reader's nose before. Consider the ingeniously conceived scene on the lawn at the country house when the children are strolling up and down in the distance, while the governess and Mrs. Grose, the house-keeper, speculate on their conversation. If I may say so, I found the scene so ingenious, so devilishly ingenious, that I in my commonplace book elaborate notes inscribed. But to go on: Mrs. Grose, true to her nature, has no theory. But the governess says with great assurance: 'They're talking horrors!' Exactly! Horrors! A suitably prudish circumlocution. You clearly might have said that the two children are reviewing and amplifying their precocious information on *les choses génitales.*"

"My dear doctor, you have, as it were, inflated with vivid and unexpected gas the rather vacant word, *horrors.* They are speaking of genital matters, are they? I t-t-tremble on the verge of astonishment to hear it!"

"But of course. What could those horrors be but those smutty words for daring to echo which Master Miles has from his school been sent down? And for what purpose other than to initiate his small sister, Flora, into this precocious knowl-edge? What you intuit, science amply confirms." Freud beamed like a bright student who has pleased his teacher. Henry James appeared to ponder Freud's gloss on "The Turn of the Screw." His eyes twinkled.

"Hmmm. How obtuse I was not to have seen this connec-tion, dangerous though it might be to dwell on scientific theo-ry whilst writing. Creation, as I needn't tell you, herr doctor, demands a certain divine vacancy, a certain naiveté; it is as a child that one enters that kingdom, you see. But science will surely reshape our vaguely apprehended world, as nothing since our primal parents et the forbidden fruit. You neurolo-gists will speak and suddenly all will be clear."

Freud paused, not quite sure of the drift and tone of what James was saying. Could he be teasing? Freud stirred his tea and looked out into the garden. He dabbed his beard with the nap-kin. Perhaps he had run on a bit and stumbled into a pratfall?

"Shall I," James asked, noting his guest's discomfort, "repay your generous analysis with a shamefaced confession?"

Freud nodded.

"You see, my dear doctor, we poor writers, denied access to the mysteries of the consulting room, are pitiably reliant on the mere imagination, ours and the reader's. As you indeed have suggested. We rely upon the reader's uninstructed surmise to fill the gaps in our stories. So that when one writes of the over-wrought governess that she believes Miles and Flora are 'talking horrors,' one writes, I fear, in perfect ignorance of what content our readers may inject into the words.

"In short, Freud, we who sit in scientific darkness must rely on the inexplicit, the unspoken. Just as our master Sophocles may not have realized when he was writing his play that he was limning the Oedipal idea before its time."

Freud was no longer quite sure what his host was saying, or suggesting. It was like a melody with many sharps and flats and chromatic chords. Tone; yes, that was the key to Henry James's elaborate and unctuous style of speaking. Did he at times detect more than a grain of irony in the flow of words? To his relief, the conversation shifted to a more mundane subject.

"Shall we cycle up to Winchelsea tomorrow? It is Rye's sister city. The two old towns have been looking at one another over the marshes for centuries. Do you cycle, by the way?"

"A bit, but not expertly, I fear."

"Ah," James said. "It is a simple art, once you get the hang of it. As you see, I am no agile youth. Noakes will give you a tutorial before we set out, whilst I undertake my morning stint of dictation in the Garden Room. And now. This has been most pleasant, but it will soon be time to dress for dinner."

Very late that evening, Henry James wrote a preliminary report on Freud's visit to Edith Wharton:

My dear Edith,

Since you abandoned me to my peril, soaring off in the char-iot of fire, the Viennese sage has descended & is ensconced in my spare bedroom. You know how I loathe resident company, so that is one measure of my hospitality. Yet I confess, all shame-facedly, that I find Freud more agréable *than I had dared hope. Yes, I was quite right in guessing that William had sent him here on an errand of medical rescue from my follies & frailties—obsessional, I think their term is. Freud, however, is playing his cards with suavity, & with a bedside manner honed to a fine edge at the couch of "hysterical" ladies in Vienna. He avoids the term but bends a kindly ear to my "neuroses," the ones hypothetically mentioned to him by William. He questioned politely my dedi-cation to the gospel according to Dr. Fletcher & could hardly have avoided the subject since, between tea and dinner, we have been at table much of the time since his arrival. I explained that Fletcherization has brought release from the repletion that has so long been a thorn in my flesh.*

"But why, Mr. James," he asked, "undergo this redundant exercise of chewing each mouthful . . . how many times is it?"

I couldn't resist a naughty exaggeration & replied, "one hun-dred & sixty nine times, Herr Doctor," but gave the joke away by laughing. But I don't think he quite grasped the exaggeration.

"So much mastication," he said, as solemnly as a priest through the confessional grill, "is redundant, Mr. James, & I speak of this on the basis of years of clinical experience with the anatomy of the digestive system. Many fewer than a hundred of those chewings *(that was his word & he is fluent in our blessed tongue, though the stray oddity now and then escapes him, espe-cially when it comes to verb order) are too many. Had you joined in as many dissections as I have done as a medical student & practitioner & had witnessed the power of the digestive acids, you would take Dr. Fletcher's edicts* cum grano salis.*"*

We both chuckled at the Latinity. "Cum grano salis," said I.

"Very good; indeed, we strive to season these gospels of alimentation with the shaker of common sense. But my dear doctor, you must allow me my eccentric faith, heretical though it be according to the true gospel of digestion!"

But my dear Edith, this was hardly the summit of our talk, this dreary subject of the "chewings." Freud is certainly a devotee of in medias res & we had no sooner sat down to tea than he broke into praise of such extravagance as would have crimsoned the Bard's own cheek. On the silvery wings of his encomium, I soared, as I shall have you know, to celestial rank with Sophocles & others whom Freud credits with having heralded, as it were from the pagan limbo, his own findings regarding the nervosi. He has read quite a few of my tales, & with disconcerting attention, albeit skewed at times by the described prepossessions. He treated me, you see, to an exposition of "The Turn of the Screw" so delicious that I wished we had had Theodora Bosanquet at hand to record the dialogue in Remingtonese! No demurrer would deflect the sage from rating my mischievous fairy tale with Oedipus Rex, though for a reason reflecting no little incidental credit upon himself & his own genius. The brilliant treatment of Master Miles and Little Flora meshed with his own "clinical" discoveries upon what he calls infantile sexuality. So that when I have the governess say that the children are "talking horrors" (having not a shred of a notion what those horrors might be, & leaving it to the reader's imagination to guess) I have all the while been psychoanalyzing, warbling medical woodnotes wild! Comme le M. de Jourdain de Molière! Freud tells me with assurance that Miles's mind is as foul as Vulcan's stithy, & perfectly perplexed with country matters.

You may be sure, my dear, that I thanked him with appropriate blushes of modesty for this elevation to Parnassus, the while protesting that we poor scribblers deal only in the inexplicit and look to our audience to supply the deficiency. Did he take my point? He is trying, I gather, but his manner of literary con-

struction is a bit Procrustean, as you see, & there was a constant naughty temptation not only to pull his leg but to make a rude bosun's knot of it. Of this you will hear more, far more, but now it is very late & I must close this first dispatch from the battlefield & rest for our cycling expedition to Winchelsea on the morrow. Freud will have a cycling lesson from Noakes in the morning before we set out & that promises to be a trifle of a story in itself. Meanwhile, believe me, ma chérie, yours most constantly, Henry James.

Dear Henry [Edith Wharton answered],

Your early report on Dr. Freud's arrival followed so hard on my heels as to leave me lagging in my thanks for a splendid luncheon. Please do tell Mrs. Paddington how much I enjoyed her leg of lamb. Your note gave me great merriment and I laughed aloud at that Freudian gloss on "The Turn of the Screw." Yet I confess myself a trifle alarmed, Henry, that your persiflage may become so transparent, even violent, as to break through even the carapace of Germanic solemnity. And then where will you be? If you do not alienate the alienist and drive him away, you may reduce him to a sullen silence and you will have missed a splendid opportunity for character study. Do then pay out more length to him—more "scope" as I believe the mariners call it when they cast anchor: 7 x the depth? Pay out your capacity for listening and see what comes of it. I know that you contain your mirth with difficulty when such feasts of literary overinterpretation are laid before you. I know your wit, but your guest does not. But enough admonition. Incidentally, I shall forward such advice as Cooper may have on the care of herbaceous borders, as promised.

Otherwise, I shall be brief for Mr. Trollope's swift couriers impend. The Kiplings came last evening and were altogether congenial and in good form. Rudyard took up the dinner hour speaking volubly, as is his way, of the oddity of Mr. Cecil Rhodes and his diamond and gold fortune which, by testamentary will, is even now flooding Oxford with young men from all over the Empire, and even from America. (He is one of the new-minted Rhodes trustees, you know.) He says the dons are appalled about the Americans and Germans, but he finds their worries nugatory and laughed and laughed. Yours ever, Edith.

It was a spectacle: the master of Lamb House in his corduroy plus-fours and other riding gear with cap and goggles making his stately way down the steep and winding cobblestones of Mermaid Street, followed by a worried and diminutive Burgess Noakes wheeling James's bicycle down to sea level. Often, some guest at Lamb House would be in train. Henry James the bicycle rider was a familiar if improbable figure to his Rye neighbors.

Dr. Freud's recruitment as a cyclist, however, posed special problems. The father of psychoanalysis had so rarely ridden a bicycle as to rank as a beginner; and he had brought no suitable kit. Noakes escorted Freud down to Johnson's haberdasher's on the High Street, where he purchased plus-fours of a bright greenish velvet, and long hose. Otherwise, Freud could not be persuaded to relax the formality of his wardrobe, and the new knickers formed an incongruous ensemble with his woolen jacket, waistcoat and tie. When topped off by the new bowler hat—no one had told him it was usually the headgear of clerks in the City—the effect was outlandish. Then, there was the cycling challenge. Noakes took the now outfitted doctor out into the garden for a few trial runs. As Horace watched from the windows of the Green Room, Dr. Freud, with muted Germanic oaths, attempted to keep the machine upright and under control, weaving and wobbling among the bushes and flower beds and finally toppling into a cushioning bed of nasturtiums. "Gott in Himmel!," he cried, as Noakes sprinted to help him to his feet. The lesson went on for most of the morning but for a time things went so unpromisingly that Noakes took it upon himself to ask Freud if he wished to postpone the expedition—it had already been understood now that Dr. Freud's visit was to extend beyond the weekend. Freud had telegraphed his kinsmen in Manchester that his stay in the south would be prolonged at James's invitation. But Freud firmly rejected a postponement; he was not to be cowed or intimidated, he declared, by a "demon of two wheels"; and that was that.

Henry James, emerging at noon from his morning of dictation, stood on the steps of the Garden Room watching the ongoing tutorial as Dr. Freud gradually learned how to balance himself. "Good! Good!" he called out in hearty appraisal of the final trial run. Noakes, with a certain reserve, had certified Dr. Freud as a qualified cyclist; but he had his doubts.

The household, including Theodora Bosanquet, James's secretary, assembled for a light luncheon. The journey had been scheduled for two o'clock and Henry James expounded at length on the history of the two old towns, Rye and Winchelsea, speaking of their long record of smuggling in defiance of the Crown monopolies.

"Ah yes, my dear doctor," James said. "If, after luncheon, you should care to scan the map of Sussex in the telephone room, just across the hall, you will find a circular spot out at sea marked, with imaginative melancholy, *'Old Winchelsea Drowned.'* Winchelsea was essentially destroyed by the great storm of 1287. The Crown then decreed that Winchelsea must move, bag and baggage, to another and safer place. We owe to the Plantagenets the geography we shall examine today."

"Remarkable," Freud said. "You know, Mr. James, I am myself an amateur of archaeology. Herr Schliemann and Professor Evans, in their diggings at Troy and Knossos, have revealed tales of even greater antiquity beneath other surfaces."

"Am I given also to understand that those—what is it you

so colorfully call them? those 'repressed episodes' of which we become aware only as they are excavated—that those are, as it were, the mental analogue of buried cities?"

"True, Mr. James," Freud said hesitantly, still struggling to tune his ear to the high tone of Uncle Henry's sallies, with the subtle persiflage against which Edith Wharton had warned. "I am fond of archeological comparisons. Just as Schliemann and Evans transformed our sense of antiquity, the techniques of the psychoanalytic movement will be revolutionary excavators of the sediments of early life. *Ach!* What we in the unconscious find would astonish you, Mr. James."

"The thought chills me to the bone," James said. "Doesn't it you, Horace?" Horace pointed to his moving cheek. The real reason for remaining silent was that Uncle Henry was in a playful mood and Horace was afraid of misplaying a card.

"Yes," James resumed, gesturing with his knife. "Didn't Schliemann find more than a dozen Troys, stacked like sardines on top of one another, before he guessed that the right one was 11B? At least, as I recall. How far, herr doctor, do you archaeologists of lost memories, of *temps perdu,* have to delve before you find your own 11B?"

"Very far. But the analogy is inexact. We don't grasp the repressions before they are brought up to light in the analytic work. The unconscious is by definition inaccessible, unlike the layered Troys. The search is often prolonged, and becomes the more difficult as we approach the deeply repressed, *la chose génitale.*"

Horace watched Uncle Henry's face register the French phrase. Freud spoke as casually as one might say "headache" or "cramp," but the words rang out in the dining room like the vibration of a dinner gong. Everyone glanced quickly at Theodora Bosanquet, the only lady present. She coughed softly and touched her napkin to her lips, darting a bland look at Uncle Henry, who blushed.

"Resistances. Hmmm," James said, trying to deflect the force of the artlessly sounded unmentionable. "To be sure. But no doubt you can depend on your, as one might say, tongue-loosening couch at Berggasse 19?"

"Ja, Herr James," Freud said, uncertainly, still groping for a key to his host's high conversational style.

While Horace and Theodora stayed behind—Horace, famished as he was for female companionship, welcomed her invitation for a long walk—the cycling expedition to Winchelsea proceeded as planned. It went without mishap but for a wild moment of which they would hear later.

As they were walking the links and laughing over the luncheon episode, Theodora confessed to Horace that Freud's clinical language made her blush, but not for herself.

"Mr. James," she went on, "is so fearful of indelicacy when he is dictating that he blushes at words that would pass muster in a Wesleyan Sunday School. The other day I was taking down a travel essay on the Remington when he mentioned the word 'navel' in connection with a Florentine statue and crimsoned like a schoolgirl!"

Her cough at the table had been intended as a cautionary signal to Dr. Freud. But he had failed to notice and, for all she and Uncle Henry could do to pull him back from the precipice, he had launched into an account of how as a student at the Salpetrière in Paris he had heard his teacher, the great Dr. Charcot, say of the origins of hysteria: *'C'est toujours la chose génitale. Toujours, toujours.'*

"You're right Theodora," Horace said. "Uncle Henry's manners are delicate. But I can tell you that he has a robust curiosity about all sorts of earthy matters, including 'the genital thing.' Mrs. Wharton told a funny story the other day: She and Uncle Henry had once visited George Sand's country house in France. As they walked in the back garden, gazing up at the windows, she said it would be interesting to know in which bedroom the great authoress slept. 'Far more interesting, my dear,' said Uncle Henry, 'would it be to know in which bedroom she did not sleep!'

"But of course, Theodora, you and I are ignoring the really startling development of the day—that they are becoming friends. Of a sort."

"I would have given odds against it," she said.

"So would I, having listened to all that grousing from Uncle Henry before Freud came."

The yet more startling news was that the master of Lamb House, after urging Freud to stay on for a few days, had enlisted for what Freud called "a short-term analysis." Horace had overheard the exchange in the hall just after luncheon and had recorded the discussion in his journal. It seemed to mark a turning point in what he and Theodora Bosanquet jokingly called "the clash of the titans." Uncle Henry was standing with his hands in his pockets, jingling the coins, and Freud, about to go up to his room to slip into his cycling kit, had his hand on the bannister.

Uncle Henry [wrote Horace], *in a continuation of the luncheon conversation, said, "I suppose, herr doctor, that you rarely cure your patients in fewer than many months, or indeed years, since there are so many sediments to delve into and 'resistances,' as you call them, to penetrate."*

SF: "Indeed, Mr. James. Many cases are intractable and require all but interminable analysis. Yet on some occasions the work can be done much more rapidly. Once on holiday in the Alps, I encountered a young serving woman at an inn where I was staying who complained of being haunted by the smell of burnt pudding. On its face, the symptom was baffling; but I was able to relieve it in a single conversation of an hour or so, no more. That was exceptional, of course. On the other hand, I completed a training analysis, as we call it, of my colleague Eitingon during a week's visit to us in Vienna. Of course, he was already conversant with our science. The term 'cure' is misleading, since one is often grappling with aspects of the human psyche that may be brought up to consciousness with hard work but in the nature of the case can no more be banished with some magic wand of a 'talking cure' than what the men of God call our fallen state. The best one hopes for is enhanced understanding."

HJ: *"You tempt me to apply for a 'short term' analysis of the sort you performed on your colleague and the servant girl, although with respect, sir, I cannot yet claim to be a devotee of your theory."*

Freud, as usual, did not quite catch Uncle Henry's teasing tone [Horace noted].

SF: *"Do you mean that, Mr. James? It would an honor be, albeit intimidating. In the absence of clinical contact with Shakespeare or Sophocles, you, sir, would provide a temptation for any analyst!"*

HJ: *"Well, since you again flatter me so extravagantly, my dear doctor, why on earth not? When shall we begin?"*

Horace, having recorded the exchange, lamented that there was no equivalent of musical notation in which cruder writers (he included himself) could signify what in Uncle Henry's talk was loud or soft, presto or andante or largo, what was said in a light spirit and what was solemn and funereal. "My impression," he wrote, closing out the entry, "was that the two great men were negotiating a dance card for a minuet—or is it a *pas de deux?*—of which neither had rehearsed the tempo, the melody or the steps."

Perched unsteadily on a bicycle rented for the day from Mr. Doyly's shop in the High Street, and conditioned by repeated tumbles into the Lamb House flower beds, Freud followed Noakes and James along the marsh road to Winchelsea. They paused several times to enjoy the sea view, took early tea and walked about the quaint old town for an hour or so. At four in the afternoon, as planned, they retrieved their machines and prepared for the return journey to Rye.

"Now, herr doctor," James said, pointing down the steep hill that led toward the intervening marshes, "this is a quite challenging leg of the journey. I usually walk my cycle down the incline because it can be difficult to control one's speed, and I recommend that maneuver, inasmuch as you are a beginner at cycling. Others, more daring, sometimes risk the descent by wheel. Noakes, who as you can see is a very athletic lad, may precede us."

Freud frowned and exhaled a cloud of cigar smoke, as if in defiance. "I shall chance it, Herr James," he said; and without another word hitched up his plus-fours, mounted his machine and flew off down the hill. James and Noakes watched with breathless horror as Freud whizzed down the 20-degree slope like a circus daredevil and flew as if catapulted onto the flatness of the marsh road half a mile below.

"*Crikey!*" cried Noakes. "He's a bloody fool, he is."

"Now, now, dear boy, he is our guest and we must indulge his whims."

Uncle Henry later reported the incident to Horace: "You are familiar, my dear young sir, with the treacherous hill that offers a straight shot down from our sister city to the Rye road? I warned him, but our m-m-magisterial friend from Vienna seemed to take it as a challenge, dubious cyclist that he is, and I feared that we might not see him again alive and that I should be pilloried the wide world over as the assassin of the budding science of psychoanalysis. But no! The gods watched over his rash Icarian plunge and when Noakes and I made our more cautious way down we overtook him, standing there beside his bicycle and still smoking his cigar as if nothing had happened.

"'You are quite the daredevil,' I said, relieved but a bit irked.

"'No,' he said, 'No daredevil Herr James. But I sometimes

fancy myself a *conquistador,* an adventurer in untested terrains, a taker of chances. It has been my way, whether out of doors or in the light of the lamp. So far, my luck has held.'

"I wondered, Horace, what other chances he takes and whether, *entre nous,* William was right in speculating that some of his papers have been written under the influence of cocaine. I am told that he has experimented with that new 'miracle drug,' and has written much about its beneficial effects. Do you suppose he was under its influence this afternoon? His only visible addiction appears to be tobacco. I am relieved to have him back here and safely tucked away in one piece!"

The report was rendered as Horace and Uncle Henry were turning off the lights downstairs. The great bell of St. Mary's was striking midnight when Henry James sat down at his desk in the oak bedroom to compose his nightly report to Edith Wharton.

. . . The calamity you foresaw, my dear Edith [he continued], *has come to pass. In a weak moment this noon, just after luncheon, I said to Freud: "You are most welcome, herr doctor, to stay on here for another week or so if your schedule permits, inasmuch as our conversations have barely moved beyond the larval stage." He laughed at my little jest & immediately took up my invitation; so there we are. I am not sure I would have issued the invitation had I witnessed the little cycling episode in leaving Wilchelsea. But in truth, I continue to find myself liking him & enjoying his company, if not his pretense as a daredevil on wheels. But here are significant* nouvelles*: As we were revising his schedule, he suddenly offered to perform a "short-term" analysis of your dull & uninteresting friend, the undersigned. I had suggested in jest that I might be a candidate & he immediately took me up. Just what he expects to find in the way of repressions in my banal cranium I can't guess. I have been pronounced* mens sana, *etc. etc. . . . by Dr. William James, with cer-*

tain exceptions. But Freud merely smiles, puffs at his cigar as he did this afternoon on the summit of the Winchelsea hill, & insists that he would be honored to psychoanalyze me as prox-ime accessit *to Shakespeare and Sophocles! (I doubt that he quite feels the idiomatic weight of such flattery in English.) He says he "will prefer" me—his idiom—to all other masters of the tongue now living. Thus, my dear, I am to be elevated to the Pantheon; & accordingly you are to genuflect in this direction at regular intervals during each workday & twice on the Sabbath.*

As for the arrangements, we must improvise. Freud tells me that in his consulting room at Berggasse 19, he usually sits out of view of his patients, who lie recumbent upon a couch & report to him whatever random thoughts and dreams steal into their heads, however fragmentary. He calls this "free association" & tells me he first stumbled upon the technique in the case of a young Viennese woman he calls "Anna O," not her real name. Her neurosis was relieved by what she was the first to call, inventively, "the talking cure." If Freud is right, it is the ultimate in mind-body connections and interactions, though I confess myself skeptical. We are to approximate the setting at Berggasse 19 in the Garden Room by shifting the sofa just a bit away from the bay window. He will sit behind me & I shall be staring at the bookcase. So you see, dear girl, that I have taken to heart your warnings & have not, so far, aborted our collegial communings by incontinent teasing. Rather the contrary. You seem not to credit me with the genuine deference I feel towards the diminu-tive Wizard of Berggasse 19. As we talk on, I find that he has astute things to say (I should have supposed as much from my too-cursory reading of his dream-interpretation tome—he writes limpid German but I fear my reading of it is less so). But the deuce of it is that like dear William he fondly believes in the effi-cacy of the "science" of dream intepretation as the "royal road" to the unconscious. So it may be. But mind you, the route is sur-passing odd. He stipulates that what is "manifest," which is to say obvious, in the stuff of dreams is merely a veil or screen for the "latent" meaning, which is not only abstruse but open to readings that are, to say the least, paradoxical. The new and prodigious Joseph at the Court of Pharaoh he may be; but the lean and fat kine are anything but plain old cattle! Be well assured, nonetheless, that I am eager to learn what prodigies of ennui the talking cure will dredge up from the "unconscious" of your devoted friend, Henry James.

2

Baltimore, Maryland, December 1941

From the moment Horace Briscoe dropped the letter to Anna Freud into the post office mail slot, it struck him, too late, as impudent. Right in principle, certainly, but hardly *suaviter in modo* and, worse, dripping subtle hints of journalistic blackmail. Hothead! he muttered as he climbed into his ancient Oldsmobile. He was not surprised when the letter elicited no further communication from London, where Sigmund Freud's effects were still being sorted and classified after his recent death. To complicate matters, young Winton Towson of the Baltimore *Sunpapers* soon appeared at his doorstep—or rather, his office at the Johns Hopkins English Department—where Miss Bladen kept her formidable vigil.

Towson appeared two days after Horace had mailed his brazen declaration of independence from what he now categorized as the Maresfield Gardens cabal. From behind his half-opened inner door, where he sat amidst a clutter of books and papers, Horace could hear the exchange. The dependable Miss Bladen said that Professor Briscoe was up against a tight lecture deadline (true enough) and hadn't a second to spare (preposterously untrue).

Horace recalled the spare, tall, inquisitive Winton Towson from the Henry James seminar ten years earlier—not only the best among fifteen good students but a youth of sometimes irritating persistence, never to be fobbed off with a casual response.

"Why is it old Marcher sees May Bartram as silvery?" he had

asked one day when they were discussing "The Beast in the Jungle." Horace had been reading and thinking about Henry James for almost forty years, but he hadn't a clue—guesses, yes, but no fixed answer. And then there was the unanswerable question inspired by yet another of the novellas: "Why did Henry James change the old maid's name from Tita to Tina in the New York Edition of 'The Aspern Papers'?" Who the hell knew? That was the answer, but hardly suitable for an English Department seminar filled with the young and earnest. The insistent voice could be heard again. "Can you tell me, Miss Bladen," Towson asked in his rattling bass voice, "whether the professor has received a copy of the 'case history' of Henry James he was expecting when I wrote my first article? The piece Dr. Briscoe believes was written by Freud himself?"

Miss Bladen had been told to shade the truth, as need might require, but to avoid outright lies.

"Professor Briscoe gets a great deal of mail," she said inventively. "I don't see it all."

"But how can I ask him without seeing him? Isn't he in there now? I can be in and out in five minutes."

"He's writing a lecture. Do you want an appointment? How about February 25th at 4 P.M.?"

"That's more than a month and there's a war on," Towson persisted. "Do you mind my saying all this is very weird? Professor Briscoe helped me generously with my first piece, but how suddenly the curtain rings down and it's all very hush-hush. As he used to say, 'something's rotten in the state of Denmark.'"

Horace, listening from the shadows of his office, chuckled. Towson had it right, except that the odor emanated from the Freudian citadel in London, not Denmark. And it was the smell of book-burning, made infamous some years before by Hitler's thugs. With sudden resolution, Horace pushed his swivel chair aside and opened the inner door.

"Oh Towson," he said, pretending surprise. "To what do we owe this pleasure?"

"I was on my way to a lecture, sir, and I thought I'd check on the Henry James matter—that Freudian 'case history' you told me about."

"Oh *that* . . ." Horace pretended to muse. He was trying to be a good actor, but that had never been among his talents. Towson was on the scent of a dangerous secret and, as usual, there was no brushing him aside. "Yes?" the reporter said.

"You might as well come in for a moment, Towson. Thank you, Miss Bladen." He led the way in and shut the door.

"Can you keep a secret, Towson?"

"To be honest, Professor Briscoe, we newspapermen aren't celebrated for our buttoned lips—secrets aren't exactly our stock in trade."

"I'm aware of that, but unless you can tuck this matter under your hat for a few days I can't talk to you at all. End of conversation."

"All right, sir. I promise. Word of honor."

"Then the answer to your question is this. I do have the case history and it's clearly authentic. And extremely interesting. Unfortunately, it's in danger of going up in smoke like Coventry and Rotterdam."

"*Jesus!* Why?"

"Because the Freudian inner circle has been spooked by some of the old man's remarks about the future of psychoanalysis—*obiter dicta*, as the judges call them. I don't think they're half as explosive as the Old Guard seems to think. But I can tell you I'm worried. The case history may be destroyed . . . burned."

"Holy cow," Towson said. "Like Jeffrey Aspern's love letters."

"Clever parallel. Life imitating art for about the millionth time."

"So the story is going to end with a Jamesian twist?"

"Not yet, if I can help it. Not while I have a copy of the translation and photostats of the manuscript. But I have to say, Towson: It never occurred to me when I decided to become a James specialist that I would be playing God in a plot in which the Cher Maître himself is a character!"

"What will you do?"

"I've told Anna Freud—and through her the other keepers of the flame—that I won't collaborate in vandalism. If they expect me to be a party to the suppression of a document of historical value they've got another think coming. To me, Towson, it's a basic question of intellectual integrity. How could I live with myself as a scholar if I rolled over for what those scaredy-cats in London are threatening? Especially now! What would separate it from Nazi book-burning, can you tell me?"

"Nothing, sir." Towson said, visibly startled. "Nothing," he said again with emphasis, then continued: "Gee, you seem really wrought up, Dr. Briscoe. I haven't seen you this mad since that dumb-bell in the James seminar asked you whether Hemingway and Fitzgerald hadn't 'eclipsed' Mr. James. All of us around the table held our breath, especially when he went on, 'I know you worship old Henry, Dr. Briscoe, but in my view it's high time the old boy just faded away. Who reads him anymore?' What was his name? Acheson? Anyway, he won't soon forget the roasting you gave him. It's a wonder you didn't kick him out. Did he get an F?"

Horace drew a deep breath, astonished and amused by Towson's powers of recall.

"I never give F's in seminars, Towson, but I give plenty of C's."

Horace realized that he *was* wrought up, and needed to calm himself. His agitation over Anna Freud's letter had already caused enough trouble for one day, including an uncharacteristic breach of collegial manners.

"Again, I've said no to London. That's as far as I've gone, but that's pretty far when you're dealing with the prophet's intimate circle, especially Ernest Jones and Marie Bonaparte. Matter of fact, I met Jones once in London when I was about your age. But that's another story. You'll have to sit on this till I decide. If I go ahead and publish, assuming you keep your promise, you'll have an exclusive. The scoop of a lifetime."

"Meanwhile, you'll let me see the old man's '*obiter dicta,*' as you call them? The case history—especially the passage where the old boy went over the hill?"

"Maybe. That's the carrot, my boy. But for a week or two you'll have to trot along with the carrot dangling before you. Now leave me alone to think." They shook hands and Towson turned to go, calling behind him, "Good luck, Dr. Briscoe."

Horace watched the young man vanish, with his peculiar loping stride, and was reminded, in a flood of nostalgia, of that far-off summer at Lamb House when he had witnessed the remote origins of the document he was now trying to save from the flames. What storyteller would ever have expected such an outcome? Art was never so wildly inventive!

The offending correspondence with Anna Freud had been relatively brief, and on the surface quite civil:

Dear Miss Freud [Horace had written on October 10, after inspecting the "case history of a great literary artist" she had sent him]:

I write first to say that it is easy to authenticate the "fragment of a case history . . ." Its subject is Henry James beyond doubt. In fact, the disguise is so thin that one needn't be a James authority to see through it. My guess is that your father wrote the fragment quite a few years after he visited James in Rye (note the reference to the "yellowed" state of his notes) and perhaps intended to expand it later. I can say of my own personal knowledge that the references to events and circumstances in Rye at the time are exactly as I recall them from the late summer and autumn of 1908. During my stay at Lamb House, I kept a diary and I also wrote regularly to my late mother in Newport. I can draw on those corroborative materials if necessary. I enclose a formal note of certification for whatever use you may care to make of it.

I may say that I do understand your uneasiness about your father's remarks on the prospects of the psychoanalytic movement, although they strike me as understandable if they reflect his intellectual collision with someone as formidable as Henry James. I gather that your father constantly revised his views about the movement—your movement—as differences inevitably arose. As I am sure you know, he doesn't say anything here about the relationship between science and art that he doesn't say at greater length and with more consideration in, for instance, the essays on Jensen's "Gradiva" and Dostoyevsky. I am sure you are aware, Miss Freud, that this greatest of themes—which in shorthand we call the relationship among science, art and religion—is as pertinent today as it was when your father and Mr. James met in Rye thirty-three years ago, and will continue to be years and even centuries hence. All three, as Freud and James fully understood, can be bent into dangerous absolutes, and all three, even science and art, into fanaticisms. Especially by followers of inferior intellect and sensibility. Need I instance the grim present? It is full of ominous signals. Mr. Churchill has recently said to the House of Commons that Hitlerism is made 'the more sinister by the lights of perverted science'—I believe those were his words, or a close paraphrase. And I hear rumors around this English department that Ezra Pound, in his Italian exile, is being wooed by the Fascisti to broadcast passages from his Cantos that condemn "usura," as he calls it, and are so loaded with crank funny-money theory as to be understood as reinforcing Nazi anti-Semitism. We'll see. At all events, as these two examples suggest, we are besieged by perversions of art and learning that remind us of the importance of such magisterial discussions as took place in Rye in 1908.

Accordingly, I propose to write an article or monograph about the Freud-James encounter, making use of the analysis itself but, if you wish, I can suppress any specific references to Dr. Freud's remarks on the future of psychoanalysis. Obviously, to this purpose, I would be grateful for your permission to quote from the case history. Wishing you the best of fortunes in these dark days for civilization, I am,

> *Yours truly,*
> *Horace Briscoe*
> *Edel Professor of English*
> *The Johns Hopkins University*

Dear Professor Briscoe [Anna Freud responded, two weeks later],

Thank you for your authentication of the "fragment of a case history . . ." I fear that I have imposed on your good time, inasmuch as a decision has been reached here to omit the document in its entirety from the archive of my father's writings. It clearly does not represent finished or considered work and there is no evidence that my father wished it to be preserved. Accordingly, the manuscript and the translations are to be consigned to the flames here at Maresfield Gardens. I feel quite sad about it. For some reason, Marie Bonaparte is especially keen that this "aberrational musing . . . so full of heresy," as she calls it, be blotted from the annals of psychoanalysis; and in this is supported by the others of the Committee, especially Dr. Jones. And since they played such a big role in getting my father and his family out of Vienna, I must consider their views and therefore ask that you return your numbered copy of the translation and, with regret, I must ask you not to quote from an artifact of the Freud Archive which, officially, will no longer exist. Yours faithfully,

> *Anna Freud*

Dear Miss Freud [Horace Briscoe wrote on November 20, 1941, in the letter he regretted as soon as he had dropped it in the mail slot]:

Believe me, I understand the worries that drive your colleagues into a state of panic. But aren't your father's remarks about the future of psychoanalysis typical of the gloom that Great Men occasionally feel about the fate of their movements? Dr. Freud's brilliant analysis of Michelangelo's "Moses" stresses Moses's self-possession at a moment of rage when he sees the Children of Israel worshipping the Golden Calf. The tables of the law are not yet cast down and broken. Your father clearly identified himself with that Moses of sober second thought. Hence in my view his musings deserve better at the hands of his disciples than that they should be dashed to smithereens like the first draft of the Commandments!

Confident as I am in your assurances that you, at least, dissent from this act of historical vandalism, I herewith serve notice that I shall preserve my copy of the case history in the name of Henry James studies, to which it is an invaluable addition. Moreover, an act of impulsive arson there in London would look very bad in the press. Even in the parlous state of the world, the news that the original has been burned would leak out and would place me in a very awkward position. The matter of its submission to me for authentication is already in the news here. What could I possibly say to enterprising reporters, especially Mr. Winton Towson of the Sunpapers *(whose preliminary article I sent you some weeks ago), when he calls to ask how the authentication is going? He was a student of mine some years ago. He is bright and tenacious and when he sinks his teeth into a subject he doesn't let go. Shall I be forced to tell him that a cabal of the Freudian Old Guard has lit a Nazi-like bonfire? Not even the war news could eclipse such a story! Hence I am strongly urging you and your colleagues there to reconsider. You have said already that certain of the Freud papers are to be locked away for years. Perhaps the escape from your current dilemma is to say that the case history manuscript has been placed among them, but that you are leaving it to me to authenticate the Henry James connection.*

Yours very truly,
Horace Briscoe
Edel Professor of English

Act of historical vandalism . . . Nazi-like bonfire . . . Those, with the blatant threat that he might spill the full story to the press, were impetuous and ill-considered touches in his last letter to Miss Freud, as yet unanswered. Those regrettable words still buzzed in his ear, even as he drove home to Roland Park that evening after Winton Towson's visit. To accuse Miss Freud and her colleagues, and she a refugee from the Hitler horror, of imitating their thuggish persecutors! No wonder Anna Freud was silent.

It was cold and rainy, and depressing, as he parked the car in the driveway and passed up the soggy walkway into the warm entrance hall, stomping the gathered wetness from his shoes. It was good to be home but not even the agreeable aromas from the kitchen relieved the gloom.

"Why so pensive?" Agnes asked, as she placed the roast on the table and poured the usual fragrant glasses of cabernet.

"It's that case history business," Horace said. "Young Towson—you know, my former student, the reporter who wrote the first story—dropped by the office this afternoon. He talked me into telling him at least part of the story. But a bit of publicity won't hurt if it heads off a bonfire in London."

"Is he going to print what you told him?"

"I've sworn him to secrecy. But I more or less promised him a scoop in exchange for his temporary silence. What do you think, dearest?"

"I was thinking how history repeats itself."

"What history?"

"Ours, Horace! You remember from back then how Uncle Charles and Henry James got into that ridiculous quarrel over the article in the Rye *Register*, the one implying that 'Uncle Henry' had gone bonkers and was being nursed back to sanity by Freud. Don't you remember how you three—Uncle Henry, Freud and you—marched down to the editor's office with blood in your eyes to demand a retraction? Could it really be thirty-three years ago?"

"*Tempus fugit.* How could I forget? What a time that was!"

". . . And Uncle Charles and Freud got into that shoving match in the foyer at Lamb House, with me waiting like a vestal virgin outside in the carriage."

"We all learned a lesson or two," Horace said. "Mainly, how hard it is to pin down the truth about anything. It made me a permanent skeptic about personal accounts of history. Everyone was wrong, as it turned out. Uncle Henry, who was anything but crazy, thought your Uncle Charles, who was anything but improper, had been defrocked—whatever the word is . . ."

"*Deprived,* dear . . ."

"Deposed, deprived, defrocked then—in effect, fired—as Archdeacon of Wells for some sort of sexual escapade. And your uncle thought Freud had come to town to 'cure' Uncle Henry of madness. Now we have the mystery of what Freud said about the future of psychoanalysis. At least that's how the faithful see it."

"*C'est la guerre*, Horace."

"*C'est la* fog *de guerre.* But now I've played the fool by writing that rude and belligerent letter to Miss Freud, the one I should have let you read before mailing it. Maybe, though, I didn't want to be prudent because I hoped I would have the guts to do what I'm doing."

"Which is?"

"Defy Miss Freud and print the case history. What do you think?"

"You know without asking, dear. You're the one who's always quoting what you call the Duke's rule: *'Publish and be damned.'* That's my position."

"I think I'll just do it. But I'll sleep on it first."

That night Horace Briscoe dreamed vividly; and in the best Freudian fashion the residue of the day took his dreams back to that colorful summer of 1908 when things got so comically mixed up and yet the world had seemed, as it actually had been, a great deal younger.

As usual, Horace's early evening dreams had a cinematic appearance, as if presented on some sort of screen. And as usual, when he was agitated, the vivid scenes had to do with Agnes, whom he had met there in Rye in 1908 and married two years later. He glimpsed her dimly as she was then, youthful, radiant, beautiful and soft-voiced. In the dream she was reclining on a couch that vaguely resembled their living-room sofa and seemed to stretch her bared arms in distress to a shadowy, bearded figure seated near her who puffed furiously on a long cigar. "Ve have many such instances seen, my dear," the bearded figure said in fractured English. "No vone else need ever know . . ." At that point Horace awoke with a start, calming himself with the recollection that he and Freud and Agnes knew that Henry James was not the only player in that far-off summer drama who had been analyzed. Horace turned on his pillow, smoothed the rumpled bedclothes, and listened for a few minutes to the wind and rain rattling the window-sash, then gradually subsided into less troubling dreams.

3

RYE, SUSSEX, ENGLAND, LATE SUMMER 1908

T he next day Horace carefully posted himself after lunch in the telephone room. He made a show of minding his own business and, to conceal what he was up to, hummed a tune from *The Mikado*, the Lord High Executioner's Song—a song he couldn't get out of his head. Maybe it had something to do with what he was about to witness. He picked up *Classic Crimes* by William Roughead and thumbed idly through it, keeping an eye furtively peeled on the scene in the hall where James and Freud were waiting for their food to settle. Uncle Henry was shifting his weight from foot to foot and jingling the coins in his pocket, glancing frequently at his watch. Freud paced in small circles, puffing his cigar and exhaling clouds of bluish smoke. Theodora Bosanquet passed along through the hall, adjusting her hat for departure. She peered into the telephone room and winked at Horace, as if to say, "What a notion!"

The grandfather clock chimed two and Henry James again consulted his watch. "It would seem that the rendezvous with my 'unconscious' is at hand," he said. He disinfected the world "unconscious" in his usual way with silent inverted commas.

"Yes," Freud said. "Would you allow me to describe this as an historic moment?"

"Historic? my dear sir. That is perhaps extravagant."

"On the contrary, Herr James. For the first time, so far as I am aware, a great writer is to be psychoanalyzed, and not from

a text or a painting or sculpture. Who knows what the repercussions will be in ages to come?"

Horace listened to the exchange, guessing that Uncle
Henry must be amused by Freud's self-dramatizing view of
himself. But then, hadn't he called himself a *conquistador* after
he shot down the hill in Winchelsea?

"Certainly, it will be a princely expenditure of time," James
said dryly, "and who knows but that it will yield a princely div-
idend?"

With that, the two of them marched through the dining
room, where Smith was removing the last of the luncheon dishes, and out through the open double doors into the garden.
Horace watched them cross to the steps of the Garden Room
and disappear. Oh, he thought, to be a fly on that wall! He pictured the drama he could not see or hear—the furniture being
shifted so that Uncle Henry could recline in the approved posture on the sofa, while just behind him Freud would draw up
one of the side chairs and sit in the bay window with his notebook. Then Uncle Henry would begin talking—he was a brilliant talker when he got wound up and would hardly need special arrangements to inspire him. Horace could hear the drone
of his voice, punctuated with rising exclamations of excitement
or amusement. Horace fought the urge to wander over to the
closed door as if strolling in the garden and try to hear the
voices through an open window. But Noakes and the other servants would notice. He told himself that Briscoes were gentlemen born and bred and did not eavesdrop, but still . . .

Horace, fascinated as he was, had to make do with imagination. He thought of the "publishing scoundrel" in Uncle
Henry's story, "The Aspern Papers," creeping around the
damp old Venetian palace and spying on the ancient Miss
Bordereau, once the mistress of a famous poet, with the obsessive aim of obtaining a cache of love letters. He recalled an
amusing Max Beerbohm cartoon that Uncle Henry loved. It

showed Henry James kneeling at the bedroom door of a country house looking with a magnifying glass at two pairs of shoes, a man's and a woman's. Prurience, Horace assured himself, is universal, along with other unattractive appetites. But Max Beerbohm's point might well be that Uncle Henry could reconstruct an intrigue without coarse intrusion, imagining the beast from a single thighbone, like the legendary dinosaur. His genius for inspired inference. When a friend told a choice anecdote as the seed for a story, and began going into detail, James would raise a cautioning hand; he could do without the mundane and smothering details. The hint, the germ, would do! His rich imagination would do the rest, would clothe it in vivid circumstance. *Go thou and do likewise,* Horace told himself. If he couldn't see or hear, he could at least envision.

. . . *The key to the whole business* [he wrote in his journal a few moments later], *is what I shall call—in my as yet unwritten thesis—the "Jamesian silence," the name I give to the implied and inexplicit: how under Uncle Henry's hand mere surmise is calculated to fire the reader's imagination. It is the concealed "figure in the carpet" where the bumptious and credulous young critic assumes that there must be some starkly obvious "key" to unlock the theme of the master's work—if only he could find it. It becomes an elaborate literary comedy. And of course there is the priceless illness from which poor May Bartram suffers and finally dies in "Beast": a "deep disorder in the blood." Surely it's art to go no further and let the reader fill in the blank. Kipling, by contrast, would spell it out to the last clinical detail of blood chemistry. H. G. Wells also. But not Uncle Henry, much as he admires and praises both Kipling and Wells. He is the Occam of artists, sparing all redundancies.*

But before this digression [Horace continued], *I was describing how the two sages, the scientist and the artist, processed into the Garden Room for the first session of Uncle Henry's psychoanalysis. I go off on this tangent because the two of them are so*

far apart, temperamentally: the master of suggestion with his par-
simonious hints that probe to the heart of any matter, and the
alienist who will no doubt line the royal road to Uncle Henry's
unconscious with garish signposts and mileage markers, inscribed
in bold letters. A high priest of philosophical realism.

Horace laid down his pen and laughed aloud at his flight of
verbal melodrama.

Well might Horace Briscoe wonder what was unfolding in
the Garden Room. Time and chance would seal the scene for
decades, though not forever. The encounter that Sigmund
Freud called "historic" was being independently recorded by
three brilliant hands, in revealing triangulation: Henry James
was writing every evening to Edith Wharton (who by then had
left England for her house in Paris); Horace, as we know, was
keeping a journal; and Freud himself was keeping voluminous
"process notes" about the analytic sessions that would be discovered, along with a partly written "case history," among his
papers in London after his death thirty-one years later.
Moreover, those notes had an uncharacteristic stylistic polish
about them, as if Freud knew and intended that he was writing
for the ages. But it would be a long time before Horace could
collate the recording intelligences.

Freud's first notes were dated August 24th:

I have written that men who were the favorites of their moth-
ers are imbued from the outset with a sense of destiny, of living
under a lucky star. Mr. J, as I shall call him to disguise his iden-
tity, is a writer of exceptional gifts and accomplishments and cer-
tainly answers to that typology. He was, he tells me, clearly his
mother's favorite among five children, four boys and a girl, and
she never bothered to make a secret of it. I became acquainted
with Mr. J through the good offices of his brother, a distinguished
colleague of mine in America, with whose writings (setting aside
the deplorable family preoccupation with "spiritual" phenome-

na) I have long felt a close affinity. It was he, for instance, who at an early stage postulated a theory of universal sexual ambivalence; and readers of my *Three Essays* will recognize that postulate as central to my own analysis of the etiology of the neuroses. The writer's brother had expressed anxiety to me on a number of scores. He felt Mr. J to be sliding into that melancholia (as he called it) which may be an inherited family susceptibility. The only sister of the four brothers, a brilliant woman who died ten years ago, appears to have been the victim of a crippling depressive neurosis, possibly also organic in its end stages (she died of cancer), which for no clear physical reason induced a semi-paralysis of her legs. She was bedridden for the last decades of her life and had moved after their parents' deaths to London with a female companion. She was dependent on that woman's faithful attendance and a bath chair for mobility. It seems to have been what the Americans sometimes call a "Boston marriage," of suspected sexual overtones. The father, a theologian and a man of independent wealth, had lost a leg by accident in youth and in his adult years had suffered what he strangely called a "vastation," an attack of utter desolation, in which he sensed a "fetid" presence "squatting" near him and somehow presenting personal menace. After months of depression the father had fought his way out of melancholia only by adopting the strange precepts and delusions of the Swedish spiritualist, Emanuel Swedenborg. He spent much of the remainder of his life writing vast and unreadable Swedenborgian tracts on universal love, poor man. My colleague, the writer's elder brother, suffered himself from a similar depression in young manhood. Two younger brothers fought in the American Civil War. One was severely wounded in the South while leading a troop of Negro soldiers and later became an invalid. He is now deceased. The other, while living, suffers from depression and alcoholic addiction.

Given this family history, would it be surprising if the writer, my host at his house in a small coastal town in southern

*England, were in fact predisposed to "melancholia"? I rather
expected him to be a recalcitrant analysand, heavily armed with
resistances, but so far to my surprise the case is otherwise. I have
rarely encountered a supremely gifted and serious man (other
than the Zuricher, Jung) who gave the appearance of being so
jolly. That is not to say that Mr. J's defenses are other than ingenious! His brother worries that he may be slipping into melancholia as the result of a variety of personal "crises." He has never
been married; his "late" writing style seems to his brother—
though I suspect fraternal rivalry here—so cumbersome and
indirect as to baffle ready understanding. He is at present in the
"perverse" process of rendering his earlier works into this same
late style; and he has sought relief from the chronic costiveness
that plagues the family in the dubious theories of a Dr. Fletcher,
the author of* The New Glutton *and* Epicure, *and accordingly
believes that every mouthful of food must be chewed dozens of
times. All of these signs indicate a predisposition to obsessional
neurosis with both oral and anal features (my own preliminary
speculation). Naturally, when Mr. J rather flippantly offered himself as a candidate for short-term analysis and invited me to stay
on with him for a while, I eagerly accepted. Not only was I eager
to see for myself whether his brother's worries are warranted; I
regard Mr. J as perhaps the supreme living storyteller, whose
inventiveness has given me great pleasure. It had not been my
intention to conduct a formal analysis. For many reasons the
analysis of a master storyteller has its complications, although it
promises to be worth the hazard.*

*Thus the present situation, as we commenced the analytic ses-
sions. I came down to R—by train on a Friday in late August
and was met at the station by his valet N, a diminutive and
amusing person, and a young American literary scholar, HB,
some sort of old family connection who is living in the attic and
who, I must say, watches me as if I were an exotic circus animal.
Our first session today took place in the writer's large writing*

office (once a mayor's banqueting hall, he tells me) and did not go very deep. Shortly after luncheon, the two of us moved to this "Garden Room" where Mr. HJ plies his craft with the aid of a tomboyish secretary, a Miss TB. She sits at a typewriter, while he "prowls," as he puts it, dictating to her his sinuous sentences which are, however, sown with the same abundance of homely metaphor as Shakespeare's plays in the ripeness of his tragic art. (Nothing like Hamlet's ribald punning, to be sure!) We shifted some of the furniture about so as to reproduce the usual analytic configuration. I assured Mr. J that we could sit face to face if he wished, although I had found in my usual practice that analysands find it easier to speak candidly if they cannot see reactions which, however unwittingly, spring to the analyst's countenance. He readily agreed that he wished to do the thing comme il faut (as he put it).

Mr. J has the unsettling habit of parrying serious and probing questions with facetiousness, and it is not easy to put one's finger on the exact tone in which he says anything. At one point, I grew impatient with the flippancies and evasions and proposed a deliberately provocative hypothesis, involving his own possible sexual repressions as reflected in his novels, and as expected he reacted angrily.

I asked, as casually as I could manage: "Why is it, Mr. J, that in so many of your recent stories people are having marital troubles?" That touched off a fencing match in which he exhibited many of the classic resistances. I tried to take him in flank, as it were, by putting to him the case of his heroine Isabel Archer in The Portrait of a Lady, *asking him why she rejects the suit of two virile men only to wed the effete narcissist Gilbert Osmond. My suggestion that it was perhaps a displaced fear of sexuality now drew a heated reaction. He became so angry that he sat up and glared at me. I thought he might call off the session and stalk out but I simply waited and he soon reverted from the tone of irritation to his usual urbanity. I have not yet mastered the arch-*

ness that is so often his conversational style. Many of his respons-es suggest that he is witholding secrets, some of them concealed by repression from himself. As I have observed in The Psychopathology of Everyday Life, *tics and motions of the fingers as they fiddle with the patient's watch chain (as he did throughout our session) speak eloquently of what is being verbally denied. In my account of the Dora case, I pointedly recalled the significance of her continued insertion and retraction of a finger into and out of her reticule. I have reserved the mention of such obvious symbolism to another stage of Mr. J's analysis . . .*

* * *

My dear Edith,

I must give you a glimpse of my first "analytic" session with the sage of Vienna. He is an homme formidable, *and amiable as well, however prey to the delusion that he has discovered a "science" of the human personality.* C'est trop fort! *His method is called "free association," through which, and through dreams, he purposes to retrieve scars from the oblivion of the "unconscious."*

Withal, given that he is persuaded of the "sexual" basis of neurotic complexes, he is not without humor & he is a painfully earnest reader & interpreter of my tales. As a mere tease, I asked him to read the manuscript of a story called "Fordham Castle" that I have just sent to Harper's magazine. When we had secluded ourselves in the Garden Room and arranged the settee so that I could face away from him and "free associate," I asked him what he made of the story. "If you please, Mr. James," he said sharply, "I would like you to do the talking." Then he turned the tables. He asked me what aspect of my life the story seemed to me to represent. Dear lady, he caught me off guard— be hanged if I know just what it was in my so-called psyche that yielded that slight harvest from a mustard seed. Social climbing of a frantic stripe had moved these deplorable women in my story to ditch their respective mate and mother so as to make their way up the slimy pole of "society," as they so narrowly conceived it. Simply, I said that such treachery seems to me grotesque. This social strife was a misery to which you were not condemned, given your exalted birth at the very tip top of the NY *quatre-cent, nor was I, though you were destined, alas, to be climbed upon.*

A silence then fell—Freud seems to regard silences as part of his technique—and both of us felt some awkwardness. I know from our informal talks that Freud longs to induce me to speak of my interest in—fascination, he calls it—"victimized" women and girls. He is, as I say, an assiduous student of my tales & regards them as "prime material" for psychoanalysis. When the silence grew unduly long & heavy, he came to my aid by suddenly saying, "Isabel Archer!."

"What about Isabel Archer?" I asked.

"Mr. James," quoth he, "what is so very striking about your admirable heroine in The Portrait of a Lady *is her obtuseness in judging men. She rejects both the fine English nobleman & her virile young countryman, to marry Gilbert Osmond, a cold, sordid, egotistical rake! What are Hamlet's words, ' . . . to decline upon garbage'? Why was it so important that she make herself miserable?"*

"Is it misery," I countered, "to feel an obligation to the child? But . . . important? Not in the least. It was merely my sense of her destiny, sheltered as she had been, that she should entangle herself with Osmond and fail to grasp betimes that Madame Merle was Osmond's mistress and the mother of his child and that both were practicing upon her."

"Destiny?" Freud persisted. "Could it be that she struggled against her destiny, which was to be a sexually fulfilled woman? Indeed, to touch the very bottom of this inquiry, Mr. James, is it perhaps your own fear of robust sexuality that is reflected in Isabel Archer?"

When he said that, my dear, I came quite close to bringing this "analysis" and the visit itself to an abrupt end on grounds that it was a front for mere prurience! I sprang bolt upright and turned to glare at Freud, who affected composure and refused to glare back. He assumed an air of urbanity, avoiding my eye, and gazing from the bow window, as if he had speculated on my favorite color. It came to me that he will say provocative things to test my limits & try to put me off guard, that it is an important part of his procedure, & that I must meet him on that turf without undue reserve or hotheadedness. I lay back and girded myself for his eternal preoccupation with "la chose génitale." I admit, under the seal of this confessional, that his choice of this rabbit hole for access to the nether world of my psyche took me by surprise. But I am determined not to be outfoxed. Meanwhile, pray that your supine Rye-bird will emerge from the auto da fe as more than a bare handful of ashes! Ever your overanalyzed, Henry James.

* * *

Throughout the summer idyl, Horace lost no chance to keep the company of Theodora Bosanquet. Unfortunately, however, Theodora was ten years older and treated him as she would a younger brother. And cordial as she was, she struck him as spinster-like and remote in the English way, and above all fiercely devoted to Uncle Henry. She placed being the great man's secretary above all worldly diversions. Horace had, in search of more eligible companionship, formed the habit of attending Sunday morning services at St. Mary's, whose lovely west façade, with its large lancet windows, towered just up the shady incline of West Street. It seemed a good place not only to seek spiritual guidance but to view pretty girls. He would have been embarrassed to say—to himself or to anyone else—which of the two appeals was the larger on Sunday mornings.

He had grown to like the services, with their flavor of Oxford ritualism, with a good deal of chanting and colorful vestments on festival days, usages that were a far cry in their opulence from the high and dry churchmanship of the Episcopal parishes of his Rhode Island boyhood. Horace admitted to himself in candid moments that a taste for Puseyism was creeping over him, and that his low church kin back home would be shocked if they knew it; but the allure of ritualism, he also acknowledged during the Confession of sins, was an inescapable concomitant of an eye for the young women of Rye.

Horace had formed the Sunday morning habit, moreover, of stationing himself at the door of Lamb House half an hour or so before the bell tolled for the morning service. He was to be seen standing there, in his top hat and frock coat, idly twirling one of Uncle Henry's walking sticks, pretending to enjoy the morning air but in fact keeping an appraising eye on arriving families that included young women as they passed along.

It was on just such a fresh midsummer Sabbath, a few weeks before Freud came, that he had spied for the first time a stunning girl in a blue smock with matching broad-brimmed straw hat and ribbons, dark hair and glowing complexion, accompanied by a tall, fierce-looking clerical figure in black who wore gaiters. That gentleman turned out to be an acquaintance of Uncle Henry, who recognized him easily from Horace's description. But Uncle Henry's reaction was qualified by subtle signals of wariness. Horace did not tell Uncle Henry exactly why he was asking about the figure (who turned out to be none other than Archdeacon Fengallon). The tall clergyman with the gorgeous girl on his arm was not among Uncle Henry's favorite fellow townsmen. The nagging question, therefore, was how Horace might arrange to be introduced. The English, he knew, were sticky about such things. The Archdeacon was that dissident at St. Mary's who could usually be heard, as the parishioners filed out of church, rallying the rector in a booming voice, and with apparent good nature, on the "romanizing" tendencies of the St. Mary's service.

I attended matins today [Horace wrote in his journal] *and as the choir processed in I saw again that radiant girl, that true Petrarchian Laura, I first spotted walking up West Street last Sunday morning. She is one of the choristers. But how to meet her? Uncle Henry, sympathetic as he is in most matters, apparently gives her uncle a wide berth. The uncle looks about as welcoming as a snow-capped alp. Is it sacrilegious to pray for an introduction?*

On the very next Sunday, it seemed that his prayers had been miraculously expressed by the recording angel to the throne of the Most High and speedily answered, as if by telegram. Horace became aware that the girl at whom he had been secretly stealing glances from behind one of the old tombstones had returned his gaze, smiling! She had spotted him, as he lurked on the fringes of the crowd and—yet more miraculously—she was now marching determinedly toward him.

"You are an American, I can tell by the way you move," she proclaimed, smiling cordially, "and a stranger here in Rye. Why are you staring at me like that?" Horace's tongue was paralyzed—what was the biblical phrase? It *clove to the roof of his mouth?* It was not merely his tongue that seemed stuck; it was as if his entire physical self were frozen like a still image cast by one of those magic lanterns which were said to be becoming so popular on the other side of the Channel in France: the sort that projected colorful, even mobile human figures on the wall. And thinking of tongues, her voice seemed to him no less than angelic—melodic as a flute and . . . (he groped for the texture of it) . . . yes, *silken*; that was it. It sounded the soft, sensual music of delicate fabrics rubbed together. As he stood there, stricken dumb and red-faced, he knew that he must at least try to pick out her singing voice when next there was a choir processional. Was there evensong on this Sunday night? If so, he would be there, come hell or high water! At the moment Horace could think only in banalities, and found to his astonishment that he didn't care.

"Y-Y-Yes," he at last stammered. "I *was* staring; if you are offended I do beg your pardon." He looked dizzily into her green eyes and for a moment words failed him. Then, in a voice choked with nervousness, he elaborated. Yes, he was an American, a student of literature, working on a thesis about Uncle Henry, er, Mr. Henry James, who lives, you see, just there, down West Street. He pointed down toward Lamb House, whose façade could be seen from the churchyard.

"Oh, everyone here knows Mr. James," she said. "He and his little dog, Max, pass my window on Mermaid Street almost every day. I sometimes come out and pet Max." Yes, obviously, Horace reminded himself: As the owner of the town's principal residence, its architectural showplace, Uncle Henry would be known to everyone. And that he was a guest there might be a passport, a *laissez-passer,* to who knew what sheltered places, including hers.

"I am Agnes Fengallon," she said. "You must come to tea, Mr. Horace Briscoe. I shall ask uncle to invite you. Is Mr. James really your uncle?"

"Not literally; I am told to call him that as a courtesy because my best friend, Billy James, is in fact his nephew. He lives in Boston. And who is your uncle, if I may ask?" Horace inquired, as if he didn't know—anything to prolong the encounter. Surely, the God who had answered his prayer so quickly would forgive him this tiny pretense.

"He is just there," she said, pointing across the churchyard, "the tall man in gaiters, Archdeacon Fengallon. He is jolly controversial." As usual, the Archdeacon appeared to be "wigging" two clergymen, literally shaking his long hair in disapproval. "He used to be dean of Wells, and before that a fellow of Exeter College in Oxford. You will like him, Mr. Briscoe, and he will like you. He is forceful, but a dear man. He is my guardian. My momma and papa are in Kenya with the Colonial Service."

Horace, now inured to English reserve, was astonished by the young woman's bubbling friendliness. But above all, he was lost in giddy admiration of her sparkling eyes and dark hair, with its faint coppery sheen, glowing in the sunlight, and a figure to match.

"Well, goodbye, Mr. Briscoe," she said. "I must rescue Father Morris from Uncle." Opening a blue parasol, she turned to go, leaving Horace with a promise that Uncle Charles would send a card—an invitation—to him at Lamb House. That had now been many long days ago, and every postal delivery brought Horace dashing to the door.

Meanwhile, Horace found that his concentration had been shattered by the mood of dreamy distraction that he had read about in books, wondering whether he would ever experience it. Now here it was. He sat upstairs at his desk, staring at the pages of Uncle Henry's story "The Death of the Lion," in a recent number of *The Yellow Book*. He could see the words well enough but they transmitted little of the comedy to his smitten brain. "Agnes," he kept repeating, "*Agnes, Agnes, Agnes . . .*" Wasn't there a saint named Agnes?

That scene in the churchyard had preceded the arrival of Dr. Freud and the beginnings of the "short-term analysis," already described. Horace's initial urge to eavesdrop had subsided and for the first time since the encounter with Agnes Fengallon, he actually became absorbed in a book—the "true crime" volume he had pretended to read while furtively watching Uncle Henry and his guest disappear for their consultation. Absorbed as he was, he became dimly aware of voices only when the two sages re-entered the house and passed briefly in and out of the oak parlor, where James apparently wished to show Dr. Freud one of the paintings. It was about three fifteen. Horace put down the Roughead book, marking his place, and listened. James and Freud had come out into the hall and were each bowing and taking leave of one another. The former looked slightly disconcerted, his feathers ruffled. Freud seemed preoccupied and headed for the stairs with his notebook in hand.

"Shall we see you again at tea-time, herr doctor?" James called, as Freud reached the first landing.

"By all means," Freud called and closed his door. James crossed the hall and peered into the telephone room. He silently beckoned Horace to follow. "Shall we walk a bit in the garden?" he asked, fastening a leash to Maximillian, the little dachshund.

James remained silent for some minutes, then broke out.

"Horace, what do we really know of our guest's theories? Are they within the compass of civilized discourse, or is the man to be regarded as a mere p-p-pretentious, p-p-prurient charlatan?"

Clearly something had been said in the Garden Room that Uncle Henry considered out of order. "I haven't the least idea, sir," he said, naturally giving no hint of his unworthy urge to eavesdrop. "I have heard your brother Dr. James speak of him with great interest. But, as you know, his theories are Greek to me, except insofar as they have to do with 'infantile sexuality,' whatever that is."

Horace was dissembling. His grasp of Freud's theories was firmer than he admitted. Why then did he play dumb? He did not like to face the likelihood that there was a trace, a mere smidgen, of duplicity and pretense in his character; so he assured himself that it was a question of deference: He couldn't see it as his role to lecture Henry James on any subject. Part of it, however, was an instinct to bide his time, look and listen. So far as the growing distraction of Agnes Fengallon allowed, his summer's mission at Lamb House was to garner materials for his thesis. If he wrote it well, that paper could make his reputation; and he was not without ambition. Yet another part was a sense that Henry James filled an emotional emptiness left to Horace in mid-adolescence by the sudden death of his father: a remote figure to him now, ever more dim in death. John Leppard Hopkins Briscoe had been a remote and elderly figure, more grandfatherly than fatherly, a decade and a half his mother's senior. His father's health had been undermined, his last years darkened, when the Harvard Press canceled its agreement to publish his life's work, a 1500-page historical work called *Raleigh's Innocence: The Ultimate Vindication, With Personal Addenda.* It was to prove that Sir Walter Raleigh had been framed and imprisoned by the manipulations of his arch-enemy Robert Cecil, the adviser of King James I. But by the time his father had at long last begun the final polishing, after 20 years of work, his diligent researches had been upstaged and the publishing contract revoked. That it was eventually published after his father's death with family funds was, of course, no consolation to the deceased historian. As for the "personal addenda," they had to do with the claim, traditional in the Briscoe family, that they were descended from Raleigh, the Elizabethan adventurer who had planted the first English colony in America, at Roanoke Island. His father's sad story was a parable, Horace deeply believed, of the perils of perfectionism. The yellowing manuscript still lay in a bank vault in Newport, and like the limited published edition, long forgotten. But among the factors that had distanced his evanescent father from Horace lay the sense that Briscoe senior had been as worn in spirit as in years: tired, depleted, the Briscoe blood, even if there had been an early infusion of the buccaneer, dwindling to a trickle. Horace had read in his recent researches that Freud, too, was the late son of an elderly father and a young mother, and the latter's favorite: her "golden Ziggy." That, by fascinating coincidence, made three of them—himself, Freud and Henry James—united by the common bond of fathers aged, damaged and daunted before their time. But there was one difference. Aesthete and cloistered gentleman historian that Horace's father was, he had not been a disciple of Swedenborg like the elder James. Decidedly not.

Henry James's accelerating pace and a sharp outcry jolted Horace out of his reverie. "Confounded little beast!" he shouted, tugging at Max's collar, although the small dog, feeble with age, was as docile as usual. Max had clearly become a very unlikely scapegoat for James's agitation.

"Dr. Freud," Uncle Henry said, stopping and addressing Horace face to face, "is urging this so-called 'short-term analysis' in exotic directions. Does he consider that he is analyzing the m-m-mad, b-b-b-bad and dangerous Lord Byron or, God save the mark, Casanova rather than a sheltered old storyteller?"

Horace could not think of a reply to this outburst that seemed other than silly and merely stood there looking, he was sure, quite blank and imbecilic. Uncle Henry was using him as a sounding board, however, and no answer was expected or required.

"Soon," James said, "he will be probing the question of my . . . my . . . amorous secrets! As if I had any worthy of exploration! He will be quite bored."

"I am sure nothing you say will be boring," Horace said, not intending flattery. He was surprised to hear Henry James disclaim "amorous secrets." With his keen longing to hear from Agnes, a romantic condition he had not yet discussed with anyone, he now imagined that everyone must have amorous secrets, and plenty of them. He had heard Henry James speak fondly on several occasions of a lady, a writer, a Miss Constance Fenimore Woolson, who before her death in

Venice some years earlier had been a great friend of his—
"great and dear friend" was the phrase Uncle Henry used.
Horace's casual reading of these scattered confidences was that
James might well have been in love with Miss Woolson, and
might even have been intimate with her. After all, they had
once shared a house in Florence for some months. And there
was, too, the question of Mrs. Wharton. She was, of course, a
married woman, though bonded to an invalid from whom she
was estranged. She had often visited for tea or luncheon,
accompanied only by her chauffeur, Cook. Was that friendship
free of amorous overtones? Edith Wharton was a vigorous and
attractive woman, much younger than Uncle Henry, with a fine
figure (especially in the bust). It was hard to tell whether her
blend of veneration and teasing might have romantic overtones. But Horace had not been invited to go with the two on
their motor tours of Sussex and Horace attached little importance to his idle speculations. Now, as they paced through the
garden with Max tugging at his leash and Uncle Henry plant-
ing his cane emphatically at every other step, the agitation
seemed to subside. Uncle Henry was preparing to resume his
"social simper" in time for tea.

Between bouts of lovesickness (as he now called it in his
journal), Horace continued to *ache* to know more of what was
going on in the Garden Room during the analytic sessions.
Uncle Henry was now taking the ordeal in stride. His mood
had brightened remarkably; and when Horace asked how the
"analysis" was progressing, he merrily said "better, much better," but did not elaborate.

It was all Horace could manage to keep his mind on the
work that had brought him to Lamb House, with this priceless
dispensation that he was living in proximity to his subject.
Henry James, Horace was well aware, vehemently opposed
biographical investigation of writers, himself in particular. Still,

he reserved the right to expose the lives of others; and he was weighing an invitation to write an "appreciation" of Mrs. Wharton for an "obscure transatlantic rag" (Uncle Henry's term). He would ordinarily have dismissed the invitation out of hand, he said, but for his affection for Edith Wharton and his sense that she would relish such a profile by his hand. But the audience would be tiny.

"If one is to make the effort," he announced to Horace, "of which, to be sure, she is beautifully deserving, one would hesitate to bury the glowing talent of tribute in so deep and dark and indeed misplaced a hole." Horace had added the remark to his collection of the writer's pithy metaphors.

My dear Edith [Henry James wrote on the day of the foregoing exchange with Horace],

Behold the Rye-bird fluttering on the limed twig of Dr. Freud's inquiry, of which I must tell you the latest. The man is a sort of wizard, with a genius for invading one's privacy. I complain, but I have stopped asking myself why I agreed in the first place to submit. Perhaps because I am that queer monster the artist, & who knows what strange grist to my mill may result? There is, moreover, some mysterious benefit. I have rarely felt so much lightened of cares. It is as if some devot of the old faith dutifully trekked every day to the confessional to be purged of his sins. In our conversation today Freud pressed me to discuss my friendship with Fenimore Woolson, a story which you of course know well.

The result was shocking in the extreme, though not in the way he supposes.

I grovel in shame to tell you with what schoolboyish naughtiness I behaved, but it seems to me a good way of dealing with his everlasting prurience. I retain a growing affection for Freud, all 135 enviably diminutive pounds of him, but he pushes me to the limit of patience with his infernal probing for "la chose géni-

tale." So I contrived today to lay a trail beneath his nose, giving him just what he is looking for in tantalizing dollops and rations, & largely making it up as I proceed. It is, I must boast to you my dear, a masterpiece of fictionalization. The fish nibbles eagerly at the hook, takes it in his mouth as one gives the twitching twine all the play it needs. The Viennese sage is very curious about poor Fenimore; and I sense that he is fixed on the idea that your ultra-celibate Rye-bird will eventually confess to having been drawn to her bedchamber. Et pourquoi pas? *Our sessions are supposedly confidential, although today I threw up to him the instance of his clever little "fragment of a case history" of the girl called Dora. He said by way of justifying his exposure of it in print that it was a special case but I said, "all your cases seem special, herr doctor." He speaks of secrets of the alcove, as he calls them, in general terms; but I suspect that he is bent on discovering the secrets of* my *alcove! So today I said, not very seriously, that "a certain literary lady" had tried on three occasions to seduce me: once in Florence at the Villa Bricolli; once at a wayside inn on Lake Geneva; and a third time in Paris. I said that I was at times sorely tempted; but that such a liaison would have been quite unfair to the maiden, inasmuch as I am married to my work & have no intention of practicing* polygamy—or even bigamy! *I thought surely that the little joke would signal to him that I was teasing. But no! So I proceeded to the most preposterous fable: I could not resist feeding him the comic absurdity that I "buried" poor Fenimore's dresses in the Laguna at Venice after her death. It is a tale of such patent implausibility that when I first invented it years ago I never dreamed that anyone but a little girl might swallow it whole; and in the beginning it was not associated with Fenimore at all. You recall the gist of it—that after Fenimore fell, or threw herself, from that window in the palazzo when she was so very ill, I had myself rowed out into the Lagoon with a bundle of her dresses and tried my best to sink them into the depths. I set this little fable afloat for the enchant-*

ment of little ears, just whose I long ago forgot, but chiefly to mock those who think that all writers are half mad. Certainly I did not intend to add another layer of mystery to the sad tale of Fenimore's demise. So far as I recall the remote inception of this fable had nothing to do with her at all—nothing!

Indeed I feel foolishly supererogatory reminding you, my dear, who were once a moppet yourself, how entranced little ones of your sex are by dolls and such, including their miniature dwellings and wardrobes. As I recall, I was once spinning out a fable about brilliantly sequined and spangled dresses of a fairy princess who had fallen asleep for want of a prince to kiss her, when the child piped up, "But then what became of all her pretty things?" and on a moment's naughty inspiration I said: "Why, dear child, they were too beautiful to be stored and forgotten in a dusty old attic and so a kindly knight-errant took them far, far into the lovely Venetian waters, where even now they may sometimes be seen on nights of the full moon glowing luminously on the surface for the pleasure of children who believe in fairy tales." I drew upon this inspired little tale in romancing about Fenimore. I was carried away, I suppose, may the Author of Peace and Lover of Concord forgive me!

My dear Edith, the affair is bizarre in the extreme. As I now explore its remotest origins it began as the inane donnée *of a possible little "ghost" story. A man whose wife displeases him with her puritanical abstentions and her pthistic physique seeks, when she finally fades away, to blot out all memory of her. He has himself rowed out into the Venetian Laguna with her tiny, doll-like dresses, with the idea of sinking them from sight. But a breeze comes up, the first breath of the dread Sirocco, and inflates them with air. Try as he may to push them under with the aid of the puzzled gondolier, they stubbornly float. Finally, overcome with disgust at the oddity of the business, he gives over & is rowed back to the piazza. There he orders a bottle of Pinot Grigio & waxes very drunk. He persuades himself that he will never see the dresses again; & yet months latter he receives a package at his palace. To his horror he finds that some kindly soul has taken it upon himself to return the dresses to him, having found a label carrying his name! . . . I never took the story beyond that point & have no recall, really, of how this silly yarn became enmeshed with the story of poor Fenimore. Yet there it is again, reborn in this confounded "analysis." As the tease went on this afternoon in the Garden Room, with your Rye-bird stretched out on the set-tee, I asked myself silently out of what perversity I draw it out. Is the question answerable? Perhaps not, or perhaps Freud with his new science will dredge up the answer from my "unconscious" before I make a full breast of the prank . . .*

Notwithstanding this admission of mischief to you, I fear this fable may lead an afterlife, even if I should repudiate it and try to stamp it out. And that is why I regularly weed all telltale documents from my archives, any that may absorb the pointless curiosity of future "publishing scoundrels."

Incidentally, Freud tells me (not in our analytic session but at tea) that he also is dedicated to a similar biographical prophylaxis: He destroys papers & notes wholesale, he says, but imparts to the act a characteristic egotism. He speaks of "cheating" future biographers who, he is confident, will inscribe reams & reams of paper & print with the chronicles of his genius. I do wonder if he weeds well. He thinks of himself as the new Copernicus, reordering the heavens. It grows late & the candle flickers in the breeze of early morning. Ever your devotissimo, Henry James.

From Freud's process notes for the same occasion:
. . . Today Mr. J seemed preoccupied and I immediately asked why. He said he was very worried about his friend Mrs. Wharton, the novelist, who is just now in Paris.

"She and I are not intimes," *he said, using the French term, "not so as to tell all but . . . There is the question of poor Fullerton." The name was strange to me and I asked who the*

gentleman might be. "He is Morton Fullerton, the Paris correspondent of the Times—*the* London Times—*and a friend . . .
We, that is, Edith and I, have been advising him on a dreadful
personal dilemma, a most disgusting threat. He is being black-
mailed by an unscrupulous woman with whom he was* intime"
(*I note the repetition of the French term; it was as if Mr. J were
handling the sexual reference with tweezers). Further silence.
"You may wonder, herr doctor,"* he resumed, *"what the connection is. You see, not even the faintest flicker of carnal or romantic emotion eludes my notice. I could see when the three of us
were together that, well, Fullerton is an accomplished seducer;
and I believe that he and Edith are* intimes *and I feel myself
much to blame."*

"To blame?" I asked, "for what?"

"For their adultery. You understand, she is not free; there is a
Mr. Wharton, who suffers miserably from gout and other ills and
thinks of me as a friend." *I could immediately guess that this Mr.
Wharton is of the neurasthenic type, a debilitated hypochondriac, and I wondered what harm there could be in his lonely wife's
affair with Fullerton. If there is a case for sexual freedom, this is
certainly one of them. And to think that my colleagues in Vienna
initially questioned my theory that men also could be "hysterical," on the basis that the Greek word refers to the uterus. My
mind wandered briefly to this as Mr. J was talking and I missed
his reflection on my earlier question.*

"She is a vulnerable woman," *he said,* "though of course ever
so much more gifted and less isolated and lonely than poor
Fenimore Woolson."

"Tell me about poor Miss Woolson," *I said, imagining that
she must be a character in one of the novels I had not read.* "You
call her 'poor.' Why is that?" *His excited reaction, flooded with
affect, told me that I had touched the emotional trigger for which
I had been groping.* "Ah," *he said, sitting up and turning to me,*
"it is not a matter for casual causerie," (*more evasive French*).

He paused. "She died in Venice years ago, in the oddest circumstances. But this may be none of your business, herr doctor."

"If it produces such undischarged emotionality," I answered, "then it is quite the business you and I should be exploring. Anything that springs to mind in the analytical situation is my business, precisely." More silence. He lay back again on the settee, drew a large handkerchief from his pocket and wiped his forehead. "Je me répète, mon cher docteur" (the French again), "c'est secret, très secret." More silence. Then he resumed his narrative, as if he had not called it "secret."

"We buried the poor lady's dresses in the Lagoon." I thought perhaps I had misheard him, or misunderstood the idiom; or perhaps he had meant to say that the "poor lady" herself had been buried in the Lagoon, unlikely as that might be. The silence had now grown so oppressive that I feared Mr. James had become aphasic at the traumatic recollection. He blew his nose loudly. Since he was facing away from me, in the direction of the bookcase across the room, I could not be sure whether or not he was weeping.

"Come now," I said, trying to maintain a tone of clinical neutrality. "How long ago was this? And could you elaborate? Nothing is clear to me."

Another long silence. Then with perfect composure he took up the story again. He said that the poor lady was a certain Constance Woolson, the descendant of an eminent American writer, James Fenimore Cooper, and an accomplished storyteller in her own right, who did not hear well—I noted the oddity of this random detail and waited for its significance to announce itself.

"Deeply melancholy following her father's death," he said. "We were often together in Florence and Genoa. We lived in the same house at Florence, on Bellosguardo: the Villa Brichieri. I was writing 'The Aspern Papers,' which I believe you have read . . . "

"Yes," I said, "I read it years ago. Tell me what the salient associations are for you."

"Ah," he said, "there was the germ of a story—two stories, really—making the rounds of our little circle in Florence. It was said that the ancient mistress of one of the romantic poets, Byron I believe, had survived in great age . . . a living link with what I call 'the visitable past' . . . A sea captain whose name now escapes me tried to obtain the letters but they were in the possession of a homely niece. She offered to give them to the questing captain if he would marry her! That was the grain of sand round which the nacre gathered; hence my story. But to answer your question directly, I now associate with it the demise of privacy: what you call the secrets of the alcove, of the bedchamber. Now they are exposed and explored publicly. As an American lawyer, Brandeis, has recently written in the Harvard Law Review, they are 'proclaimed from the rooftops.'"

Of course I could hardly miss his insinuation: that those "secrets of the alcove" are the preoccupation of psychoanalysis. But I did not interrupt.

"Miss Woolson did not survive," he said.

"The ancient mistress?"

"No, Miss Woolson, my friend, the writer."

"Yes, you were speaking of her dresses—their burial in the Lagoon. What happened?"

"Alas, her melancholy overcame her one night in Venice when she had been very ill. She . . . fell from the upper story of the palazzo where she was recuperating. She did not survive."

"A suicide? I seem to recall reading of this."

"I balk at the word suicide, herr doctor. There was no proof of that. It is possible that she was simply taking the night air at her open window and lost her balance."

"Is it important to you to think that her fall was accidental?" I asked. The question administered a visible shock; for again Mr. James fell silent and the silence persisted.

"*Important? Yes, I suppose it is, in a measure . . . Self-slaughter is not a charge to be bandied lightly about . . . *"

"*And because in that event you might have felt some responsibility?*"

He ignored my question; so I changed tacks. "*What do you now feel, now associate, with the event? What, for instance, are your associations with water, with the Lagoon where you say you buried her dresses?*"

"*Water. Hmmm. Styx. Lethe. Oblivion. The crossing over from life to the kingdom of the dead. That sort of thing. But on second thought not oblivion. Merciful heavens, I did not wish to forget. Never that.*"

"*You do agree that it is quite uncommon to be rowed out into the Venetian Lagoon for the purpose of 'drowning' or sinking a lady's dresses?*"

"*Did I say drowning, herr doctor?*"

"*Perhaps that was my word, Mr. James. My notes on the last session are not at hand, but could there be some resentment? Some unadmitted dislike of her? Some reason for trying to extirpate her memory?*"

"*That, sir,*" he said in a stilted tone that is the telltale of unease or concealment, "*that is an impertinence.*" I could see that we were making some progress, however qualified.

I pause here to note that I had detected some dawning signs of the approaching transference. Today, as I was reiterating a brief outline of psychoanalytic theory he said: "*Just what are we—are you—seeking? Sometimes I feel like our friend Prince Hamlet, when he complained of being played like a pipe. I was once before deluded by the bootlegging of 'scientific' ideas into life: My brother William became a devotee of the idea of entropy as applied to us. The human being was like a fine engine which if too passionate might burn itself into a cinder: a reduction of the incalculably human to mechanics. It seems to me that your* 'science' is also mechanistic in essence, a hydraulics of the mind. To what end?"

"To no especial end," I said, "if you have in mind some ultimate enlightenment or conversion. I don't pretend to a vision of the good life, except as it might be promoted by enhanced consciousness, by dragging up to the light of day the deeply repressed matter that stealthily controls our behavior without our awareness. Even yours, Mr. James!" I added, knowing that he is a superbly intelligent man with deep intuitive insight. I was careful not to labor the little tutorial.

"Your outpouring of affect suggests that you are in denial; that your relationship to this "poor lady," Miss Woolson, was more complex, more ambivalent shall we say, than you admit— even to yourself. I must add, Mr. James, that it is wholly immaterial to me that you deny this."

Just now, in these random notes, I alluded briefly to the transference, as we call it, in which the analyst becomes a sort of stand-in or impersonator for authority figures in the patient's past, most often the powerful imago of the father. In Mr. James's case, however, I am at a loss to identify the slightest sign of a transference, usually so obvious. I cannot doubt that his parents, whom he evidently revered, were very strong and benign influences—benevolent remembered ghosts, as it were, who require no strenuous laying. So far, then, in conventional analytical terms my sessions with Mr. James must be accounted a failure, inasmuch as he does not seem to identify in me any reimbodied imago from the past, infantile or later. He does readily accuse me, constantly, of a prurient desire to peer into his "secrets of the alcove" (he has picked up that term from me, and relishes it). I am beginning to ask myself, however, whether such secrets even exist. Either they do not or my methodology and authority are too crude to bring them to light when they are harbored by genius.

*

"Bosh!" he exclaimed, when I accused him of denial. "I deny nothing! I have told you already of the lady's efforts to seduce me. But I must say, Dr. Freud, that you dredge deep."

"'Bosh'? Do you mean nonsense? It can't be nonsense if you react so emotionally. But do continue," I said; he did so, and it was as if a dam had suddenly burst and spilled tons of backed-up water.

"Poor Fenimore. She had suffered unbearable earaches in Oxford in that autumn of 1892. They brought on fearful attacks of melancholia and I visited her regularly at her rented flat in Beaumont Street . . . My sister Alice had just died and Fenimore and I were counting our losses, coming to terms with bereavement. Then she was prostrated in London, although finally the removal of some horrid eardrum prosthesis relieved the pain and in May she was able to go to Venice. We met in Paris. I had been in Switzerland, writing . . . "

"Yes?"

"You speak of dreams, herr doctor. This had been a nightmare, in some ways it became a comic nightmare. She summoned me to Paris. We dined at Fontainebleau, then returned to her small hotel. Paris was at its most beautiful—the flowers, the chestnut trees in bud and small leaf. It was, again, late April or early May. Who would not feel a surge of romantic feeling? . . . But no, I shall stop there. The poor lady is at rest now in the Protestant cemetery at Rome, near Shelley, as she would have wished . . . "

It seemed to me that we stood on the brink, some threshold at which he balked, and I wanted to help him pass over it. "What you say, Mr. James," I reminded him, "is confidential. As in the Roman confessional. You need have no fear . . . "

"But that little 'case history' of yours, the case of your patient Dora. Was she aware that she would emerge as a character in your little tale? Shall I, one of these early days?"

"You must resolve that worry for yourself, Mr. James," I said. "I am an honorable man and a physician. But you follow the rules of psychoanalysis too selectively; you hover at the edges of your memory and decline deeper exploration. I do not understand. Ex hypotesi, as we agreed earlier, only puritans divide human lives into higher and lower segments, spirit and flesh, and condemn the latter. We are all of the kingdom of Dr. Darwin, working our way by slow recapitulation toward fuller consciousness of our impulses . . . "

"Ex your hypothesis!" he exclaimed, then resumed on a different tack. He began to speak of his youth and of what he calls his "obscure hurt," some sort of mysterious physical insult that kept him out of the army and the American civil war. He is still embarrassed by it. I wondered what link might exist between the two associations, Miss Woolson's memory on the one hand and his "obscure hurt," his physical debility. I was about to ask when I realized that we had run some minutes beyond the hour.

"We are making progress," I said.

"Progress?" he retorted. "Or is it regress? I thought that was the object, herr doctor."

As usual, I admired the devilish quickness of his wit. But there is no doubt in my mind, as I sit recording these summary notes in the privacy of my Lamb House chamber, that our session touched the quick of Mr. James's unconscious. Water is always a telling symptom. He spoke with suspect fluency of that odd business of the dresses in the Lagoon! His associations with water, however, are distinctly literary and defensive. When I asked for associations he mentioned Lethe and Styx. He said nothing, significantly, of baptism or swimming or any of the other mundane uses of water. One may suppose that his Swedenborgian father, mired in his mystical muck, may not have believed in the orthodox rituals of religious faith. In any case, I never believe the assertion of analysands who claim cognitive recall of infant expe-

rience. So where do we stand now? Still at sea (to speak of water) but I see land-ho! in the distance . . .

* * *

Horace found, to his disgust, that he had slipped into a distracted mood ascribed to the sappy lovelorns who figure in bad romances. But what could be done? He spent many vacant hours staring out the window over the marshes and trying to think how he could arrange to call on Agnes Fengallon without an invitation from the rather forbidding Archdeacon. His only amusement in this unaccustomed moodiness was observing Uncle Henry's changing demeanor as his closetings with Dr. Freud continued. There had now been at least three, on successive days, and the master of Lamb House, usually as solidly earthbound as the nearby chalk cliffs, seemed to float about the house on a cushion of air. He spoke in a way that Horace would have called "manic" if the idea hadn't been absurd. But Horace wouldn't have been surprised if Uncle Henry had clapped him on the back at breakfast as if they were the fraternizing members of some ridiculous civic club. One morning James was whistling one of the popular Gilbert and Sullivan tunes as he came across the garden, leading Max, something, Horace recalled, about *my object all sublime / to make the punishment fit the crime.* Either Dr. Freud had worked a miracle cure of astounding swiftness of Uncle Henry's depression (occasioned in the main by the laggard sales of the New York Edition, to which he had attached such high hopes and on which he had lavished such toil). Or, more likely, James's instincts as a tease had been mobilized and were being indulged at Dr. Freud's expense. And there was the steady outpouring of daily letters to Mrs. Wharton, suggesting that there was a waiting audience for whatever tease Uncle Henry had concocted. The theory found support in Theodora Bosanquet's confidential comment that Uncle Henry was writing almost daily notes to Edith Wharton in his own hand, rather than dictating them to her at the Remington, as he did his other correspondence. "It all adds up," Horace wrote in his diary.

In fact, Edith Wharton, from Paris, was contributing her own comments on the unfolding analysis. She had recently written:

Dear Henry,

I am relieved that you seem to be taking my counsel and giving Dr. Freud "scope" to disclose himself and his "science," even as he explores your fathomless psyche. But I confess that another alarm went off when I read, in your latest, that you are teasing him with fables, however preposterous, in connection with your cherished memory of poor Constance Woolson. I am sure that you mean no harm—au contraire!, but that talk about the dresses in the Lagoon (of whose remote origins you give conflicting accounts) is so very bizarre that it is likely to take on a life of its own. Some stray letter or note of yours or Freud's might leak into the archives; and as you know archives, however carefully winnowed, can be treacherous. And there is always hearsay. In that case you may find that some credulous chronicler of your genius has erected upon this silly fable a quirky theory of your relationship with Fenimore that goes miles beyond the facts. Beware, Cher Maître! Moreover, your query to Freud is much to the point. That is, if these analytic sessions are as confidential as the Roman confessional, as he claims, why then has he been so inconsistent as to write them up in certain instances as "case histories"? That he cloaks the subjects in pseudonyms is, I fear, tissue-thin protection. You may well find yourself at some future hour quite transparently "done" (as you would put it) as a "case." I can hear you scoffing at the possibility. But remember: We two as tellers of tales should be the last to doubt the ruthlessness of any writer when tempted by an intriguing subject! And do not

doubt that Freud is a creator himself. You are warned!
Devotedly, Edith.

One morning Horace descended for breakfast at the usual hour to find Henry James sitting alone. Freud's seat was vacant.

"The doctor has gone for a walk," James said in answer to Horace's interrogatory glance. "He begged off breakfast saying he has been too well fed by Mrs. Paddington and he would make do this morning with his elevenses." He paused; Horace caught a glint of mischief in his eye. "Perhaps we may plot and plan a bit in his absence."

Horace began to eat his poached egg. The dry toast crunched and crackled audibly in the silence.

"I say, plot and plan," James insisted. Horace waited, not knowing quite how to react. He indicated his moving jaw. The earliest rule of American table manners he could remember was that one never spoke with a mouthful of food. Besides, chewing in itself was a good defense. Uncle Henry always deferred to chewing.

"Freud is very persistent in probing my secrets, boring as they are. I exclude the incidents I have made up of whole cloth. I wonder if Freud may have secrets of his own." Horace realized that James was driving at something; since he himself was usually busy Fletcherizing his food and was not given to idle breakfast-table chatter.

After a short silence, James spoke again. "Dear boy, what would you say to a small errand of *lawful espials?*" Of course, Horace knew that was what old Polonius had called his prurient prying into Hamlet's mood.

"What could I say, beholden as I am, sir?"

"Freud, I believe, has an eminent disciple in London, a Dr. Jones, Ernest Jones, a Welsh physician. William has met him and thinks him very able."

"Dr. Jones, yes," Horace said.

"Perhaps, Horace, you would be so good as to go up to town and interview Jones. Noakes can make an appointment."

"What would be the substance of the interview?"

"You are hardly unresourceful, Horace. Notwithstanding your playacting"—Uncle Henry spoke with unusual sharpness, as if weary of collaborating in Horace's pretended innocence—"but if I might suggest: You might say that your host, Mr. James, feels himself at a loss for ways to divert Dr. Freud—that in our rural quietness and ignorance of the larger latitudes of science, we lack the diversions of a great metropolis like London or Vienna and fear that we may be boring our great guest. That would do for an entree, then perhaps a morsel or two of gossip would transpire."

And so it was arranged.

From Horace's diary:

Here is the episode from my stay at Lamb House of which I am least proud—a mission of espionage or "lawful espials," as Uncle Henry called it, echoing snoopy Polonius. No savory model. I was sent yesterday to London to see Dr. Ernest Jones of King's College, an eminent convert to Dr. Freud's psychoanalytic science. Burgess Noakes somehow made the appointment. I never cease to wonder at his efficiency, because he seems so stolid and impassive and when Uncle Henry makes a request he usually registers no reaction. But, as usual, he succeeded and Dr. Jones invited me to meet him at noon at the Garrick Club, a quaint old place just off the Strand in the West End, once the home of David Garrick the actor, Dr. Johnson's friend. Dr. Jones turns out to be a spry, wiry, balding fellow, quite young, with a professorial air about him. He took me upstairs to the club room and we took a table by the windows overlooking the street. He offered me a shandy and we ordered roast beef sandwiches. Dr. Jones kept eyeing me with a combination of curiosity and sur-

prise, as if he couldn't quite make out what I was doing there or why he had agreed to see me. It soon came out that my access to him was simply in deference to Uncle Henry. He mistook me for Uncle Henry's "confidential clerk," and I thought it pointless to correct him.

"You are a very youthful confidential clerk, Briscoe," he mused. "I had pictured you as middle-aged, when Mr. James's man rang me up."

"Yes, I am lucky to be at Lamb House. A family connection. Mr. James's nephew is a close friend."

"I see. As it happens, I am a fervent admirer of Mr. James as well as of his brother, the eminent philosopher. The Ambassadors, for instance. Such a brilliant story, and so funny at places. You must have been in on the writing?"

"Oh no, not I, not the writing. But you are quite right, sir. Odd to say, Dr. Jones, you are among the few readers of that novel who detect the comic strain. Mr. James is among the supreme comedians, but even close readers miss much of the fun. They mistake the tone, you see."

"What a funny twist, at any rate," Jones remarked, "that Mr. Lambert Strether turns out to be a sort of voyeur. Perhaps the term is harsh, though of course he does journey to Paris to spy out the young man's life and loves, Chad's that is. And his reward for luring him back from the tents of wickedness is to be the hand of Chad's mother! What else would you call it, pray tell, when Strether skulks about at a distance watching the young man rowing on the little river with his Parisian mistress?"

"A conversion experience? It makes Strether feel how much he has missed in life . . . "

"Indeed, Briscoe, damn this everlasting repression of ours— of the English-speaking tribes, I mean. 'Live all you can!' Isn't that the first and greatest commandment? Strether tries to pass it along, having realized how he has wasted his youth. But yes,

my dear Briscoe, after these agreeable preliminaries, what may I do for you exactly?"

At that point, having so far acted my part with aplomb, even with a certain swagger, I was at a loss and I fell back on prepared lines.

"Mr. James is fearful that he will bore Dr. Freud, our life in Rye being so drearily provincial. We have taken him biking, but now what? No doubt his life in Vienna is quite racy, a regular Schnitzler story."

"A Schnitzler story? Do you mean Arthur?" Jones seemed thunderstruck. "Hardly, my dear Briscoe! Freud is a great admirer of his stories, and no less their confirmation of certain clinical findings. But he is scarcely a Schnitzler character."

"I had imagined," I said, trying to control a telltale quaver in my voice. "I had imagined that so bold an investigator of irregularities, if that is the word, had himself led quite a merry life after-hours."

"Freud? On the contrary. Freud is a model of bourgeois regularity. A regular old stick in the mud, I should say. Actually, a bit of a puritan."

"I simply thought . . . that is, I had supposed . . . "

"I can imagine what you might have supposed, Briscoe. Many do—thinking that because Freud traces the neuroses to repression he himself is a great old libertine and advocate of free love, a figure out of Krafft-Ebing. Nothing could be farther from the truth. He is proper to the point of stuffiness."

"Not, then," I said, cautiously tendering my most provocative card, "even so much as a whisper of scandal."

"Nay. I wouldn't say that, Briscoe. Geniuses always stir up scurrilous rumors. Freud's enemies whisper against him night and day, unceasingly."

"What could they whisper, then?" I said, trying to imitate a suppressed yawn behind my hand, a feigned indifference to a trail that was growing quite warm.

"*Just for instance, though you must not repeat this, they—Freud's detractors—have circulated the rumor that he is intimate with his sister-in-law, a maiden lady, a Miss Minna Bernays, who has lived in the Freud household for more than ten years. I have met her; she is an intellectual. No Magdalen.*"

"*Still, that is quite a whisper,*" I observed.

"*Indeed, but Freud is too great a man to stoop to such mischief, and under the noses of his wife and children.*"

"*Naturally! But why such malice?*"

"*Freud has spoken of it to me at length, how scornful some of his colleagues have been about his findings.*"

I was still pretending indifference, while wondering how to keep this stream of information in spate. "*Nothing else then? Malice seems the invariable price of being a scientific pioneer.*"

"*Well,*" Jones said, "*there was the Fliess matter . . .*"

"*The Fliess matter? Who—or what—was Fliess?*" My question sounded eager and I could feel myself blush. Surely Jones knew that he was being "pumped," to use one of those vulgarisms that Uncle Henry sanitizes with inverted commas. But to my surprise Dr. Jones was not reluctant to confide.

"*A who, Briscoe, a Berlin physician of rather odd views whom Freud was close to a few years ago, when he was developing his theories. Odd chap, Fliess, one of those Teutonic types who swathe everything in billowing clouds of vague theory. He had the curious idea of a male sexual cycle of twenty-three days, as I recall. I rather think old Freud was infatuated with him for a time.*"

I tried, by pretending to tighten the knot of my cravat, to disguise the bobbing sensation I felt in my Adam's apple. I asked, "*But what was the 'matter'?*"

"*The sober truth is that Freud and Fliess bungled an operation and nearly killed one of Freud's patients. Not the least crazy of Fliess's theories was that one could relieve hysteria by surgery on the nose. There was some imagined link with the genitalia. Not my line of thought, to say the least.*"

I was astonished that Jones would speak so freely. "Of course," he said, wagging his finger at me, "you can't repeat any of this, even to Henry James," he said.

"Of course not," I lied, "since you regard it as confidential." Jones grinned. He knew I was lying and would repeat what he told me. But why did he tell me all this unless my being an emissary of Uncle Henry's conferred a sort of nimbus?

Then Dr. Jones suddenly said: "Now, Briscoe, kindly remind me of the exact nature of your errand from Mr. James"—as if we hadn't been gossiping for more than an hour about Freud and I so riveted that I had eaten only half of my sandwich. As if all our preceding exchanges had been a runup to something of real importance and not the gossipy nuggets Uncle Henry had sent me to dig out. I repeated that Henry James feared that Freud would find his hospitality inadequate.

"Not to worry, Briscoe. Freud is easily entertained. He is a wonderful listener, acutely observant, as he must be in the nature of his—I should say, of our—science. Tell Mr. James to divert him with a good yarn or two when the conversation drags."

Dr. Jones looked at his watch. His expression said that he had invested all the time he could afford in the company of a raw youth. He rose, we shook hands and went our ways—he to greet some friends of his at the long club table in the middle of the room, I to Victoria to catch the 3 P.M. train to Rye.

As I returned, I reviewed the conversation with Dr. Jones. Had I grasped the errand? Why would Uncle Henry send me all the way up to London merely to spy out Freud's personal secrets? It seemed uncharacteristic, and indeed what secrets had I discovered? They were paltry gossip—that Freud's enemies in Vienna whisper maliciously about an affair with his sister-in-law? Pure slander; the usual envy of brilliance. That he once swallowed whole the bizarre theories of a Berlin doctor, possibly a charlatan, who thought women could be cured of hysteria, so-called, by surgery on their noses? And whose assumption was *that noses and genitals were connected? This seemed uncharacteristic of Freud, although genius is not proof against gullibility: witness Uncle Henry's staunch faith in Dr. Fletcher. There must be some other explanation of the Fliess matter and Jones hinted that it stemmed from a temporary personal infatuation on Freud's part. I find it hard to imagine why Uncle Henry would stoop to petty gossip (unless he plans to build a story around it). In a momentary surge of megalomania, I began to feel that I might be the true adult in this curious threesome at Lamb House. I hesitate to tell Uncle Henry that my talk with Dr. Jones came to so little, but I'll sleep on the question. During the journey from London I was so mesmerized by the rocking of the railway carriage and the vast sheep herds that whiten the Sussex terrain that I nodded off and nearly missed the change of trains. When I finally got back here, in the dead hours of the evening, dinner was over and no one was to be seen in the common rooms. I went back to the kitchen and begged a sandwich from Mrs. Paddington, who as usual teased me mildly about Agnes, then crept up to my room (where I am writing this). If Uncle Henry asks for an immediate report tomorrow, I shall beg off and say that Dr. Jones had little to report that was useful and that I need to review my notes.*

But Horace found next day that he felt no hesitation to tell all. When Henry James seized the first moment of privacy to ask Horace what he had learned, he gave James a nearly verbatim account of the interview with Ernest Jones.

From Freud's notes:

Today's was surely one of the oddest of our analytic sessions. Mr. James was in a strange mood, which I took to be a continuation of that in which he declines, frequently, to distinguish clearly between fact and fancy, protesting that literary men move in and out of parallel universes of their own. I caught a gleam of mischief in his eye before we began, and knew that we were in for something unusual. I was not disappointed.

"Let us," he said, "resume for a moment our suspended consideration of Hamlet."

I asked what relevance it had. "After all," I said, not for the first time, "this is not a colloquium but an analysis and you, Mr. James, must do the psychoanalytic work. Otherwise it will be without value for you. Of course, if you feel compelled to speak of Hamlet, please do so. Perhaps we shall stumble on a nugget."

He ignored my expostulation and went on. "Of course, the heart of the matter, so far as the Prince is concerned, is the incestuous relationship between his mother and his uncle. Now, why does he call it incest, damned incest to use his very words? His father is dead and it would seem that Gertrude and Claudius have been lawfully if hastily wed. You recall, herr doctor, Hamlet's complaint that the funeral meats furnished the wedding feast?"

I murmured assent, wondering where he proposed to carry this rumination; but on the theory of free association I waited patiently for his theme to declare itself.

"I have sometimes thought," said he, "though it is scarcely in my regular line, that it would be jolly entertainment to do a sort of variation on Hamlet's *theme of incest, echoing the Bard but reversing the roles. Let us stipulate, for instance, that a King or some other male character (perhaps a 'conquistador,' to use your term) might have an affair with his wife's sister. Does this chime at all with your clinical experience, Dr. Freud?"*

Whereupon he turned his head as if to see how I might react. But I had no idea why. I looked out the window. It was very odd, this line of talk; I believe he was trying to provoke me out of the analyst's role.

"No?" he continued. "You are yourself, I believe, close friends with your belle-soeur, Miss Bernays? Not that I should for a moment drag her into this wicked little hypothesis—only that

you have perhaps experienced, as it were, the possible complexities of such a ménage."

For a moment, I sensed a sly insinuation, as if he thought Minna Bernays and I were other than good friends. Could he possibly have heard the gossip from Vienna? But it seemed inconceivable that James, great gentleman that he is, could be guilty of such indirection. "Yes," I said, "Miss Bernays does take a keen interest in the psychoanalytic science, but I doubt that she would have any reaction to speak of to your twist—your variation—on the Hamlet story. But why are we wasting time on this tangent? The question is of its pertinence to you, Mr. James. What does it mean for you? Are you *interested in incest?"*

There was a long pause. "No, I am not. Nothing," he said. "Nothing whatsoever. Let us proceed." And so we did . . .

* * *

My dear Edith [Henry James wrote later],
I have been very wicked. You have heard, possibly ad nauseam, the tales of Freud's insistent probing into my most private life—as if it were as lurid as de Sade's or as variously amorous as Casanova's & not largely a blank. On a sudden whim, I dispatched young Briscoe to spy out Freud's own secrets: what he calls "the secrets of the alcove." Briscoe met with Dr. Freud's London disciple Ernest Jones, who in a spare luncheon in the clubroom of the Garrick gushed, all unprompted, with rumors—including the rumor of an affair with Freud's sister-in-law, Miss Bernays. Having described these tales, however, Jones dismissed them as the sweepings of Viennese malice, spread by Freud's detractors, & insisted on a seal of silence—though Horace, after much humming and hawing, tells me that Jones, having been so candid, could hardly have expected him to remain mute. I appropriated & adapted them quite shamelessly today in our "analytic" session by purporting to be mulling a story of "incest" in

which the Hamlet *situation is reversed & the king becomes amorously entangled with two sisters, rather than a queen with two brothers. As I embroidered this cheap faux-donnée, I violated one of the protocols of analysis by swiveling my head and glancing behind me to see whether the dart had stung. But no, not a bit of it! When I turned my head—I was, of course, supine on the couch—I detected not so much as a hint of discomfiture on Freud's part. He is a master of the poker face. Then, there was another story, fetched back by Horace & laid before me, that Freud & one of his associates in Berlin, one Fliess, had bungled surgery on a young woman's nose & nearly killed her. But I found myself at a loss for a way of contriving a "screened" version of this scandal. In short, my impulsive little experiment in retaliation, my attempt to fight back, came to naught. And indeed, dear Edith, to reiterate the word, I feel contaminated by this sly business, into which I fear I have been lured by the climate of prurience generated by Freud's sexual inquiries. I beat my breast with loud cries of mea culpa, which you no doubt will echo & for which echo I cringingly brace myself at this very late hour. Yours ever more tenderly, Henry James.*

Edith Wharton responded in one of the occasional relics of this correspondence that survived Henry James's purges:

53, rue de Varenne, Paris

Chêrest Maître,

The penitent tone of your confessional letter seems to call out for a swat or two of the birch, but the stripes administered will be clement. I must admit not only that your escapade seems distinctly out of character, but that I find no equivalence between Freud's nosiness and your own. His interest in your private life is professional. If you weren't prepared to co-operate in his digging & delving, which you depict as an inquisition fit for Torquemada himself, why did you consent to this "analysis" in

the first place? Indeed, you & I share a robust interest in the vie
privée *of many interesting figures—you surely recall your sly
remark about George Sand's many bedrooms! But speculation
long after the fact is a far cry from espionage and you have confessed that your exemplar in this business is horrid old Polonius,
who does not shrink from setting spies on his schoolboy son in
Paris nor thrusting forward his innocent daughter as bait in aid
of the unspeakable Claudius and his nefarious plotting! "Lawful
espials" indeed! The mere lawfulness of any patently immoral
act is, as I need not tell you, the first plea of the scoundrel. But
some rough justice, as it strikes me, has been rendered since the
little conspiracy came to naught (except in soiling the innocent
hands of your protégé, Briscoe). Even if it should prove out that
Freud did or does have a dalliance with his sister-in-law Miss
Bernays, what is that to you? You, cher maître, would ordinarily
be among the last to exploit such an embroilment and the first to
seek out its finer shadings, not reduce it to a purée of gossip. You
would worry that the poor wife should have caught wind of the
scandal, and yet for the sake of the children—several, I seem to
recall your saying—would have to endure her fate in pained
silence & take what crumbs from the table of affection might fall
to her. Thank heavens you passed up the Fliess matter altogether. There, the stripes have now been administered, but gently, as
always with continuing affection.* Je vous embrasse tendrement,
Edith

It had occurred to Horace, even before he went on the
strange mission to London, that it might be humane to offer
Dr. Freud a friendly warning that his patient had a streak of
mischief. It would help Henry James as well if Freud understood his manner and tone of voice more fully since Horace
believed that Freud would probably write something about the
encounter, perhaps one of his "case histories." How could he
resist?

Did Uncle Henry share his suspicion? Horace thought not—in fact, there were times when Horace wondered if he weren't playing the umpire between two monumental inno-cents who for all their intelligence (or perhaps because of it) sometimes seemed blind to the obvious. They resembled two magnificent ocean-going vessels, passing each other with fog horns blasting unheard. Not long after the journey to London, Horace was walking Max in the garden and encountered Uncle Henry, opportunely, as he was making his stately progress to the Garden Room for a morning of dictation. As Uncle Henry approached, Horace tentatively ventured the obvious. James was startled, incredulous.

"I? The subject of a case history? It is the height of d-d-derangement, Horace, so much as to imagine it. Freud puts pen to paper only to write up hysterics and paranoiacs and such fry as that. I would be a psychic subject so boring as to break the very point of his quill! Dismiss it from your mind, dear boy. Why it would be next door to one of those—ah—so silly deco-rative volumes that one sees on ph-ph-philistine bookshelves: 'The Full and Candid History of My Flaming Love Affairs,' say, which, being opened, consist of b-b-blank pages. There are some who find such fripperies amusing in these pursy days. I thank you for your warning, but do not worry yourself, Horace, that I shall be slow to detect so sly a purpose."

Uncle Henry protests too much, Horace thought to himself as Henry James spoke this fervent denial; the very suspicion has occurred to him! And he doesn't mind!

"Forgive me, sir, I spoke out of turn," Horace said. "It was a frivolous thought and I shall dismiss it from mind, as you urge."

But the possibility remained in his thoughts. As did the belief that Sigmund Freud, despite his own indirect hints, might remain as deaf to the intricate music of Uncle Henry's ironies as Uncle Henry was to the possibility that he might someday join "Dora" or the "Paranoid Dr. Shreber" in the gallery of famous case histories. He had very possibly failed in his role as Cassandra with Uncle Henry; but perhaps it would be otherwise with Freud. Horace was sitting in the oak parlor, pretending to peruse the latest volume of the New York Edition but thinking dreamily of Agnes, when he saw Freud walk through the dining room into the garden. Now, he thought to himself, is the right time. To give himself an excuse for approaching the formidable doctor, he fastened the leash on Max. Freud had been walking vigorously up and down near the greenhouse, his hands clasped behind him, dressed as usual as if for a Viennese winter.

"Hello, sir," Horace called out from a distance. Freud in his concentration had not seen him emerge.

"Oh, Mr. Briscoe," Freud said cordially. "*Ça va?*"

"*Oui, ça va,*" he responded—that had become their customary greeting.

"Aren't you absolutely baking in your wool suit?" Horace asked. Freud seemed surprised, as if he hadn't noticed that it was mild—about sixty degrees—with a bright sun and a pleasant southerly breeze off the Channel.

"Ja, come to think of it, it is *jolly* warm." The English adjective was Freud's little joke.

"You are picking up the spoken idiom, sir," Horace said, grasping the opportunity. "How is it coming along—your psychoanalysis of Mr. James?" Freud wagged a finger at Horace in admonition, but as if in fun. "We do not talk out of school about an analysis," he said. Horace felt himself reprimanded. He changed tacks.

"Oh, I didn't mean to pry into the substance," he said. "I know that is confidential. I had in mind the feeling, the ambience, of your sessions. But everyone in England, everyone literate anyway, would pay handsomely to listen in if they knew of your Garden Room sessions. The preeminent alienist of

Europe closeted with the greatest writer of the age: a matter of remark in itself, whatever the excuse. *The Times* would love to know of it, but I shan't tell."

"The *ambience*," Freud mused thoughtfully, giving the word a French intonation. "*Ambience,*" he repeated. "Hmmm."

Horace pushed on—after all, he was doing Dr. Freud a favor. "I am sure you are finding, sir, with your powers of perception, what a tease Mr. James can be. As you know, I am writing a thesis about his tales of art and artists, especially the comedies. The element of teasing is as obvious as it can be."

"Teasing? Please explain, Mr. Briscoe."

"Well, the best place to look is that story called 'The Figure in the Carpet.' I assume you know it, sir?"

"I have read it," Freud said. "I suppose one would naturally expect that those of us who are professionally involved in 'detective' work, so to say, of whatever sort, are interested in unriddling 'the figure in the carpet,' the design, the theme, deeply encrypted as it was in that tale. But remind me, what *was* the figure in that carpet?"

"In my view, Dr. Freud—and *entre nous,* I would never test it on Mr. James himself—the jest is that there simply isn't any such figure, or thematic skeleton key that would unlock Hugh Vereker's stories. For his own perverse amusement, he encourages the notion that there is such a key to bait critics who in their zeal for 'meaning' miss elements that are as plain as the nose on your face. You saw right through it. That's why you don't recall the 'figure,' no doubt." Horace plastered on the flattery, hoping he was not overdoing it.

"Hmmm," Freud mused again. "I take it you are saying that Mr. James, like his figure Vereker, is capable of the same sort of foolery?"

"Exactly, doctor, although I would shy from the word 'foolery.' It is more in the nature of a jest. But we all must be on the *qui vive* with Uncle Henry."

While he stood there wondering if the point had sunk in, Max tugged at the leash and lifted his little hind leg at Dr. Freud's trouser. Horace quickly led him to a safer target and by the time he returned to resume the conversation, Dr. Freud, saying "most pleasant to visit with you, my boy," had walked on. Well, I tried, Horace thought.

In fact, Freud had been more interested in Horace's little parable than he had let on. When he returned to his room some minutes later he sat down immediately and added a reflection to the process notes for what he was already calling "The Case of Mr. J":

A disturbing talk in the garden just now with Mr. James's other guest, Mr. Briscoe, the young American who is writing a doctoral thesis about him. He happened to be walking the little dog and spoke to me about our host's sense of mischief, as reflected in certain of his tales of art. Well, Ernest Jones warned me that the Anglo-American sense of humor can sometimes baffle others, even students of the subject (see my Jokes and Their Relation to the Unconscious*). The clear division that we solemn old central Europeans draw between the serious and the unserious may fail to cover all cases—as in that interruption of the gruesome Macbeth by the drunken porter, with his jokes about drink and sexual potency.*

Does Briscoe's warning relate to our analysis? Yesterday, Mr. James began to speak of a youthful physical disability about which he is both sensitive and secretive, an injury to the groin. He was part of a fire brigade and in passing a heavy bucket of water he suffered an "obscure hurt," as he calls it, that made him unfit (so he says) for the Union Army.

I said that it was interesting that he called it "obscure," not a term familiar to clinical anatomy. I asked if he had sought a diagnosis and he confessed that he had not "crossed that threshold," even though the accident occurred many decades ago. I was aston-

ished. I said that perhaps one of my colleagues in Vienna would be glad to examine him, next time he came that way.

Instead of responding directly he lurched back to the subject we had been discussing, his friend Miss Woolson, the writer, and her death in Venice in 1893. I detected in his voice a controlled anxiety that is familiar to me from my consultations with mild hysterics.

"We met often," he said. "She was . . . she wished to be . . . she wished me to be . . . her lover! I often ask myself whether I made the right response. It was . . . It was decent enough, herr doctor, my deportment. The gentlemanly thing, but was it right? I wonder now if she felt rejected."

"My dear Mr. James," I said, "how can I answer that question? It is you who must answer it. That is precisely the psycho-analytic work of which we have spoken: pushing against resistances piled up over time by the censor to disguise the repressed matter, which as I have told you is always sexual. Always. This would appear to be a classic instance."

"You do assure me of confidentiality? If you must know, it involves what you call the genital thing—literally."

I told him again that he could rest assured of that.

He continued: "It was at an hotel at Paris. She invited me to her suite—the French, so blatant in their assignations, scarcely turn a hair at behavior over which in this country the constables would be summoned . . . "

I waited. "She had asked me to her suite, saying that she would need five minutes to change into something more comfortable. I walked about the lobby for a while, then took the staircase to her floor. She opened the door wearing only a negligee and a billow-ing kimono. She had let her hair fall . . . I was astonished . . . When I hesitated, she reached out a hand and pulled me by my coat sleeve into the room—she was a strong woman, then, before illness began to undermine her health—and closed and bolted the door. She then began to fumble with my cravat, panting at my ear . . . 'Henry,' she whispered, 'I know that you are not the marrying sort but please don't force me to end my life as a virgin. You know that I love you, love me now!' She was clearly inviting me to initiate what is vulgarly called a conquest . . . "

"Did you oblige?"

"Yes," he said, "or rather yes and no." There was now a pause so lengthy that I became aware of the birds scratching in the gutter over the bay window. " . . . But you see," he finally went on, "I could not . . . that is to say, herr doctor . . . that I was as a maiden myself. That is where the obscure hurt as I call it came into play—or rather did not, since I could not maintain the necessary virility for all of my affection for the poor lady. The seduction was foreordained to fail—even though we went to the length . . . the length of occupying her bed sans vêtements." (His French, I find, is a defense, invariably.)

Mr. James is an exceedingly private man, and I was embarrassed for one of the few times in my practice. If he is not worldly, there is no worldliness; yet in this he seemed abject and I felt sympathy and wondered what I could do to alleviate his distress.

"This need not be a permanent condition, even at your age," I said. "At least if this obscure hurt, as you call it, is not organic. Or perhaps even if it is."

"How could it not be organic?" he asked.

I said that he would be very surprised at the handicaps the mind can impose on the body. Only clinical examination, I said, could isolate the root of the complaint . . .

"Root?" he exclaimed, and to my astonishment laughed. I could not see his face, but then I caught on: "Root," I recalled, is an English vulgarism for the penis. Again, this incongruous Anglo-American sense of humor!

"Impotence," I said, ignoring the mirth, "is not so very rare as you might suppose. Virile men sometimes suffer from it." Then, to my surprise, he once again seemed to reverse himself and draw back from his candor like a circling fox.

"Does this tale," he asked, *"sound too much like those penny dreadful romances, vended in Paris and London, in back-alley shops of the sort that figure in dear Joseph Conrad's novel last year, in which bodices are ripped in uncontrollable excitement? You see, herr doctor, my storytelling impulse is so compelling as to make me reluctant even to read the fumbling efforts of my confrères. I no sooner open them than I begin revising, rewriting, as I think the thing should be done . . . Indeed, as I have told you often before, in the devious world of my imaginative economy I cannot always distinguish the 'real' from the fabulous—an inconsequential distinction for the artist. Do you see, Dr. Freud? You may have read my sad little tale 'The Real Thing,' in which professional models of the working classes pose for a magazine artist more plausibly as aristocrats, than aristocrats properly so called. What was it you were saying the other day as we walked the golf links? That business about how you had second thoughts about your 'seduction' theory?"*

I felt a bit like a traffic policeman at a busy confusing intersection; but with a gentle reminder that it was he, not I, who was under analysis I once again described to him my recent epiphany: how many if not most of the hysterical patients who claim to have been sexually molested by stepfathers, brothers, uncles, even fathers, are in fact fabricating—fantasies in most cases, woven of whole cloth in others. I had stumbled upon what I call my Oedipal theory. These tales had to spring from the repression of incestuous impulses!

"Ah yes," he said. *"Exactly! The real and the unreal; the true and the fabricated; the remembered and the fantasized; the experience and the illusion. How thin is the membrane between them! Ah, the whims and wiles of human memory!"*

Putting all this together now with what Mr. Briscoe had to say as we walked in the garden just now, I caution myself. What am I really to make of what Mr. James tells me? Could these tales of his be fables? Could I be the butt of a grotesque practical

*joke? Or is it that he honestly disclaims the capacity to distin-
guish in his memories between what is real and what is imaginary, as I have tried to do in modifying the seduction theory?
Did I foresee such complications when I agreed to conduct this
short-term analysis? I think not!*

 My dear Edith [Henry James wrote to Mrs. Wharton at
about the same time],

 Your note stung and I grovel under your lash. Of course *one
shouldn't disclose intimacies to a third party and I am at a loss
now to think why I did it, in connection with poor Fullerton,
save that this daily psychoanalytic fencing with Dr. Freud is
weirdly exhilarating and produces odd effects. I haven't felt so
lightheaded in many moons. Yet all the while, the Viennese sage
remains so earnest, not to say solemn, as to fill me with guilt
over my fantasizing & the guilt is all the more onerous (curse this
"free association" business) inasmuch as I found myself dragging
poor Fenimore into the picture. I grossly exaggerated the carnal
dimensions of our friendship. Of course I needn't tell you, lady
of the deepest perceptions, that it is a rare friendship that is without some element of the erotic. I always felt that Fenimore
longed for a lover & further that the lover she longed for was,
improbably, your determinedly celibate old friend. As I wove my
tall tale under Freud's prodding and probing, I plunged suddenly over the precipice into gross indiscretion. What he makes of it
I have no idea but I am satisfied that, all in all, it is a case of just
deserts. He pursues the sexual aspect of things with the zeal and
bugling of a pack of beagles, and I rewarded his expectation in
due measure. You rightly decline to assist in fleshing out any
such fable; & I may already have stretched it a step beyond cre-
dence. Toward the end of the latest session, I tried to warn Freud
that for a storyteller the membrane separating history from fantasy is thin & porous. Whether he took the warning to heart I
don't know, though he seemed to me to be gulping eagerly from*

my tainted chalice. But then, he tells me that he has had to become expert in distinguishing the sexual fantasies of his young "hysterics" from actual fact, when they speak to him of seduction. No doubt he has heard enough from them to suspect my feeble fibbing! Moreover, he has been in consultation with Horace & I suspect the kindly young man of trying to forewarn Freud against the wicked devices of your fedilissimo, Henry James.

The truth was that few conversations, with Dr. Freud or Uncle Henry, interrupted Horace's preoccupation with Agnes Fengallon, who had failed to write to him as she had promised that earlier Sunday in the St. Mary's churchyard. If he were back home in Cambridge or Newport he would march directly to her door and leave his card, with the edge bent. But he was still unversed in English manners and was beginning to wonder whether his impressions had been wrong, or whether Agnes had simply forgotten their recent conversation and with it her pledge that her Uncle Charles would invite him to tea. Agnes now haunted his daydreams. He kept recalling, in his mind's eye, the wonderful colors of her face and cheeks, her riveting green eyes and amber hair. And was there a mind's ear as well? How else hear, as he did in imagination, the silken voice? And the torture merely intensified when he tried resolutely to ignore these daydreams.

Why did he not hear from her? Might Agnes already have her eye on someone else? He tried not to think about it—the thought of rivals tormented him, though he realized that he had, so far, no claim to be rivalrous over a girl he had hardly met and had not been formally introduced to. But he hadn't thought it wise to mention his infatuation to anyone at Lamb House. Noakes seemed, however, to be aware of it, as well as Mrs. Paddington, the cook, a maternal woman on whom Uncle Henry had perhaps modeled the guileless housekeeper Mrs. Grose in "The Turn of the Screw." "I hear that Cupid shot an arrow," she whispered as she passed him in the hall, "and I can see who was hit, right enough. Poor Mr. Horace!"

How she knew or guessed this Horace couldn't imagine, unless the staff were somehow mysteriously permeated with Uncle Henry's intuitive powers, and the contagion extended even into the kitchen. He smiled at Mrs. Paddington's words but did not respond.

Horace was sitting one afternoon staring at the empty tea cups and the devastated pastry platter that now held only an assortment of crumbs, and suddenly resolved to act. The resolution had been building for days and Horace finally said to himself, "Enough brooding; act! Faint heart . . . etc." Agnes and her uncle lived five minutes' walk away, around the corner and down the hill in an ancient half-timbered dwelling on Mermaid Street. Putting on his soft hat, Horace bounded out of the front door and walked rapidly in their direction. The Fengallon dwelling stood cater-cornered across from the old inn where Uncle Henry often lodged his visitors, a building of the Tudor period with a red slate roof, in common with many of the older buildings in Rye. Perhaps because it had stood precariously poised for so long on the steep street it seemed to Horace to tilt to one side, like the famous tower of Pisa, as if weary of standing upright and wishing to lie down. He stole a quick glance at the Fengallon house as he walked rapidly past it, trying not to trip on the cobble stones. Could it be, he wondered, that his perception that the house was off balance reflected his own agitated state of mind? His plan was to walk up and down Mermaid Street a few times, casually passing and repassing the Fengallon doorway, and hope to be seen without making his purpose obvious. He kept facing forward, not daring to peer, though it was very tempting, into the large front bay window. As he was passing the house for the fourth time his strategy was suddenly rewarded.

"Mr. Briscoe!" he heard a woman's voice call from above.

"Hello, Mr. Briscoe." He looked up, pretending surprise, and saw Agnes leaning from an upstairs window. She was wearing a low-cut dress and looked as bewitching as she had that Sunday in the churchyard.

"Miss Fengallon!" he called, snatching his hat from his head, and bowing. "What a surprise to see you again. I had no idea . . ."

She smiled radiantly down and shook her head. "Oh dear," she said. "I had planned days ago to have you to tea. But uncle had to go to London on boring old church business." She leaned farther out the window, so as to be able to speak conversationally, and for a moment Horace worried that she might fall. He moved forward just in case she might lose her balance. She was some ten feet above him but otherwise they were now almost face to face.

"I can't imagine that church business would be boring," Horace said awkwardly; it was the only thing he could think of. He was a bit dizzy.

"Well, maybe not exactly boring. Uncle Charles says the church has been going to the dogs for years—ever since Mr. Pusey began preaching those popish sermons. That was ages ago, but he can't get it off his mind. If he weren't my uncle I'd call him fanatical." She paused. "But wait, this is silly. Why don't you come in? Mrs. Brown, the housekeeper, is downstairs. She will act as our chaperone."

Would he come in? Horace's heart jumped. A few moments later, an elderly woman in a cap and apron opened the front door. "Miss Agnes will see you in the parlor, sir," she said. "You are Mr. James's house guest, aren't you? Please say hello to him. He and his little dog visit us quite often." The greeting was cheerful and with an equally cheerful "Certainly" Horace followed this Mrs. Brown through the entrance hall and into the parlor—reminiscent, Horace observed, of the oak parlor at Lamb House, though smaller. Agnes rose from her seat, her green eyes reflecting the late-afternoon sunlight. He bowed again and kissed her hand. That seemed the courtly thing to do.

"Why all the ceremony?" she cried. "You must do better than that!" Horace wondered what "better" meant. Agnes threw out her arms and hugged him and soon they were kissing, passionately. Horace had had some experience back home with "fast" girls. But Agnes was setting speed records; never had matters proceeded so quickly from casual greeting to—to, what was it? Certainly he had never before found a kiss so delicious or stimulating.

Agnes drew back. "Dear me," she said, breaking off. "I forgot myself. You are certainly the most delicious man I have met, or kissed!"

Horace was breathing hard. "You take my breath away, Miss Fengallon," he managed to say, and immediately regretted that he had called attention to her forwardness.

"I find you fascinating and fetching, Mr. Briscoe," she said. "Exotic as well. American young men are so . . . warm! But you must sit down and tell me all about yourself." She patted the sofa cushion on the love seat under the bay window, which, rather like the bay window at Lamb House, projected out over the street. Horace glanced nervously out, wondering if they might have been seen. Agnes laughed frequently as they talked, opening and closing a small Japanese fan, and fluttering it from time to time before her face, which looked wonderfully pink and moist. Horace never once broke off his gaze; surely Dr. Mesmer's mysterious force of animal magnetism was at work.

"I want to know all about you, Horace Briscoe. All I know is that you are Mr. James's guest and you are so . . . so very American. But I could tell that when I saw you at St. Mary's. I love America. I want to go there so much!" It was a gush of words and Horace was charmed. Horace explained that he had come to Rye to do research for a doctoral thesis about Henry

James's "artistic" fiction and was living in the attic at Lamb House, along with the servants.

"But I thought all Mr. James's stories were artistic," she said. "That's what Uncle Charles says. He reads all the time when he isn't engaged in church business. He is so pleased to be Mr. James's neighbor. He reads all Mr. James's stories as they come out, even in the American magazines. Would it offend you if I say this?" She paused. "Uncle Charles doesn't always understand the stories. That's what I heard him say when he was reading 'The Gilded Vase.' Oh dear, I can see that I have the title wrong. Let's see. It isn't the Gilded Vase now, is it?"

"I think perhaps you meant *The Golden Bowl*," Horace said with a tone of instruction, which he quickly regretted. "But your title is close. It wasn't golden, you see, the bowl in question, it was gilded to look like gold and had a hidden crack, a flaw, in it. That's the point. You see, it's symbolic of the ancient Italian culture as embodied in Prince Amerigo . . . Gilded but flawed and of uncertain substance . . ." Horace stopped in mid-sentence, feeling idiotically pedantic. "Not that any of this matters one bit, just now." Limited though his experience with the opposite sex was, Horace had noticed that young women weren't always aware, as most men were, that casual talk between the sexes tended to run at two levels, the more important of which was sub-verbal. At least, when the women were as beautiful as his hostess. Later, relishing the encounter in his literary way, Horace thought of Miss Jane Austen's memorable heroines and wondered just where Agnes—certainly the bloom of English girlhood in this modern century—might fit into that delightful array. She seemed as lively and witty as Elizabeth Bennet and less credulous and calculating than Emma Woodhouse. As for the meek, mild Fanny Price—well, the distance separating Miss Fengallon from Fanny was absolutely cosmic. And none of these heroines had anything like her physical warmth; it would have been condemned in that sedate age as unladylike, or something. Well, he thought, it had been a century and doubtless Agnes was something quite new, a new girl for a new age.

". . . I love to hear you talk, Mr. Briscoe," Agnes said, as they sat there in the parlor on Mermaid Street. "Do go on. Do you plan to be a don?"

"We don't call them dons in the States," he said, "actually. I believe the term is special to Oxford and Cambridge, what you call the ancient universities. Some think it comes from the word *dominus*, master . . ." That pedantry again! Horace silently cursed himself and bit his tongue.

"Well, what would you be called?" she pressed.

"Professor, probably," he said. "But enough about me, dull as I am. Tell me more about yourself."

"My father, Uncle Charles's younger brother, is in the Colonial Service, in Kenya. They, my parents, sent me back to live with him and be 'educated.' Besides, the climate in Kenya wasn't suitable. But I haven't learned very much and what I have learned is very boring. But if I don't know much, I am easy to know," she laughed, "Even! . . ." She did not finish the sentence and laughed and fluttered the fan.

The following morning, Horace tapped softly at Freud's bedroom door. He loathed the idea of bothering Henry James's guest but, as he told himself, this was an emergency. Uncle Henry had disappeared, as usual, for his daily stint of dictation to Theodora Bosanquet and Freud had retired to his room following his after-breakfast stroll in the qarden. The house had fallen quiet.

"Ja?" Freud called out. "Please leave the tray outside the door, Noakes, and many thanks." Freud thought he had been brought his elevenses, his biscuits and coffee.

"It's Horace, Dr. Freud. Please pardon the disturbance."

"Ah, Briscoe," Freud said, opening the door. "Come in." He pointed to a chintz-covered reading chair and pulled another chair from the small desk where he had been working. Horace felt a sudden and foolish impulse to flee. He wished he could melt into thin air. "I . . . I . . . that is, I . . . " he stammered.

Freud smiled. "I can see that you are on urgent business. Take your time. I hope you don't mind the smoke." He blew a thick cloud of blue cigar smoke toward the ceiling.

"Oh, not at all, sir," Horace said, feeling stupidly tongue-tied. "I wonder if I could ask you a question or two, Dr. Freud. Hypothetically, of course."

"Certainly," Freud said. "I have asked you no end of questions since we guests here together have been. Fair play is turn about." Horace couldn't help smiling. Dr. Freud's progress with English idiom was slow, given his acuteness and fluency.

"Thank you, sir. I have questions . . . about women," Horace managed to say. "Theoretical questions about women, or rather *a* woman." He knew that Freud would see through the ruse; but he was a courtly man and a doctor, after all, and perhaps he would spare Horace the embarrassment of saying so.

"A complex subject—women," Freud said dryly. "Or, as you say, a woman."

"Yes, complex. May I submit a hypothetical case, doctor? Suppose a certain young man were to meet a certain beautiful young woman, a ladylike young woman, indeed a chorister at the church . . ."

"Capital luck, I should think."

"Yes. Or rather, yes and no. Suppose that there were anomalies."

"Anomalies?"

"Anomalies, yes, in the sense that—in this hypothetical case, you understand—the young woman were to seem, well, surprisingly warm-blooded. Suppose that this girl, this dazzling girl, were to ignore the usual social expectations and to kiss the young man passionately, in their very first private encounter. And were to intimate that, with more privacy, the relationship might go even further. Much further."

"Alas, I claim no authority on social manners, Briscoe. By the way, may I call you Horace? We seem to be friends becoming."

"Yes, please do."

"You may call me Ziggy, that is what my mother called me when I was a lad."

"Oh, no sir. I feel a bit awkward, you see, calling my elders by first names. We don't do that in America."

"Very well, as you wish, Horace. As for women, they vary with time and place and class. Is this young woman English, or American?"

"English, sir." He paused and then went on. "I realize that as you say, women vary. But you are . . . you are, so to say, an authority on male-female relations. On sexual matters." There, he had managed to spit the embarrassing word out.

"I don't understand. Your hypothetical case is a bit bare of circumstantial detail. Was there some timidity on the part of the young man, some reluctance with this bewitching young woman to respond to her advances? In the hypothetical case, of course. Perhaps the young man sensed that the woman is what we in psychoanalysis call the devouring female?"

"No sir, doctor, not that . . . not really. No. She is very feminine."

"Then perhaps the young man in this theoretical situation is not of sufficient ardor? Unsure of his prowess? He should not worry about conflicting urges. In my *Three Essays* on sexuality I have dismissed the superstition of sexual absolutes, in sexual orientation. I have proclaimed universal bisexuality! Perhaps that would throw some light on the young man's dilemma. In the hypothetical case."

"Oh no, Dr. Freud. I am sorry to say that I have muddled the matter thoroughly. There is no lack of ardor on the young man's part. Indeed, the problem may yet be to control the ardor, given the inducement. You see, the young man is very much in love—theoretically—with the 'bewitching young woman,' as you call her and fears that if he yields to her impulses it may compromise her and spoil his prospects, which are entirely honorable."

"Yes, I see," Freud said. "What then precisely is the dilemma?"

"I suppose it comes down to this, Dr. Freud. How could the young man in such a case be sure . . . how could he be sure what the young woman really wants?"

"Oh, my dear Horace, that is the great question of all questions."

"And what is the answer?"

"There no one answer that I can discover is. No answer that covers all the cases, which are many." Freud's voice dropped to a confiding tone, and he glanced across the room as if he feared someone might be eavesdropping.

"You are a studious young man and know your Latin?" he whispered, leaning forward confidentially. Horace nodded.

Freud now brought his chair closer and resumed in a soft voice. "I shall give you confidentially the outline of a case of mine. A troubled young woman sought analysis in Vienna, a married woman suffering from the usual hysterical symptoms. As we talked she disclosed, to my astonishment, that her husband had left her *sine consortio* for years. The etiology of her disorder was clear, as was the cure."

"What was the cure?" Horace asked.

"As I told a colleague later, the cure clearly was *penis normalis, dosim repetetur!* Alas, such remedies aren't to be had by prescription at the corner chemist's."

"I see," Horace said, puzzled. He wondered what the case

had to do with his own. Fifteen minutes of consultation with the great man had produced no useful "cure"; and indeed the "dosage" Freud had recommended in the Vienna case was precisely what worried him, and in repeated doses!

"What has baffled the young man in your hypothetical case has baffled men since the Garden of Eden," Freud said. "But perhaps he has some pleasant choices to make."

"Indeed, sir," Horace said, rising from the chair. "I am grateful for your time and advice. I hope it hasn't been a bother."

"No bother, not in the least," Freud said. Even so, Horace felt that he had wasted Dr. Freud's time and had absorbed more cigar smoke than wisdom.

He had no sooner bowed out of Freud's presence, however, than he kicked himself inwardly for his timidity. The consultation had been stupidly aborted. He had danced as daintily as a vestal virgin around the subject that was actually consuming him. Fool! he muttered to himself as he stood in the hallway, shifting his weight from foot to foot. He heard Freud cough and the chair scrape on the floor as the doctor seated himself to resume his writing.

Why had he shrunk from asking the questions he wanted to ask? Horace had posed as the ignoramus, but he knew enough about Freud's theories to believe that if useful counsel was to be had, here and now, Freud was the source at hand.

He touched the doctor's doorknob, then quickly drew the hand back as if burned. Yet if burned it burned to knock again. He felt perspiration pop out on his brow.

He knocked. It sounded thunderous.

"*Ja?*" Freud's voice was now faintly edged with irritation; at least it sounded so to Horace.

"Begging your pardon, doctor, for another interruption," he called out, pressing his mouth to the door crevice, "but could you spare me another minute or two? I failed to ask a key question."

Footsteps approached the door; each resonated like a pistol shot and when the door swung open Horace felt as if he were staring into the mouth of a cave of unmeasured depth and dimness.

"Ah, it is you, Briscoe! I supposed as much," Freud said in a merry tone. He chuckled. "To tell the truth I could see that you were your true intent screening. I mean no insult, but long clinical experience has taught that when romantic links are at issue young people are to be direct sometimes disinclined. Oh, but I see I am lapsing into the wrong verb order."

Horace tingled with relief. Freud pointed and he sat down again in the same chair. He drew out his handkerchief and mopped his wet brow.

"I am glad to hear you say that, sir. I nearly ran away."

"I am glad you didn't, Horace. I can guess what brings you back. I sensed that the beautiful young woman of whom you spoke earlier is, in fact, your own love object?"

"Right, sir. You save me the embarrassment of admitting that. I must tell you, sir, that while I have had my crushes I have never felt this way before. I get dizzy when I think of her. But what I said about my worries"—Horace swallowed hard—"what I said about my worries, that also was true." He felt his face blaze. "What if she pushes our embraces so far that . . . that . . . ?" He left the question hanging. "One might lose control."

"If she is a well-bred young woman, as I suppose, I don't imagine she will test that limit. Unless . . ."

"Unless what, Dr. Freud?"

"Unless the warm nature you so vividly describe is rooted in some disorder, some 'neurosis' as we say in our deplorable jargon. I am compelled to ask: Is this ardor of hers so aggressive that it seems to you to reflect some traumatic experience?"

"That is far beyond me to say, Dr. Freud. When I am with her I am not quite sane myself. She is well bred; that is to say, she mentions the proprieties but whispers of exceeding them, of, of"—he stuttered—"unexplored pleasures. Erotic pleasures." There, he'd got the word out.

Freud rotated the cigar in his mouth; there was another silence.

"I fear that I can't give you any reliable sense of the young lady without the young lady myself seeing. Perhaps that could be arranged?"

Horace, stunned, gaped in spite of himself. The implications seemed so vast as to be unmanageable. But he plunged on.

"It might be arranged," he ventured, "but of course I shall have to ask her. That will take some doing. Her uncle, you see . . ."

"Her *uncle,* did you say?" Freud broke in, pronouncing the word with a certain emphasis.

"Yes sir. She lives nearby, just a few minutes away, with her uncle, a high Anglican official known as Archdeacon Fengallon. Her parents are in Kenya with the Colonial Service."

"Hmmm," Freud repeated. "The family constellation of relationships is suggestive. Uncles are often significant."

"If I could arrange to introduce you, sir . . . Her uncle is away just now on church affairs in London and we have an hour or more before luncheon. The house is a brief walk from here." Horace cringed as he felt the deep water lapping about his chin.

"It would be a pleasure to meet so bewitching a young lady, Horace."

Horace seized the moment. He ran down the stairs to the first landing and called to Noakes who, as usual, was loitering in the foyer.

"Burgess, would you do me a huge favor? Could you take a note down to the Fengallon house and wait for a reply? It's just across from the Mermaid."

"Righto, sir," Noakes said.

*

Meanwhile, the psychoanalysis that was keeping Dr. Freud at Lamb House seemed to be approaching a crisis; there was tension in the air. The following afternoon, after his consultation with the great doctor, James, Horace and Freud were sitting at tea, and as usual eating their way through too many of Mrs. Paddington's scones with butter and jam. Uncle Henry seemed ill at ease, toying with his watch chain. Horace was not surprised, a short time later, when Uncle Henry looked at his watch and, standing abruptly, announced that he had pressing work. A preface to the latest New York Edition volume must, absolutely must, go in the mail the next day. He excused himself with elaborate apologies, then raced through the double doors and through the garden and mounted the steps into his office.

Freud watched James walk away and then said in a conspiratorial tone, "Could you spare me a moment, Horace?, as I did you yesterday?"

"Certainly."

"That little talk in the garden, when we discussed Mr. James's teasing. You recall?"

Horace nodded, pretending nonchalance; he certainly would not confess that it had been so interesting that he had written about it at some length in his diary.

"You spoke to me of Mr. James's lightheartedness. Or rather, his tendency to place the writers in his stories in the position of teasing the critics. A reflection of his wish to keep critics at arm's length, to guard his tales against clumsy dissection? I believe that was how you put it."

"Correct," said Horace breezily. What was coming next?

"Well," Freud said, "I am still wondering, and I almost brought the subject up when you came to see me about the beautiful young woman and her friend's dilemma, which led to our morning expedition to Mermaid Street. Were you warning me?"

"Why should I warn you?" Horace toyed with his teacup. "I was speaking of the stories." He blushed at his disingenuousness and was certain Freud noticed.

". . . Mr. James might speak with every appearance of candor and yet—what is the English slang?—and yet might pull one's leg?"

"Oh," Horace said, "I see what you mean, sir. How could he pull a leg as firmly planted as yours, Dr. Freud?" But Freud's suspicions were aroused. "Are you worried?"

"I cannot divulge the substance of our analytic session, Horace, but toward the end of yesterday's sitting Mr. James began to remark on the 'osmotic' border—membrane, he called it—his speech is always wonderfully precise—that separates the real from the fanciful. Indeed, he said that the 'membrane' is always 'crudely porous,' in the case of storytellers. He claimed that he sometimes finds himself unable to distinguish between fact and fancy. Do you suppose he meant to put me on the *qui vive*, Horace?"

Horace took a confidential tone. "I thought your system made every allowance for the human disposition to fantasize. Surely you have tried and true techniques for distinguishing fact from fancy? As you demonstrated so well this morning when you saw clean through my clumsy evasion. Only a fool would try to deceive you!" Horace observed that a small dart of flattery had struck home. Freud's robust vanity was never far beneath the surface.

"I feel reassured," Freud said, rising from the table. "I think I am now in the garden a short stroll taking. Will you join me?"

"With pleasure," Horace said; and they moved out into the sunlight.

"I had wanted to ask you, sir, in any case, what conclusions you reached this morning during your visit with Agnes—when I left the room."

"She is a lovely creature, Horace, but I must tell you that I fear she is troubled. It is mere intuition at this point, but you see I have interviewed many young women much like her. I told her of a friend of mine in London—Eliot, by name. He is brilliant. If I were you, my friend, I would press her to visit him for a consultation."

* * *

Although Freud had limited himself to the brief advice about his colleague Dr. Eliot, he had assured Horace that Agnes was a pleasant problem to have. Now he knew what it felt like to walk on air, as the cliché had it. He came floating through the hallway, and was about to levitate to his room when Uncle Henry called out from the parlor.

"Do join us, Horace. Dr. Freud is elaborating on his theories." As he entered, Theodora rolled her eyes as if to say, *This is as far-fetched as anything you've ever heard.* Freud, with his usual expression of serene interest, was probably thinking, again, *These English make a joke of everything, just as Ernest Jones warned me.*

"And so," James resumed, as Horace took a seat, "one gathers that we are deluded in assuming the innocence of children, as you were saying apropos of my 'Turn of the Screw.' Like the fleshy putti in Titian's naughtier canvasses these naïfs are little engines of carnality." Horace wondered if Uncle Henry had been drinking something stronger than barley water. Freud chewed at his unlit cigar and then shook his head.

"I know you are joking, Herr James, but your picture of the Oedipal situation is ridiculously flippant. What could be more obvious? Consider the orality of the suckling infant. Surely this early feeding function is surcharged with libido, as we call the sexual energy."

"Ah," James said. "Light begins to dawn. Does it not,

Theodora?" She shrugged. "I fear not for me, Mr. James. But no matter."

Horace wondered what had brought on this new round of mockery. But just then "Enough," James said, turning to him. "I called you in, Horace, because rumors reach me that you are under attack by Cupid." The words were exactly those Mrs. Paddington had used. "Do confess, my boy. Own up." Horace, blushing, saw no point in concealment.

"I met a lovely girl at St. Mary's a couple of weeks ago and since you ask, Uncle Henry, I don't mind admitting that I am somewhat smitten. She lives just down the hill in an old Tudor house called the Old Hotel. With her uncle, a clergyman. Her parents are in Kenya with the Colonial . . ."

"Merciful heavens," James exclaimed, interrupting. "Not Agnes Fengallon!"

"Yes," Horace said. "She, that is Agnes. Is something wrong?"

"Fengallon!" James repeated. "A name to be spoken cautiously hereabouts." But he smiled, as if to soften the exclamation. Horace readily identified James's expression. It was the "social simper" Uncle Henry often mentioned in his stories— a mask of social politeness from which the telltale eyes of a very different mood peered out. Theodora glanced at him with sympathy.

"What do you mean, sir?" Horace asked. The question was awkwardly phrased; it sounded challenging and had popped out of his mouth.

"Dear boy, let us not pursue this. I am delighted by your good fortune. *Chacun à son goût!*" Uncle Henry had punctuated and closed down the discussion, as he had a way of doing. But his reaction to Agnes's family name was too puzzling to leave hanging and Horace resolved to probe the mystery at the earliest opportunity. When Uncle Henry rose, pleading the need to write a letter before they changed for dinner, Horace followed him.

"Sorry to persist, sir," Horace said. "But what did you mean, each to his own taste? Is Agnes Fengallon an unsuitable . . . friend?"

"Horace," James said, "it is a longer story than I—than we—have time for just now. I cast absolutely no aspersions on the young lady. She is beautiful and so far as I know very nice. You should merely be aware that her Uncle Charles is controversial. He meddles in all sorts of business not strictly his own and is constantly writing to the newspapers and hectoring others on every imaginable subject. He has bees galore in his bonnet. And there is said to be a—shall we say?—a shadow. It is said, Horace, though I have no direct knowledge of it, that he was deposed as archdeacon of Wells when he, when he t-t-took l-l-liberties with the choir mistress. And I hear that something not unlike got him cast from his fellowship at Exeter College in Oxford. Naturally, you are not to repeat this paltry tittle-tattle. I tell you only because you insisted."

"Liberties?" Horace asked.

"Must I spell out to your subtle understanding, dear boy, what latitudes of deportment are sometimes to be discovered among the foxhunting clergy? The archdeacon is notoriously unreconciled to the increasing sobriety of the church by law established and that may account for his louche reputation. They say it runs in the family, this taste for mild outlawry. His brother was nearly cashiered from the Colonial Service for some picayune indiscretion. The tendency no doubt exempts the females, and Agnes is a lovely girl." And with those words of warning, Uncle Henry mounted the stairs to write his daily letter to Edith Wharton.

That afternoon, after their psychoanalytic session, Freud recorded his impression of the incident:

Mr. James let the cat out of the bag, as the English say, today after lunch. As I already knew, his young guest, Briscoe, is smitten by a young lady, a Miss Agnes Fengallon, who lives nearby.

I have met her; she is lovely but troubled. When Mr. James heard the name of his protégé's sweetheart, he began to quiver with a surprising overflow of excitement and affect. At the risk of putting him on guard I later inquired about it, having myself made the maiden's acquaintance. Of course I did not say so.

Perhaps the mood in the Garden Room today was to some degree set by the stormy weather. There is a rainy gale, sweeping up the hill, and it was rattling the windows so violently I feared they might break. Mr. James got up from the couch to see that they were secured. He said Noakes could be trusted to do the same in the main house. "Smith, alas, will by now be too drunk to notice," he added, referring to the butler. Perhaps Smith should be fired once again—after all, he was, once before. But Mr. James is very tolerant.

"Permit me," I said, "to raise the matter of Mr. Briscoe's romance with the young woman he met at church. You reacted vigorously to the name."

"As usual," he said, "your memory is acute. But you missed the key modifier. I said, 'mixed company.' In this country we do not speak of indelicate matters before ladies—as I believe you do in Vienna."

I laughed at his little joke, although it is a miscarriage of analytic procedure to react. "I thought we were agreed, Mr. James, as confederates in deploring the legacy of—what to call it? Victorianism? Prudery? I am not aware that women dislike plain talk about every sort of matter."

"Touché," he said.

"Within these four walls," I asked, "would you mind saying more of your associations with the name, Fengallon?" Henry James was too acute to miss my purpose. "You mean," he said, "the archdeacon's louche reputation."

"Your associations, Mr. James. Speak as it comes to you."

"Oh, these infernal associations! The association in my mind is with a certain shade of indelicacy. I have heard it meanly whis-

*pered roundabout Rye that Agnes may have absorbed the man-
ners of her lascivious uncle—lascivious by sly report. But you
tempt me to common gossip, Freud. For shame. I do hear that
the girl is quite forward—*fast, *as used to be vulgarly said in New
York—for a well-bred young lady. But Horace will perhaps discover this for himself."*

I smiled to myself. I did not tell Mr. James that Briscoe had
sought my counsel regarding this "forwardness."

"As for the Archdeacon," James continued, "As Trollope in
his Barsetshire stories showed, our reverend clergy share human
characteristics common to any official service. Indeed, the dear
fellow told me on more than one occasion, may he rest in peace,
that he had learned much about church politics from observing
the inner workings of Her Majesty's postal service.

"Which is to say that the perquisites attaching to the church
attract the worldly as well as the spiritual. And such, by all
report, is the whilom Archdeacon of Wells, Fengallon. I believe
it was Disraeli who appointed him to that post, though one
would have thought that a man of such bellicose temper would
have joined the Army.

"As the story comes to me, Fengallon became a fanatical
detractor of the so-called Tractarians, who sought to re-establish
the forgotten links with the early church and Apostolic fathers.
And when I say fanatical, Freud, I speak literally. A bigot, one
might even say. I have seen hot letters of his to* The Times *on
such issues as whether some unoffending rural parson dare face
away from his parishioners when celebrating the Holy
Communion, or has ventured to put waxlights, that is candles,
on the communion table or, far worse, performed his hocus-pocus
at the altar, also a controversial noun. There is no doubt of his
learning and zeal; but one could winnow his sulfurous broad-
sides with the finest comb in search of charity. As for that, Herr
Freud, while I take no part in the internecine church wars and
whilst, moreover, the fires have cooled, I do sometimes look in*

on Father Morris's services at Saint Mary's. That old edifice is at hand, as you know. Morris is a saintly man of the Anglo-Catholic persuasion, but no zealot. He observes the forms revived by the Oxford apostles of decades ago, including the abundant use of candles and incense. It is a wonder to me that Fengallon ever darkens the door there, since he clings to the stripped-down eighteenth-century forms (high and dry but especially dry!). But I do believe he is there every Sunday and feast day; I see him occasionally as his walk to church passes our door. I suspect that he attends only to carry on his tiresome quarrel with Father Morris as stand-in for the Catholic party. Morris tolerates his taunts in good cheer, although he reacted furiously when Fengallon made off with a eucharistic vestment from the altar rail, on some antipopish pretext. It was said that he had been drinking that day, and not merely the sacred blood.

Such, Freud, are the oddities of the cure of souls today."

"But," I prompted, "you insinuated some scandal . . . not these obscure and outworn church wars."

"All in good time, herr doctor. I am now at the portal, as it were, of that episode of which the naughty world whispers . . . Fengallon is said to have conducted a flamboyant affaire du cœur *with the choir mistress. On the crowning occasion of indiscretion, he was seen to blow into her ear as they awaited the first notes of the processional hymn one Sunday morning. This was noted by the other clergy, who perhaps had been revolted by his poisonous militancy on issues believed to be long settled, and as to which most were prepared to live and let live. He was delated. The offense was brought to the notice of his bishop and thence to Lambeth Palace, and he was deprived. But confound this free association! You are leading me on . . . "*

I was naturally amused by Mr. James's insinuation that his eager gush of gossip had somehow been provoked by the technique of free association.

"You see, Freud," he continued, "we have only reached the

threshold. Fengallon brashly called witnesses to testify to his virtue, and they were compelled to tell all. Reports leaked, as usual, into the accursed papers, whose readers leap like gaping fish at every tidbit of bait."

"But do I understand you to say that her uncle's behavior has somehow smudged the good name of Miss Fengallon?"

James bridled. "You incite me to bear false witness?"

"Not at all, I am only interested in the excitement these and other sexual matters seem to stir."

"You play me like a pipe." But then he added, "You do recall our discussion of 'The Turn of the Screw?'"

"Of course," I said.

"Well then," he said, "with your prodigious memory you cannot have forgotten the remark of Mrs. Grose, the housekeeper at my haunted house, that Peter Quint, the reprobate butler, had been 'free' with everyone, even the children? Well, herr doctor," he said, "those who have ears to hear, let them hear."

And with this cryptic remark, our discussion turned to other matters, chiefly the interest of Mr. James's father in the theology of Swedenborg. The link eludes me. I keep these notes primarily to remind myself of the progress of the analysis. But in Mr. James's case the conversation is so intriguing that I am tempted to speculate, perhaps prematurely. For instance, the raw affect of his distaste for Fengallon, Agnes's uncle. Mr. James fastens upon that man of God's energetic distaste for the hocus-pocus of religion. I ask myself how this interplay fits into the emerging picture of Mr. James's psyche. One detects in him a comparable passion for display. Is that not evident in the New York Edition, his chief professional preoccupation? Is it not, so to say, literary ritualism? His brother, who is not free of the envy common in gifted siblings, views the "late style" and the elaborate revisions of his earlier work as a rococo cakewalk, which view is at the least imprecise; but when was Cain sympathetic to the labours of Abel?

What is this elaboration on Henry James's part, I ask myself, but a hoarding of the minutiae of his literary career, a fixing in verbal amber, which is really to say a familiar variant of anal-retentiveness?! That this is among his fixations is clear, moreover, in the redundant mastication of food. (It is supposed to relieve costiveness, a family affliction, but is all too likely to do him harm.) I would hazard that those who cherish the baroque details and flourishes of ritual are themselves of a retentive character; and while I see no evidence that Mr. James is superstitious, he is allied in spirit with the ritualists. Thus he sees Fengallon as an enemy. QED! Our session ended at precisely 2:30 this afternoon.

Henry James offered his own brief view of the day's topic in his letter to Edith Wharton:

My dear Edith,

The little plot I have been describing has now been side-tracked by an unexpected turn of events—that is, by adolescent complications. My guest Horace Briscoe, whom you met when you were here for luncheon, has been smitten in St. Mary's churchyard by a neighborhood beauty, Agnes Fengallon. She is a lovely girl, who often intercepts my walks with Max on Mermaid Street, but her own reputation is vaguely shadowed by a sort of Brontësque rumor involving her uncle & guardian, an ecclesiastic of violent outlook who was deprived at Wells (it is said) for an affair with the choir mistress. Gentlemen cannot, should not, be talebearers; but I thought it the better part of valor to run up a small storm signal regarding Miss Fengallon & her uncle. It caught the attention of Dr. Freud, who was present. He is always on the lookout for sexual innuendo. In our analytic session he questioned me closely and his reactions were predictable.

"I would speculate," said he, "that as you describe him, this pompous man of God is a perfect example of the seductive

Oedipal figure. It is not unlikely that this briest (for so Freud pronounces the word) may be of that 'dribe.'" (Why do I mock his nearly perfect English, simply because he mispronounces a few words and occasionally places his verbs in the Germanic order at the tail end?)

"But Dr. Freud," I protested, "I thought that you have largely abandoned the idea that hysterical patients have been seduced by male relatives, fathers, brothers, stepfathers, uncles, stepbrothers, et al. This would seem to be a snap judgment."

I added that I thought that his theory now assumed that many, indeed most, of the aggressions mentioned by female patients are fantasies. And besides, we had no information at all about the young lady.

"Yes, in most cases," he replied, "but when men such as her uncle are in the grip of the God-projection, and arm themselves as you say this gentlemen does with delusions of righteousness, one cannot assume that they set the usual obstacles to their own gratification."

He then mentioned, once again, the "case history" he has written of an "hysterical" young woman he calls Dora, who denied to her father and to him her sexual attraction to an older friend of her father, as well as some sort of sapphic attraction to another woman. He had apparently forgotten that he gave me a copy of this screed, and I did not remind him that I had read it. I wanted to see what the connection is, but he did not say; nor can I imagine. I must say, my dear, that Freud's unflattering speculation regarding the whilom Archdeacon has made me question my own dim view of him. But we shall see what comes of all this. I must close for now. Your faithfullest old Henry James.

In fact, Horace had detected in Uncle Henry's warning the usual undercurrent of merriment, and, besides, he did not regard Uncle Henry as an expert on matters romantic. And what he said on most matters was bent by the prism of irony. In any case, how could he act on such a warning when he couldn't get Agnes Fengallon off his mind? Her face even haunted his dreams. Suddenly wakening, he would imagine her floating up Mermaid Street in a thin gown and large hat, twirling her parasol, or reading a novel quietly in a secluded garden. These visions were a delicious torture, but moments of gloom visited him also; and lest he be seen moping about like a lovelorn in a silly novel, he stayed out of the way except when tea or meals demanded.

He had not seen Agnes since he had slipped Freud down to the old hotel to meet her in person. That had been days ago and so far no invitation to tea had arrived.

One evening after dinner, finding his impatience mounting again, he excused himself on the pretext of a digestive walk and stood looking down Mermaid Street and wondering if he were going mad. It was nearly ten o'clock and growing dark and the only light flickered dimly from the occasional window. He hurriedly passed the Fengallon house and heard, through the open front window, voices and laughter and the clink of china and glassware. Agnes's Uncle Charles must have returned from London; for some sort of dinner party was in progress. Horace moved up the street a few steps and, by standing on tiptoe, could see into the house. The room the window gave on was the parlor where Agnes had received him with such enthusiasm. Beyond it, through double doors, he caught a tantalizing glimpse of candle light and the sounds of dining. These sights and sounds whetted his need to have a glimpse of Agnes and, if possible, to hear her voice. He thought of knocking at the door. But that would be awkward at this unconventional hour. What excuse could he offer for an impromptu visit?

As he paused there, still on tiptoe, he noticed a small gate on the downhill side of the house. Might there be a garden beside the house, with trees and shrubbery affording conceal-ment? He crossed the street and slipped through the gate, which fortunately was unlocked. He threaded his way down a narrow alley and found himself at the edge of the back garden. Of course, the servants, or even the people in the house, might spot him; but in this incautious state, having already tres-passed, he darted from bush to bush and stood at last behind a tree from which he could look directly into the dining-room window. By good luck it too was open. Agnes sat at the foot of the table with her back to him, while at the head, splendid in white tie, sat her uncle. The guests, two men and a woman, were likewise dressed and completed the scene except for a footman who hovered to one side, with a platter in his hands. Horace drew his breath, stood very still and listened—fortu-nately, his hearing was acute. At first he could not believe what he heard, but it seemed that the Fengallons and their guests were discussing Uncle Henry!

"Yes," he heard Agnes say. "It is true. His young friend Mr. Briscoe was here just the other day and he confirmed the rumors."

What rumors? Horace wondered. He cupped his ear.

"Do you suppose," Archdeacon Fengallon asked in a loud pulpit voice, carrying well through the window, "do you sup-pose the poor fellow is balmy? Why else, in God's name, engage a Viennese alienist to come to him in Rye?"

Horace froze. *Uncle Henry balmy?*

"Isn't it rather obvious, Archdeacon?" one of the other guests said. "If Harry James were being treated by Freud in town—say, at the Atheneum, where I believe he usually lodges—wouldn't word of it spread? There would be whispers that the old boy is bonkers."

"That does rather make sense," Fengallon boomed. "Agnes, you see more of the great man of Lamb House than we. Has Mr. James been acting strangely? By which I mean to say more strangely than usual? He is a great eccentric, after all. You have heard of his romance with that charlatan in London—Fletcher? The 'doctor' who poses as a gourmet and recommends that every bite be chewed dozens of times?" The Archdeacon laughed loudly with much snorting and braying; it sounded to Horace like asses. The other guest joined in.

"Please, uncle," Agnes said. "You are being unfair. I often see Mr. James when he walks his little dog and he seems quite sane to me. But pray, to get back to the subject, when shall we ask the darling Mr. Briscoe to tea?"

"Why Agnes, I do believe you are sweet on the young man!"

"Perhaps. He is so interesting. You would enjoy his literary talk, Uncle. What about inviting him to tea? And why not invite Mr. James and Dr. Freud to dinner as well? You could then judge for yourself what is going on at Lamb House."

By now, Horace's heart was thumping so hard that he feared it could be heard in the dining room.

"Capital idea, Agnes, *capital!*" the Archdeacon roared.

Horace leaned against the tree to gather himself. The company was nearing the end of the meal—a savory was being served—and when the port came out and the ladies left the table they might come out into the garden on such a warm night. If they found him there, he would be compromised, ruined, a peeping Tom. His shirt was now wet. He passed, almost running and crashing into two clumps of shrubbery, behind the house and up the alley on the other side and into Mermaid Street. What he had heard surpassed his fondest hopes. It seemed not only that the divine Agnes Fengallon shared his feeling, but that Rye was buzzing with absurd speculations about the visitor at Lamb House. But no matter. He floated up the street, *back to the madhouse,* he said to himself and laughed. Looking up he sent a silent prayer of thanks to his lucky star.

*

When Horace opened his eyes, it was half past seven and the sun was well up, promising one of those glorious sunny English days. He was in danger of being late for breakfast, but lay back for a moment, his hands tucked behind his head, and savored the dangerous adventure on Mermaid Street. Certainly he had exceeded the outer limits of the code of behavior in which he had been reared. He shuddered when he thought of what his mother would say about that escapade, especially the eavesdropping. On the other hand, he relished the likelihood that he might soon sit at Agnes's side at her own dining table and kiss her hand. Who knew what might follow? He threw back the covers and, crossing the room, splashed his face with water at the basin Noakes had brought in while he still slept. Noakes and his other attic neighbors had doubtless been up and about for hours. As he was beginning to dress, he suddenly heard a resounding thump in the downstairs foyer, two stories below. When he opened his bedroom door he heard the thumping sound again and realized that it *was* the sound of somebody stomping his foot! A voice, unmistakably Uncle Henry's, could he heard shouting. *"No, no, no! A thousand times no!"*

A thousand no's to what? Horace wondered. He accelerated his toilet. When he came down the stairs a few minutes later he beheld a red-faced and agitated Uncle Henry, flourishing a small sheet of cream-colored note paper. A crest and several lines of handwriting could be seen on it. It was too early for the mail, and it could hardly be a tradesman's note. Then he quickly guessed what had provoked James's wrath.

"What is it, sir?" he asked with an air of innocence.

"What is it? The Archdeacon!" Henry James said angrily. "The cheek of the man! He has invited us—you and me and 'your guest, the honored alienist, Dr. Freud'—to dinner in Mermaid Street tomorrow evening. "No, no, no!" he said again.

"Why not, sir?"

"You know what I think of that zealot, that meddler and disturber of the peace, that l-l-lewd gentleman! I do not keep such company when I can avoid it."

"But sir," Horace protested, "May I please have a say? It is Agnes who instigated this, for my benefit. You were planning to have a dinner for Dr. Freud before he leaves, to meet some notables of the town, you said. Won't this do as a substitute? It will cause Mrs. Paddington far less trouble."

"You jest, Horace." To his relief, Uncle Henry's indignation was yielding to curiosity and kindness.

"No, sir. It is just that . . . I may as well be honest. I would give most anything to dine with Agnes."

Horace watched as the expression on Uncle Henry's face softened as swiftly as an April landscape, from distress to sudden pity. Or mercy. James rubbed his cheek, put his pince-nez on and again scanned the note. "Dear boy," he said, "I shan't thwart your budding romance. But really, must one throw oneself into such a d-d-den of d-d-degradation? In any event we must consult Freud; he may object."

"I am sure he won't," Horace said with assurance, although he dared not say why he knew.

Degradation, and with the affected stammer. The word was a giveaway. James's expression softened further into a teasing smile. Horace pressed his advantage. "I am sure you recall, Uncle Henry, that story Boswell tells of how he maneuvered Dr. Johnson into dining with his *bête noire* John Wilkes? How outraged Johnson was at Boswell's sly suggestion that, perhaps, he might not be civil enough to dine with a man whose whiggish political agitation he despised? How he scolded Boswell for suggesting that. And how much he enjoyed the evening in the end?"

"*Touché,*" James said. "How can your poor Uncle Henry resist so beguiling and noble a comparison? Wilkes was a prince of men by comparison with that clerical rascal, but you plead a case well, Horace. Perhaps you should l-l-lower your-self and become a l-l-lawyer."

After breakfast James stepped to the small desk in the tele-phone room and wrote on a note card: "Mr. Henry James is pleased to accept the invitation of the Very Reverend Dr. Fengallon for tomorrow evening. Messrs Briscoe and Freud will accompany him." He paused, then inserted the word "kind" before "invitation."

"Here," he said, handing the card to Horace, "you may be our Mercury."

Horace raced out the door and hurried with high heart down Mermaid Street. But as he neared the Fengallon house he stopped to consider. He hoped to steal a glimpse of Agnes, but if he merely presented the card at the door that would be unlikely. He knocked. No answer. He knocked again, more loudly.

A glowering figure in livery opened the door, the same foot-man he'd seen serving a few nights earlier. "Yes?"

"I am Horace Briscoe," the caller announced, extending his card. "An acquaintance of Miss Fengallon. Might I have a word with her?"

"Miss Fengallon does not receive at this early hour," the footman said, holding Horace's card between thumb and index finger as if it might infect him with a disease.

"Please ask," Horace said; and without being invited to do so stepped across the threshold. "Be so kind as to give her my card."

A few moments later, a familiar voice called down to him from the staircase. "What an unexpected pleasure," Agnes said.

"I came as a messenger," Horace said, dazzled as always by Agnes's beauty. "That is, I have come to say that Uncle Henry, that is Mr. James, would be happy to come to dinner. I shall come also; as will Dr. Freud. Is your uncle here? Would you see that he gets this—Mr. James's note?"

Agnes stepped forward with a rustle of silk, taking the note from him with one hand and with the other grasping his elbow. "This way, Horace," she said. They passed out into the garden and beyond the rose arbor reached a small summer house well screened by trees and shrubbery. When they had seated themselves on the circular bench, Agnes laughed and fixed her green eyes on him. "Do you know what, Horace?" she said. "You are found out. I saw you crossing our back garden in the moonlight last night, as Mrs. Mellon and I passed the upstairs window. I am sure it was you, there was a full moon. Admit."

"What?" Horace said. His face crimsoned.

"Don't worry," she laughed, "I'll never tell. But what on earth were you doing in our garden, gallivanting about in the moonlight? Playing the Druid?" She giggled.

"Taking a short cut," he stammered.

"A short cut! I don't believe you," she laughed. "A short cut through our garden, leading where, pray?"

"All right. I was hoping to catch a glimpse of you. I don't know what possessed me. But it had been too long since I brought Freud to call on you, and days since that visit in your drawing room. You had . . . well, you promised to invite me to tea. Don't you remember?"

"Of course I remember. Unfortunately, uncle had to go to London and our social calendar suffered. But what an odd coincidence that you should be wandering about like Moses in the wilderness when we were just discussing Mr. James at the dinner table. You should have heard."

"Oh? You were?"

"Yes. Uncle and his friends are absolutely devoured with curiosity about Mr. James's guest, the famous alienist from Vienna, as they call him. I couldn't tell Uncle that I had met him and that he doesn't bite."

"Freud, you know, is a colleague of Mr. James's brother, Dr.

William James, also a psychologist—or alienist as you say."
Horace caught himself; that was the term Fengallon and his
guests had been using as he was eavesdropping. He was conscious of trying to deflect strange conclusions and making a
flop of it. The more he said, the more evasive it sounded, even
though it happened to be true.

"Nothing more than a friendly visit before Dr. Freud goes
on to visit relatives in Manchester, who are in trade there.
What are people saying?"

"Well, Horace, if you promise not to repeat it I shall tell you
a little. Uncle thinks Dr. Freud's visit is highly significant. So
do others in Rye. Why would a famous alienist be here? They
say Freud specializes in, well . . . " she paused. "In . . . certain
mental disorders. They think that he is here to treat Mr. James.
As you know, I am under no such impression. But Uncle is a
great collector of gossip."

Horace staged an imitation of surprise and indignation. "The
very idea of those village gossips! What has happened to English
privacy? Uncle Henry is one of the sanest men on earth!"

"Please don't shout, Horace," Agnes said, tugging at his
sleeve. "And don't be upset. It's just village talk. And you
asked . . ."

"Damn village talk. It sounds vicious." He jerked his sleeve
from her grasp and began pacing around the summer house. "I
am shocked that gentlemen like your uncle would give curren-
cy to this, this talk, these rumors."

Agnes now rose also. "Horace, I can't stay here now. You
are making so much noise. The servants will hear us and think
I am being denounced. Please, don't breathe a word of any of
this to anyone. Mr. James might cancel the dinner plans, and
you know what that would mean."

"What would it mean, Agnes?"

"That you and I . . ." she said, leaving the unfinished sentence hanging in the air. She kissed Horace on the cheek and

hurried away. "Go out the front garden gate, Horace. I know you know the way. *À bientôt!*"

From Freud's notes that afternoon:

There was something unusual, a je ne sais quoi, *in the air today when Mr. James and I sat down for our consultation. "How," he asked, "do you decide when an analysis has run its course? Strictly speaking, human relations have no such terminus. As I recently wrote in my preface to the new edition of* Roderick Hudson, *the artist's challenge is to produce an illusion of closure; I suppose your science must do no less."*

"You are right," I said, "in implying that there is no obvious end point, but a skilled analyst finds milestones along the way, marked by what we call the transference. The analyst becomes a surrogate figure in a problematic psychic drama involving the patient. But these are milestones on a road of incalculable length."

Would I say that we had come to any such milestones? I replied that the question was hard to answer in a case so special as his.

"Special, Mr. James, in that you are an artist. It has been an honor to explore the unconscious with you, a rare privilege. Yet the process has been superficial and in a way frustrating. I have analyzed many, based on their works—Shakespeare's Hamlet, *the tales of E. T. A. Hoffmann, Jensen's story "Gradiva," others. You were kind enough to read my essay on "Gradiva," the tale brought to my attention by Carl Jung of a young archaeologist who falls in love with a marble relief of a young woman, and in particular with the unusual attitude of her foot. He becomes convinced that she was buried in the eruption of Vesuvius in AD 79, only to find, when he visits Pompeii, that she is in reality a living girl he played with as a boy and now finds himself in love with. But analyses of artists performed from cold print pale by comparison with the challenging privilege of speaking face to*

face with an artist of the first magnitude. Our analysis could proceed indefinitely and I hope we may correspond after I leave. But candidly, no, I don't believe we have reached any milestones. I detect no transference. You do not vest me with archaic authority!"

He pressed me for explanation. "What have I left out?" he asked, almost pleadingly. I hesitated, though I knew the answer. I said that these processes could not be rushed. "I sense, moreover, Mr. James," I went on, "that your unconscious is richly stocked with repressed materials of the greatest interest. But you have thrown up a wall of flippancy, as if it were a treasure to which you don't wish the map to share. Just for instance, while I told you at the outset that dreams are a royal road to the unconscious you have yet to bring me a single dream for analysis!"

"Oh dear," he said, "I am not an accomplished dreamer. When I do dream, my dreams are banal, unto tears."

"You don't remember your big dreams. There is no such thing as a banal dream; all are significant, however ordinary they may seem to one of a high-flying imagination."

"Perhaps there is limited capacity for work, in your special sense, distressing word, and the work in my case is so heavily invested in storytelling that no surplus energy is left over for dreaming. Perhaps, herr doctor, the fixed quantum of psychic energy is absorbed in my writing? Ergo, boring dreams."

"Perhaps, Mr. James, insofar as your censor, as we call it, allows full play to that energy. Repression is a powerful force; so are the defenses that guard it against illumination."

"What would you like to discover that we haven't touched upon?" he asked.

"In fact, I was reflecting that parental influences are crucially important. As I have said, they typically figure in the transference. I know enough of your relationship with your brother, Dr. James, cordial as it is, to see that a certain rivalry is involved. But you have said little about your remarkable father. Did he really

subscribe to the delusions, as I would call them, advanced by
Swedenborg?"

"By what warrant do you call them delusions?"

"Herr Swedenborg imagined that earthbound men speak
with personages on other planets. That to me is delusion. Did
your father believe it?"

"I can't say, and I have no idea whether such notions are
delusions or not. You recall Hamlet's admonition: 'There are
more things in heaven and earth than are dreamed of in your
philosophy, Horatio'? My father rarely spoke to me of metaphysical matters, though he and William talked of them constantly. His chief interest was in the ethical implications of
Swedenborg's system. He came to it after what he called his 'vastation,' his terrible vision of evil. Do you exclude these numi-
nous possibilities a priori? I would call that dogmatic."

"Indeed, Mr. James," I said, "I am persuaded that all deistic
beliefs, in all their bizarre variety, are what we call 'projections,'
the lingering influence of human authority figures. Usually
fathers. Consider, Mr. James, that your own transparent benevo-
lence may be a mere internalization of your father's 'hard-won
benignity,' as you called it. Indeed, your godhead."

Mr. James appeared not so much to be pondering my theory
as to be devising a strategy of resistance. I said to him candidly
that we had been digging shallow little holes at the mouth of a
gold mine, with amusing finds, but with no discovery of the
Virgilian auri sacra fames.

"I congratulate you on the metaphor," he said. "The accursed
hunger of gold! Exactly! You see, I am that queer monster, the
artist, and as you have observed in your writings on Leonardo
and Jensen, there is an enormity in the artist: lustful with curiosity, licentious, unaccountable, anarchic, at least as measured by
the narrow gauge of science. We artists contain your science,
Freud."

I said that I was well aware of that. "As I sometimes say,

before the problem of the creative artist, analysis must lay down its arms."

We had been going in circles as the hour sped by. We ended the session with Mr. James's promise: "I shall try my utmost to produce—I almost said, hatch—a dream for your dissection."

When Mr. James had left, I sat for a moment recalling his brother's rather aggressive remarks about the New York Edition. He suggests that it is an obsessional neurosis of some sort, but apart from my previous speculation as to anal retentiveness, what little he has said about the "prefaces" he is affixing to the new editions suggests to me that his preoccupations are perfectly understandable—and often brilliant—musings on his craft . . .

* * *

What an evening this will be, Horace thought as they arrived at the Fengallon doorstep promptly at seven the following night. Many days later, he pictured the evening in memory as a set piece from a Russian novel—at least in its release of boisterous passions. But what, after all, might he have expected of such a cast of characters?—the Archdeacon, with bonhomie and booming voice; the diminutive Freud, pleasant and sphinx-like; and finally Uncle Henry, ever genial and conversational but destined to be caught in the middle? As they were welcomed by the same glowering butler, Horace guessed that Archdeacon Fengallon would doubtless underestimate the subtle brilliance in Freud that he and Uncle Henry had now had ample chance to observe. And at his peril.

They stood in a polite circle, sipping Tio Pepe, except for Uncle Henry, who had asked as usual for barley water. Their host immediately began to interrogate Freud about Vienna, describing the great imperial capital as one of his favorite cities.

"I love the music there, especially Brahms. And then there

is your Herr Wagner, with his strange operas spun out of Norse myth."

Horace watched a faint pained expression cross Freud's face. *Didn't this man of God know that Wagner was German, not Austrian, and nothing to do with the south or the great polyglot empire?* Torn as he was between admiring Agnes and monitoring portents of danger, Horace was already perspiring in his formal suit with white tie and the evening was only minutes old. Nothing had yet been said about Freud's stay at Lamb House or the gossip it seemed to inspire. As they entered the dining room they passed a small *placement,* fanlike on a tray, and Horace saw with delight that he would be seated beside Agnes, who was at the foot of the table, next to Freud, who would be on the Archdeacon's right, across from Henry James. As they stood behind their chairs, the Archdeacon raised his hand and in a loud voice intoned: *Benedicite, benedicat. Per dominum nostrum Jesum Christum. Amen!* "Amen," Horace and Agnes said, with a small echo from James. Freud merely bowed his head. As they took their seats it was as if Freud and Fengallon had already identified one another as the designated antagonists of the evening. Freud was at his most Viennese, however, beaming with smiles and gestures, while Fengallon made a point of questioning Uncle Henry, with lavish irrelevance, about his current work.

"And how many volumes," he asked, "are there to be in this New York Edition of yours, Mr. James? And why are you undertaking it?"

"Twenty-three, by present plan. It is my small votive offering to the great Balzac, a model for us all who labor in this vineyard. As you know, he designed his *Comédie Humaine* in precisely that compass. As for the purpose, well, reckon not the need! A writer inevitably begins with juvenilia, and as his craft matures—well, it is as if you, Archdeacon, were forced to go back to your apprentice sermons and put them again before the public. Could you do so without blushing? No? No more can I, although occasionally I marvel at some presentable relic of my *jeunesse.*"

"And how do you decide which of your works are to be made canonical, as it were? If you are held to twenty-odd volumes, you obviously chuck quite a few. How, as we often put it in my line of work, separate sheep from goats?" The Archdeacon chuckled and Henry James smiled agreeably.

"I suppose," said the latter, "that the process is mostly intuitive and certainly subjective. I am not including *The Bostonians*, for instance, about which I seem to recall you were kind enough to write me a note."

"Indeed, sir. I applauded your satire of that skirted monster. What was her name? Olive Chancellor? A witch, born and bred! A pity to lay it aside. It should be required reading. The world needs such good sense."

"Alas, Archdeacon, the reading public in America did not share your enthusiasm. I rather liked the tale myself, though I do not regard it, as you do, as a sort of parable for our times. The sale was pitifully small. And for my troubles I was censured by the Boston *conoscenti* for allegedly taking the side of the Confederate invader, Mr. Ransom. I thought I resolved his struggle with Miss Chancellor for the allegiance of the girl strictly on the merits."

Horace was straining to listen to these interesting exchanges but his head was spinning and it wasn't the wine. Agnes, to his mixed surprise and pleasure, had let her hand wander into his lap and was exploring here and there in a way that could not be ignored. His face blazed, and he gave thanks that the others seemed to be entirely absorbed in the conversation. *Thank God,* he said to himself, *that there is little chance that we must leave the table any time soon, for in this condition I would be very embarrassed.* He struggled to engage his mind in what Fengallon and James were saying, hoping to be distracted from the dangerous sensations Agnes had stimulated. He sat rigid and looked straight ahead across the table and toward the side window, fearing to look into her eyes. The conversation rose and fell. Freud sat so contentedly silent that Horace wondered what all the fretting had been about. He tried to recall Uncle Henry's worries of the other day. It had to do, he thought, with latent explosions and discharges. He himself had said, "So you are saying, Uncle Henry, that Freud and Fengallon would be a combustible mix, like matches and kerosene, since Freud thinks of religion as an infantile survival."

"Yes," Uncle Henry had responded, "that's precisely one's fear—combustion, sudden combustion. A veritable explosion, my boy, of lurking passion! Why venture to touch matches to gunpowder?" (*Did he really say that?* Horace marveled.)

"But surely, sir," he had asked, "as a student of the human comedy you will find such an explosion revealing, even exciting?"

"Exciting? There is such a thing as too much excitement, Horace, and some settings are inappropriate—everything to its place and season. You are a dangerous influence. Still, for the sake of your love life, I shall take leave of good judgment." *Well! Who would have predicted from that sedate exchange at the breakfast table at Lamb House that for Horace, now, the potential combustion was of an entirely different order, carnal not theological?*

Agnes, noting his condition, withdrew her hand, smiled fondly at him, and merely patted his hand. The table talk gradually came back into focus. So far, the gathering had been unusually sedate and perhaps it would end without the merest pop of a conversational squib. Horace, apart from his preoccupation with Agnes, was feeling vaguely disappointed and had failed to detect the storm cloud hovering just over the upper end of the dinner table, where the host and Dr. Freud sat before the platter of mutton. The talk, so far, was bland.

"Speaking as you were earlier of sheep," Freud said, "I am reminded of the great herds of sheep I saw as we came down by rail from Ashford—clouds of them, as far as the eye could see, all glazed, it seems, in the colors of their owners."

"Indeed, this part of Sussex has been sheep-raising and sheep-shearing country since the Middle Ages, when English wool supplied the weavers and spinners of half Europe. Naturally, we also eat a great deal of lamb and mutton, out of loyalty . . ."

Horace, seeing no promise in a discussion of sheep, had dared turn back to Agnes, and as if nothing had happened beneath the table asked her with an air of seriousness about one of the paintings on the dining-room wall—probably the portrait of some earlier clerical Fengallon. Henry James was contentedly chewing according to the principles of Fletcherization when Horace saw his fork pause in midair. The Archdeacon had just said that he had been reading Oscar Wilde's *The Picture of Dorian Gray.*

"Poor Oscar," James said. "He was on tour in New York, once, when I visited. It must have been fifteen years ago now."

"A fascinating tale from the point of view of psychoanalysis," Freud said. "I have been tempted to write an essay about it."

"And what would you write?" Fengallon asked in a challenging tone.

"I would call it an example of what we call 'splitting' between the ego and the id—that is, between the controlling, rational self on the one hand and the fundamental energies on the other; all innocence on the surface, all licentiousness and contamination within. A brilliant conceit, that portrait."

"Poor Oscar," James said again, shaking his head. "That story was his autobiography."

"Why do you call him 'poor Oscar?'" Freud asked. Fengallon nodded, as if to second the question.

"Do not suppose, my dear Freud, that the epithet has to do

in the slightest with his . . . his so very exotic private habits. I was thinking merely of his vulgar displays on the public stage, the outré dress and, dear me, the lily, the lily! Irish raffishness at its worst. I can say that with authority, because my grandfather, who made our American fortune, was quite Irish, though of a more Calvinist breed. All this is quite apart from Oscar's reckless entanglement with that scamp, the young lord 'Bosie,' as I believe he was called."

"Come now, Mr. James, aren't you overlooking other associations with 'poor Oscar'?" Freud asked.

"There *are* no others," James said. "No repression, if that's what you're driving at." Everyone was listening now and it struck Horace that the veil of the Garden Room had been rent and the private conversations there suddenly exposed— "Supposing I had repressed some association, such as his involvement with the brutal Queensberry, how should I know? On your theory, Freud, what is repressed cannot be conscious!"

"In my view," Fengallon broke in, "Wilde stands as an example of the worst liabilities of the spoiled Catholic. I would say that their predisposition to estheticism in sacred matters invariably plays them false—confusion worse confounded . . ." Horace shuddered. *Here it comes,* he thought silently; the Archdeacon now had one foot in the stirrup of his hobby horse.

"Were it left to me," Fengallon boomed, "and not to his too-clement lord of Canterbury, those who even now subvert the sound Protestantism of the English church, scheming to *papalize* it, would be chivvied from it bag and baggage: by which I mean, sir, their fruity incantations and chants, their infernal bell-ringing and incense-burning, their candles and bobbing and scraping and the like. As, sir, we must put up with at Saint Mary's . . ."

He steamed on: "I don't suppose, Freud, that you are familiar with our internecine church wars—and all because the neo-papists feared having unbelievers pass on the Prayer Book and other sacred matters. An all but endless string, once pulled. Eh, Mr. James?"

Henry James cleared his throat and touched his napkin to his lips. "There is, very possibly, much in what you say, Archdeacon. But I am an unfit referee in this great matter of sacred usages. I thought we were discussing poor Oscar Wilde. I am more at home there."

"Wilde! ah yes; and so we were, Mr. James, so we were. I must say that he writes like an angel . . . a fallen angel." Everyone began to talk about Wilde at once, but Freud almost casually injected a few words that touched a match to the waiting keg of gunpowder.

"Writers of your perspicuity, Mr. James, are conscious of so much more, begging your pardon Archdeacon, than the ordinary man of God."

"You may not be aware, Dr. Freud," Archdeacon bristled, "that I was trained in medicine, at Guy's Hospital. My field of vision is not limited to sacred matters."

"Ja?" Freud said.

"Yes," the clergyman said, "you will forgive me for saying that my former colleagues, without exception, are exceedingly skeptical of the turn medical trends have taken in Vienna. They certainly would question, for instance, your competence to pronounce on theological questions."

"Please, uncle . . ." Agnes said.

Freud sniffed softly and drew a large silk handkerchief from his sleeve. "What medical trends do you mean, sir? Viennese medicine is unrivaled in Europe. I cannot imagine that I would be in the least troubled by your colleagues' ignorant opinions."

"Oh, but you would be interested, herr doctor," Fengallon said, "if you heard them. Their views flatly contradict your so-called 'science'—psyche-analysis."

"Psychoanalysis, sir."

"Very well, psych-*oh*-analysis. In any case, Gaskell, for instance, calls it '*modern witchcraft*.'"

The terrible word witchcraft resounded from the Archdeacon's lips, as if he had been waiting from the first to toss it into the mix at the earliest opening. The playing with fire had begun.

"Please, uncle," Agnes repeated. But in vain; Fengallon thundered on.

"Yes, witchcraft, sir. That was his very word. *Ipsissimus*! He tells me of your so-called 'cures' in which you induce maidenly young women to lewdly discuss their virginity and ignore the recent findings about the role of bodily chemicals. The hormones. The secretions of the ductless glands. And this quite apart from the prurience of the proceeding! They are the determinants of what you call hysteria, not the uterus!! That is medical superstition."

Freud was aroused. "I am reluctant to respond sharply to *mein* host. But permit me to say, sir, that the term 'hysteria' is merely a traditional term of art, an anachronism if you please, and implies no physiological significance. But in any case, these are strange and unpersuasive claims from a man of God. I should have thought that witchcraft, if we must resort to so insulting a term, would more closely fit the pretenses of the priestly profession. That black tide of mud! The denial of human instincts. Do not your English parsons still pray for rain during droughts? A mere step from the primitive rain dance. And your 'harvest festivals' and 'resurrections'? Again, a short jump from the days when your ancestors painted themselves blue and danced to panpipes in the light of the full moon! Believe me, as a Jew and a student of the Hebrew scriptures, I am familiar with the propitiation of crude tribal deities . . ."

James covered his mouth with his napkin, but his eyes and his shoulders betrayed him. He was unsuccessfully trying not to laugh at what he had professed to fear.

"A tide of muck? Is that so, sir?" Fengallon turned up the volume of his voice to fortissimo. "That is all you have to say of nineteen hundred years of sacred history?"

"Indeed, Archdeacon, what I have just said are commonplaces of the new anthropological science. A small thought experiment would explain your own retreat from medicine to priestcraft. Did it not occur when your father died?"

"What business is that of yours, Freud? And what is your insinuation?" The Archdeacon flourished his wine glass, and the footman hastened to refill it.

"Please, uncle," Agnes begged. In her worry, she was ignoring Horace's lap and that was a relief. But the antagonists weren't listening.

"My dear Archdeacon, what I say is not an insinuation, it is a finding, supported by abundant clinical experience. Your 'God the Father' is very probably what we call a projection of your natural father, a vestige of the latter's presence, the internalization, so to say, of his paternal dicta: his 'thou shalt nots . . .' What is it you English say, the grin from the Cheshire cat vanished? All the do's and dont's. I would include the Ten Commandments that Moses, if there was such a man—he was probably Egyptian—brought down from Mount Sinai. Surely all this is too firmly established among men of learning to be questioned."

Henry James had stopped smiling at Freud's darts, which certainly were finding their target in the hide of the Archdeacon. The two combatants had put down their silver, as if there was some danger that they would attack one another with their table knives. Horace, observing, was relieved that they did not wear swords. Once again, Fengallon waved his wine glass and tapped it sharply on the table. "Fill it," he commanded. "And Freud's. There is nothing like a rattling good debate!"

"Please, uncle . . ." Agnes repeated. "Our guests . . ."

"If I had entertained any doubts of the dangers of your false 'science,' Freud, these indecent suggestions would quiet them. Indeed, sir, you speak of sacred matters with no more restraint than your common, ranting Hyde Park Corner mountebank! Blasphemous and vulgar! What they say is true, then. Is it not your design to supplant divine authority with sexual license which, I am given to believe, you trace even to the innocent doors of the nursery? Confess, sir. You cannot deny it!" The Archdeacon was growing very red in the face.

"Please, please, uncle," Agnes pleaded. She half rose from her seat.

"Quiet, Agnes, this is a serious matter. And come to that," he went on, "I will say that decent folk here in Rye are most curious about your proselytizing mission among us. What libertine heresies do you propose to sow here?"

Horace was thankful that dueling was unlawful in England. But suddenly, as Fengallon's face darkened from pink to purple, Freud's was growing pale, as if by some subtle transfusion from one to the other as in *The Sacred Fount,* one of Henry James's stranger novels.

Freud fell silent. He withdrew his handkerchief again from his sleeve and sneezed. His eyelids fluttered and his head slumped to his chest. Henry James noticed it first. "Help him, Horace," he cried, rising to his feet. "Quickly! Bring the spirits of ammonia," Fengallon called to the footman. Freud had fainted and sat with his eyes closed and his chin resting on his chest. Horace braced him and he remained upright.

The Archdeacon sprang quickly around the table to Freud's side, taking his pulse. He looked into Dr. Freud's eyes. "Dilated," he said, "but not fixed. He will recover in a moment, Mr. James. I do hope it was not the wine." The footman returned with a small vial and Fengallon waved it with a sure hand under Freud's nose. Freud started and opened his eyes.

"Dear me," he said, "I seem to have fallen asleep. I regret . . . "

The Archdeacon smiled triumphantly. "You will recover, Dr. Freud. I fear that our friend from Vienna," he said, turning to Henry James, "is unused to the rough and tumble of our English debating!"

"If you please, sir," Freud answered. "This brief spell hardly betokens timidity or surrender. I am susceptible to such lapses when agitated, but with the substance of discussion they have nothing to do. Nothing, I assure you! I do fear, however, that our exchanges had gotten a bit 'out of hand' as you English say. Somewhat sharper than we had intended.

"You mistake me," Freud continued. "I meant no sweeping insult to Christian history as such. It is formidable and very great men have been—and are yet—given over to this mystical delusion; and, I must add, with striking benefits to the arts and letters. I have written of them—Michelangelo, Leonardo, Dostoyevsky, even Augustine. Christianity is to say the least a force to be reckoned with, although great evil has been done the Hebrew people in its name. I believe that the Jews were expelled from your land until the time of Cromwell?"

"Yes, and that was shameful," Fengallon said, in a quieter voice. "I am the first to say that our faith stands upon the voices of the Hebrew prophets, Joshua ben-Joseph among them. I dare say we both grew over-excited and I beg your pardon, Freud. It is after all my duty as host to make my guests comfortable at table. I retract the word 'witchcraft.' It was not mine, to begin with; it was Gaskell's. I merely quoted it. Johnson, do bring more wine." He signaled to the footman. "Agnes was quite right to call me down! And yet, to return to the question of the ductless glands . . ."

"Uncle!" Agnes cried. "Let us speak of something less contentious. The sheep herds of Sussex, for instance."

Everyone laughed and the tension melted. Horace glanced

around the table. Both Freud and Fengallon wore the look of serene volcanoes, silent and inactive but far from extinct.

It need hardly be added that this exercise in debate considerably shortened the dinner party. Dr. Freud cheerfully declared himself recovered, the cloth was pulled, and the male guests lingered uneasily for almost an hour over the port. Freud for his part smoked a cigar in contentment. No one ventured to renew the argument that had brought on the fainting spell. For sheer tedium (Horace thought to himself) this tranquil aftermath, the calm after a spectacular storm, took every prize. Everyone was excruciatingly, stiflingly, polite and Horace longed to be with Agnes, who, by English custom, had been banished from the table and the port and cigars.

"Gentlemen, the pisspot is under the sideboard if anyone needs it," the Archdeacon said. "It is our ancient English rationale for dismissing the ladies." No one moved.

When a decorous discussion broke out on the merits of Vienna architecture, Horace excused himself. Agnes heard him leave the dining room and came down the stairs. They went out and sat in the summer house, listening to the noises of the late twilight.

"When will we see you again?" Horace asked. "I liked what happened at the dinner table, and I don't mean the food or those silly arguments about rain dances and witchcraft. I've never felt this way before." He reached for her hand in the dim light and brought his lips to it, feeling again her softness. He was drawing her closer but just as he did so a door opened and light splashed into the garden. He heard himself summoned.

"Damn, they're leaving, Uncle Henry and Freud are. I guess I should go too, but I don't want to. Perhaps you and I could . . ."

"Not now. Goodbye, Horace. You must go, otherwise Uncle will suspect that something is happening between us and who knows? He might send me away and that would be too dreadful. I love you, Horace Briscoe. We shall find a way to be together. Alone."

* * *

Horace couldn't help feeling, the next day, that he was in a way responsible for the fiasco at the Fengallon dinner party. He had derided Uncle Henry's doubts of the wisdom of dining with the volatile Archdeacon and James had yielded out of a generous instinct to promote Horace's romance. Beyond that, Henry James's young visitor was now in solitary possession of a guilty secret. He knew that the gossips of Rye were speculating about the purpose of Freud's visit and leaping to wild conclusions. It was hardly surprising. One of Uncle Henry's favorite literary themes was the obtuseness with which the philistine world (including some critics) regarded storytellers. One could find a splendid treatment of the theme in the bitterly amusing Yellow Book story called "The Death of the Lion," in which the fashionable admirer of an eminent writer loses the dying author's manuscript on a train. If the plain folk of Rye imagined that Freud was here to "treat" Henry James for madness, well, that was perhaps among the costs of being a famous author.

Ordinary people [he wrote, patronizingly, in his journal] *have a ludicrous idea of the strangeness of writers. They are strange, but not in the way hoi polloi imagine. That's the irony. If an eminent alienist happens to be a guest at Lamb House, it follows, in their eyes, that Uncle Henry has gone bonkers, and secretive cures are being attempted. But of course the true strangeness of great writers (and in my estimation Uncle Henry is the very greatest, greater than Joseph Conrad, his only living peer) lies in the scope of their intuitive and poetic endowments. They know, from their superb intuition, all there is to know about the stratagems of humankind. If anyone had doubted Uncle Henry's capacity as a seer,* The Wings of the Dove *alone would remove all doubt. Agnes told me the other day that the Archdeacon had tried to read it, and that is to his credit. But she got the title wrong and said that he found it difficult, and that's no wonder . . .*

Then, there is the matter of the New York Edition, this 23-volume labour. Billy James has told me that his father deems it a "princely" waste of time—"princely" being an intensifier of scalding sarcasm with both James brothers. How could I agree to so philistine a view? The Prefaces alone, to say nothing of the revisions themselves, are the deepest critical writing yet to be attempted about the art and craft of fiction. It is like looking into the very depths of the sea! And it is Uncle Henry who has wrought fiction into forms that justify the term "art."

Freud seems to be among the baffled. He has confided to me his ideas about the "Collected Works" (its proper title) and who knows where he got them? He views them, he said the other day, as "anal" hoarding, or some such, which assessment has the advantage for him of being beyond rebuttal, entirely subjective.

My own notion is this: As Uncle Henry said the other evening at the Fengallons' dinner, the New York Edition is his intended monument to himself (for what writer does not covet a certain immortality?) and his tribute to Honoré de Balzac. And in a human way he hopes to make some money out of the enterprise, something his work has done too little of so far. Commercial failure has been his greatest regret, and thank God he was left with sufficient wealth to ignore the idols of the marketplace. And of course his experiment in playwriting flopped, though I believe he is working on another.

I was granted, not long ago, an explanation from the horse's mouth, when I asked Uncle Henry at breakfast whether he regarded the New York Edition revisions as "definitive." A fascinating and altogether inimitable discourse followed:

"Definitive! Why my dear Horace, never was spoken a more thunderous irrelevancy! And by you, a lad of the tenderest sensibility! When one speaks of stories—prose parables, as I like to call them, and especially those that essay some slight penetration of our queer species—nothing is ever even f-f-finished, let alone definitive! To be sure, one reaches a certain equilibrium of satisfaction at the given moment.

"Allow me to cite, for instance, a couple of examples that I have recently been working on, and will pursue in Miss Bosanquet's faithful Remingtonese. You must bear in mind, dear boy, that these rephrasings remain tentative:

"In the earlier edition of my tale "Daisy Miller," I wrote: 'Winterbourne stood looking after her; and as she moved away, drawing her muslin furbelows over the gravel, said to himself that she had the tournure of a princess.' More recently, I write: 'Winterbourne stood watching her, and as she moved away, drawing her muslin furbelows over the walk, he spoke to himself of her natural elegance.' Or in the earlier Portrait of a Lady, where before I wrote that 'Caspar Goodwood raised his eyes to her again; they wore an expression of ardent remonstrance,' as revised the sentence now reads, ' . . . raised his eyes to her again; they seemed to shine through a vizard of a helmet.' As you see, I strive for greater ease of phrasing and, in the latter case, for a figurative language that as dear old Conrad says will make the reader see.

"Thus you do realize, dear lad, that a story isn't subject to being 'done' in the way of one of Mrs. Paddington's roasts, still less in the condition of pourriture noble, like a Bordeaux grape plucked in its high ripeness from its fugitive vine; it is a living, organic thing, subject to unceasing pentimento. You know that term—meaning repentence of some previous depiction—in the work of the Old Masters of painting. We may, on occasion, whether by comparing a cartoon with the final picture or peering with a magnifying glass under strong light at an overpainted surface, see that a Michelangelo or the great Titian has been finick-

ing about some detail in the pupil of an eye or the attitude of a hand—has, as who should say, fussed with it trying to get it just so. And thus it is with one's little stories and novels. Finished is a vulgarism, don't you see?"

"Yes, Uncle Henry," said I, "but to my discredit I hadn't realized that you were so keen a student of the visual arts, although of course there is The Tragic Muse *for evidence."*

"Why, my dear Horace, you forget that in my youth I was for a time writing about Parisian art at its noblest efflorescence to the New York papers!"

It was a brilliant impromptu discourse and I have tried to record it verbatim. I did see! But many apparently do not.

Horace noticed that Uncle Henry was staring at him at the luncheon table, as if he could see through him and into the secret he was harboring. He couldn't tell, of course. Not only had Horace learned of the gossip by eavesdropping; he knew that the gossip itself would enrage his genial host. He was uneasy with his secret knowledge and was sure that James sensed his discomfort.

"Why the long face, Horace?" James asked. "You look as if you carry some burden of forbidden knowledge, as if you had joined in that ill-fated Edenic picnic with the forbidden fruit."

The words chilled Horace. Uncle Henry's perception was uncanny. He wondered for a moment if perhaps James had somehow seen what Agnes had been doing under the table at the dinner party. He dismissed it as impossible but made a mental note to record the scene at the earliest opportunity when the words would be fresh—and of course to capture their stately echoes of the King James Bible.

"What?" he asked distractedly, pretending that he hadn't heard either the question or the speculation. "Sorry, sir. I didn't sleep well. I guess it's the excitement. I was up writing much of the night."

"Writing in the wee hours? That is for old men, Horace, not for the *jeunesse dorée* who should be sleeping the dreamless sleep of innocence. Insomnia is the privilege of age; you are much too young for it. Much!" James pushed his glasses down to the tip of his nose and peered again, very hard, at Horace.

"My boy, you fool me to the top of my bent! I can see that your doleful countenance can't be explained by mere wakefulness. I do believe that you sigh for Miss Fengallon's company. I was sorry to interrupt your garden tryst last night."

"I saw her briefly on the street today, but we hardly had time to speak. She was with her uncle."

"I thought that accounted for your long face," James said. "And pray, what's the latest? Is Fengallon still gloating over his s-s-stertorous bout with poor Freud? I gather he has been in London to see the Archbishop at Lambeth Palace. I marvel that that high worthy would receive him." James spoke with vehemence, sweeping his arm for emphasis, and accidentally propelling a teaspoon from the table. It ricocheted in a corner of the dining room and everyone at the table jumped.

"Strike that uncharitable remark from the record, Miss Bosanquet," James said, then laughed at his own vehemence.

One morning as Freud's two-week visit was drawing to its close, Burgess Noakes intercepted Horace at the foot of the stairs as he came down for breakfast and pointed silently but urgently into the garden, where Henry James could be seen pacing up and down, clearly agitated. The master, Noakes explained, had sat down for his early cup of tea and opened the Rye *Register* for a brief morning glance—James reserved his ration of serious daily newspaper reading for *The Times*, which usually came by the first morning train from London. From the pantry, where Noakes, Mrs. Paddington and Smith were preparing to set up the breakfast buffet, Uncle Henry's usual chuckles at the imbecilities of journalism could be heard. Then came an ominous silence and a shout of disbelief.

"Damn their cheek!" James roared, and with a rattle of disintegrating newsprint hurled the *Register,* in tatters, across the parlor. Noakes, hearing the commotion, dashed into the room and found James brandishing a story ripped from the front page.

"Damn their cheek," he repeated in a loud voice. Henry James rarely raised his voice and for his usual breakfast companions and sedate Lamb House, his rage was the equivalent of a fire alarm. The dachshund Max, who had been resting under James's reading chair, darted away and hid under the dining table.

"What is it, sir?" Noakes asked.

James, repeating his loud curses of the *Register*, said, "Noakes, you will not believe this." He handed Noakes the piece he had torn from the front page and without another word stalked out into the garden, where he continued to stride furiously up and down. Noakes read:

FAMED VISITOR AT LAMB HOUSE
From our correspondent
Rye's most distinguished address, Mr. Henry James's Lamb House, at the top of West Street, has been graced of late by an eminent visitor, Dr. Sigmund Freud of Vienna. I understand that the famed alienist, whose theories about childhood have excited so much talk in recent years, has been summoned to treat Mr. James, the eminent novelist, in his recovery from unspecified mental disorders. I further understand that Dr. Freud was referred to the case by Mr. James's brother, Dr. William James, of Harvard, Massachusetts, USA, an occasional visitor to Lamb House. Dr. James is also an authority on alienism. Those who know and value Mr. Henry James as a neighbor and fel-

low townsman—who are legion in this city—will join this reporter in hoping for a quick recovery of his wits under Dr. Freud's care. For those wishing to send convalescent greetings to the great writer, The Register *will be glad to serve as an intermediary and will forward flowers, cards and letters to Lamb House. Call Rye 090 for information.*

The usually tranquil master had never, in Horace's experience, been so transported with anger—or any other emotion. The servants had stopped work and were stealing worried glances through the windows as the master marched up and down in the garden.

"It can't be good for Mr. James's nerves," Mrs. Paddington said, shaking her head. "Shouldn't you go to him, Smith?" Smith shook his head in terror and hurried back into the kitchen.

It seemed to Horace that a curse had descended on Lamb House. First the dinner-party disaster, now this. No writer of the age had written more sarcastically about the press than Henry James, in stinging, satirical novellas like "The Papers" and "The Reverberator." One passage in "The Papers" pictured credulous newspaper readers as fish leaping with gaping mouths at the bait. Was it possible that the local editors had read these unflattering tales? Certainly, someone had been spreading unpleasant stories about Uncle Henry. Horace had a prime suspect.

"Breakfast is served," Noakes said and rang the gong. A moment later, Freud's footsteps could be heard on the stairs. As usual he was immaculate in his three-piece suit, with not a button or a whisker out of place.

"There was down here someone shouting," he said. "Is something amiss?"

Noakes handed the story about the "visiting alienist" to Freud, who studied it silently, with the shade of a smile playing about his lips. Freud chuckled quietly, but when someone pointed through the window Freud raised his hand as if to say "let me take care of this."

He walked out into the garden, where Henry James paused, greeted his guest with a bow and began to talk and gesture animatedly. Freud, nodding in agreement, was getting an earful. A few minutes later the two of them, arm in arm, entered the dining room and filled their plates with Mrs. Paddington's scrambled eggs. Henry James seemed more composed.

Breakfast passed in silence, then Freud made a suggestion: "I shall write to the editor. I shall say that my visit is collegial and has no therapeutic purpose. The very idea is absurd, though one can hardly expect your provincial townsmen to understand that an analyst is not always on duty. This is not Vienna, or even Paris or London. Of course, it can be a mistake to deny the manifestly stupid."

"An interesting suggestion, Herr Freud," James mused. Horace thought James resembled an angry lion (was it the literary association?) who might at any moment toss his mane and bare long yellow teeth with a roar. Slapping his hand on the table, James announced a decision.

"See here, Freud. You and I must scatter this nest of village gossips, and set them straight. I trust you will accompany me on this errand?"

"Of course," Freud said, though Horace could see that Freud was more amused than angered. "Of course," he repeated. "These *schwein* must be taught a lesson. They must be made to face up to their . . . their carelessness and licentiousness. This misfire, Herr James, illustrates why I gave up on the newspapers long ago—the more sensational ones, anyway. They market the mere shadows to their deluded readers, like the projections on the wall of Plato's cave which the viewers mistake for life itself. You can't imagine how crudely I have been, as the English say, 'over the coals raked' in the shadier

Vienna papers, especially those that are anti-Semitic by disposition. It reached a height when I announced the Oedipal theory of the neuroses, which brought forward the role of fantasy
and entailed a theory of infantile sexuality. It is that which in
the gutter press is depicted as the imaginings of a dirty old
man: myself!

"But wait. I hadn't meant, Herr James, with this little outburst to steal the floor. It is you who are the target of malicious
misrepresentation."

"Ah, not at all, herr doctor. We are in this together. I have
been a contented resident of this city for a dozen years," James
said. "This is the first time I have been traduced, in print or
otherwise. You and I, Freud, shall descend like wolves on the
fold and teach these ink-stained m-m-miscreants a lesson in
manners they will long remember. *Long, long, long!*" he cried,
with some relish at the idea. "Horace, would you like to come
along?"

"I can't wait, Uncle Henry," he said.

Now that he had settled on a plan, James in the role of a
field marshal began mapping strategy. "We shall beard the editor in his den at tea-time. Noakes!" he called.

"Yes, Mr. James?"

"Noakes, dear boy, please be so kind as to ring the Rye
Register, and tell the editor that Mr. Henry James and Dr.
Sigmund Freud will wait upon him at his offices this afternoon.
Obtain a time certain. You may say that we wish to take up the
item about us published in that rag today, and that we shall be
accompanied by Mr. Briscoe."

"Very good, Mr. James," Noakes said, "but begging your
pardon, sir, I shan't call the *Register* a rag. The town folks con-
siders it a good paper."

"Of course not, Noakes, you shall choose your words. I rely
on your unfailing diplomacy. But do not fail to procure an
appointment."

In common with most of Rye's essential establishments, the *Register* was housed in a red-roofed brick building of indeterminate age and architectural provenance on the High Street. James and his guests could not see through the walls nor guess what consternation their plan had caused. But when they were driven to the doorstep in a cab that afternoon, James in his top hat and Freud looking very natty in his wool suit, Horace sensed many eyes peering out from the tawdry curtained windows. James carried his heavy walking stick. They approached the front desk. The receptionist, a pale, thin young man in a high collar wearing a green eyeshade (*as in the storybooks,* Horace silently observed) looked at the cane and bowed deferentially.

"Mr. Oliver is expecting you, Mr. James," he said. "It is an honor to have you here, sir." He opened a half gate parting the reception desk from the outer room and led them up a creaky flight of steps into a corridor also darkly floored and lined with doors with opaque glass windows. At the end of the corridor, a double door opened into a lighted room where a dozen men in shirtsleeves bent over their desks, from several of which came the clicking of typewriters. Horace knew the novel sound from Uncle Henry's daily sessions with Miss Bosanquet. There was also the faint scent, probably from a basement press room, of printer's ink. It was sharp but not unpleasant. The clerk tapped at a closed door, which was promptly opened by a large woman wearing a dark dress with severely upswept hair.

"Mr. James and Dr. Freud to see Mr. Oliver," the clerk announced. "And Mr. Briscoe."

"This way, gentlemen," she said, leading them to the door of an inner office where the editor, Percival Oliver, rose politely from his rolltop desk. Horace gasped, barely managing to stifle the sound as a pretended sneeze behind his handkerchief.

"You, sir, are Mr. Percival Oliver? The editor?" James asked. Oliver bowed slightly. "May I present my guests, Dr. Freud and Mr. Briscoe."

Oliver indicated a semicircular row of captain's chairs where, Horace assumed, the editors gathered daily to plan the day's harvest of rumor and titillation. Like most of those who had spent little time in newspaper offices, Horace believed that newspapers lie about everything and do it for no other purpose than profit. Henry James was still holding his cane, but Percival Oliver was not the sort of man one cudgeled. He was a tall, angular, and scholarly-looking fellow with a shock of graying hair, as tidily dressed as James and Freud. Horace had pictured him in prospect as seedy, but he was clearly a gentleman. Beyond that—which was why Horace had started when he saw him—he had been one of the dinner guests Horace had observed at Archdeacon Fengallon's table the night he had spied and listened through the window!

"We have come, sir, on a disagreeable errand," James said.

"Yes. In reference, I take it, to our news item this morning?"

"Just so, Mr. Oliver."

"I hope you found it agreeable to be tendered the good wishes of your fellow townsmen. In any case, it is good to see you up and about and in full possession . . ." The editor did not finish the sentence.

"Agreeable! On the contrary, sir, I found the item insolent and libelous."

"Something then was amiss in our story?" Oliver smiled.

"Amiss, sir? That would be a mild way of putting it. It was garbage. It was a feast of garbage!" He pounded the floor emphatically with his cane.

"Garbage is a strong word, Mr. James," said Oliver. "We meant to be charitable." James told Horace, later, that he had been thinking of Hamlet's tirade to his mother in the closet scene, when he denounced her shabby taste in husbands. Mr. Oliver had missed the allusion and taken the word the wrong way.

"You have said, sir, or your paper has said—has insinuated—that I am under treatment for a mental derangement . . ."

"Is it not so?"

"It is most certainly not so! How could it be so? Dr. Freud is in Rye on a social visit entirely, sent by my brother William. That is the one fact, apart from his merely being here, that your story got right."

"Ja," Freud added.

"If we were misinformed . . . " Oliver said.

"If? If, sir?" James rose from his chair and banged his cane again. "Do you question my word?"

"Not at all, Mr. James. Please let me finish. If we were in error, as I was saying, we shall cheerfully print a correction, with apologies. Errors are not unusual in newspapers. But apparently I was not reliably informed by a gentleman of the town whose report I had every reason to believe."

"And who might that be?"

"I am not at liberty to say—I never betray sources, other than to tell you that he is a clergyman of distinction, who was once trained, as I happen to know, in the medical arts and speaks with some authority there. He told me, with some certainty, that Dr. Freud's prolonged visit could only mean that you are under his care for—is it 'hysteria' they call it now? Yes, I believe that was the term he used, hysteria. Reference was also made to Dr. Fletcher and his 'modern gourmet' theories. We were led to believe that you suffer, sir, from a number of frailties. If not . . ."

Horace gasped. It was now obvious that the speculations came straight from the Fengallons' dinner table.

"Mr. Oliver," James said, "you compound the epidemic journalistic vice of inaccuracy with a willful concealment of the source of your inaccuracies. But never mind. Rye is a small place and it will not be hard to run this hare down. I already have a good notion who your source is."

Percival Oliver blushed and his bobbing Adam's apple told the story of a palpable hit. The editor of the Rye *Register* said nothing in response, but shuffled through a file of papers he was holding in his lap.

"Aha!" Henry James crowed, thumping the floor with his stick again. "My guess hit home, did it not, sir?"

"Ah yes," Freud put in; "I see that your busy hands confess what the mouth denies!"

Oliver shook his head sadly. "I may as well confess that I was at Archdeacon Fengallon's dinner table a few evenings ago, with some ladies, including my wife. You know, Mr. James, that the fair sex relish gossip."

"You take refuge from your error in ladies' prattle?"

Oliver threw up his hands. "What more can I say? We shall print a correction and apology, Mr. James. I beg you, however, to believe that we meant no mischief. I don't savor the effect if this contretemps were to be reported to the Archdeacon, who as you may know is extremely combative. It could mean holy war in our little city."

"We shall see," James said, putting on his hat. "If you print a correction Fengallon will notice and this so-called holy war may be unavoidable. Let it come! I am ready. I bid you good day, Mr. Oliver."

As they stepped into the cab, James shook his cane at the facade of the Rye *Register* building. "Fengallon shall hear of this," he said ominously.

Horace closed his eyes and fervently wished he were less deeply implicated.

* * *

From Horace's journal:

. . . I felt dreadfully guilty during our session with the editor, Mr. Oliver, since I had overheard the dinner-table talk that led to the journalistic outrage but couldn't say so. Should I now warn Agnes that a storm is brewing? I think not. She would tell her

uncle and the storm might blow suddenly up from Mermaid Street rather than down from West St., at such time as Uncle Henry wills it. At this stage, I feel like a vessel freighted with dramatic irony. I know that while Uncle Henry isn't being "treated" for any illness by Freud, it isn't strictly true that Freud's visit is exclusively "social," as he and Uncle Henry told Oliver. That would be obvious to anyone who looked at the calendar. Freud came for a long weekend, has been here for almost two weeks, and still is here—in order to conduct a "short-term analysis." I am as sure of Uncle Henry's sanity as I am of my own; but what might be the medical implications of an analysis I haven't the faintest idea . . .

Henry James wrote, as usual, to Edith Wharton:

My dear Edith,

You are as well aware as I—as all poor scribblers must be—of the dictum that truth is sometimes stranger than fiction, a dubious commonplace resting on the naïve idea that truth, so called (all of us have a touch of jesting Pilate in us!), has some fixed & independent existence apart from our personal seizure of it & also on what one might mean by "strange." There are certainly occasions when the bizarre overtakes, and rivals, one's imagination. Such has befallen us here. If I had heard the little tale from a third party, it might have qualified as a donnée, *the precious seed of a little comedy to sprout & exfoliate from it. That infernal rag, the* Rye Register, *published today a diabolical little squib on its front page. Under pretense of well-wishing, it says that I am under "treatment" by Freud for a mental disorder, and needing a "cure." You know, my dear, that the ragged sales of the NYE have plunged me of late into a rather bluish mood. But I am, happily, still far from gibbering in the streets & in want of no straitjacket. No goodnight sweet ladies or tossing of posies for me, as yet!*

This article so enraged me that the two of us, accompanied by young Briscoe, trooped down to the editor's office on High Street for a démarche. *The place is quite seedy, as I imagined it would be, but the editor, a quite presentable fellow called Percival Oliver, has agreed to publish a correction & apology. But what continues to rankle, as I sit late with candle and quill, is the role played in the instigation of this comedy by that ass, Fengallon. I believe I told you in my last note of the fiasco at his dinner table a few nights ago, when amidst a furious argument over religion— smacking indeed of the ancient* odium theologicum—*Freud passed out & thus nearly aborted what promised to be an evening of high dialectic. Now it seems that Fengallon is at the bottom of this rumor-mongering by the local rag. Were I a dueling man I should call him out,* malgré la loi. *But as I have also mentioned, Horace is smitten by Fengallon's niece, a great beauty, to be sure, but as she strikes me a quite worldly young lady—certainly less the innocent ingenue than my precious Nanda Brookenham.*

So I have settled for the moment on an irenic policy & am content to let things segatiate, pending Oliver's act of penance. On the same principle, I remain true to Strether's admonition to Little Bilham (as you know, it derives from something dear Howells said once to me) that a youth like Horace has the right, the duty almost, to live all he can while he can. I shall endeavor to see that no old man's quarrel gets in the way.

As for Freud, he is moving slowly towards departure, and for all my worry when he was impending I anticipate that I shall miss him. We both have concluded, I believe, that our psychoanalytic jousting has ended in deadlock, since I remain of the view that Freud's mental "science," interesting as its insights occasionally are, is too schematic and mechanistic to account for the infinite, intricate shadings and vagaries of human consciousness. Still, Freud is a decent sort. When we returned from our confrontation with the miscreant editor, he said, very graciously: "Mr. James, I fear that I have caused you embarrassment & I regret it exceedingly." I assured him that this ludicrous episode

*has brought no great embarrassment. I am, more than ever, your
devoted Henry James.*

Dearest *Cher Maître* [Edith Wharton replied from 53 rue de
Varenne, Paris],

*Your escapade is worthy of one of your own tales—let us call
it "The Imaginary Invalid," to distinguish it from M. Molière's
play. You would know far better than I how to give it the ingenious twist that would render it not merely true to life but deeply
instructive as to our odd nature. Say, for instance, that the victim
of the libel is a hypochondriac who has so often pretended to be
at death's door that, finally, his vexed physician pretends to
believe it. He may be so annoyed by being repeatedly summoned
to the stricken bedside that he secretly collaborates with a gossipy editor to contrive a "cure" by journalistic shock, as it were,
and prints the news that the imaginary invalid is at last dead!
The* malade imaginaire *is of course outraged, denies his death
strenuously, threatens a suit at law (thus falsifying the report)
and when last glimpsed has survived another half century, free of
all illness, real or imaginary.*

*You must pardon me, Henry, for making light of your jour-
nalistic tribulations. Righteous indignation is not your long suit,
you may permit me to say. By the time this note reaches Lamb
House you will have regained your perspective and good humor.
After all, have you not told me that you are reclining regularly
on Freud's clinical couch, even if you shrink from the dread word
treatment? No one doubts, of course, that you are perfectly sane.
Anyone who supposed you ill would prove his own insanity! You
see, my wearisome experience with Teddy Wharton, who might
well be Molière's original, has shortened my patience with all
ills, real or imaginary.*

*We are beginning to see the approaching outriders of autumn,
and Paris has lately been its blustery but always delightful late
August self. Devotedly, Edith.*

*

From Freud's notes of the same episode:

My prolonged visit has been ruffled by a strange passage. No need to recount the bizarre details, except to say that the local rag (a useful dismissive term of the Anglo-Americans for an untrust-worthy newspaper) printed an item insinuating that Mr. James suffers from a mental breakdown and that I am here to treat or cure it. An absurdity, of course. Mr. James hates publicity, especially when it invades his carefully guarded privacy. I suspect hypersensitivity on the score of his sex life or lack thereof—most secrets being sexual in nature—but that is speculation. So far, my effort to mine this buried ore has been in vain.

I did seek to use the journalistic episode as a gambit. "You and I," I said, "are at one on the maliciousness of village gossip, of the sort retailed by the Rye newspaper. But what distinction would you draw between that sort of fiction and the fiction you regularly deal in as a storyteller?" The question, I quickly realized, was maladroit; and I braced myself for a sharp retort. It was not long in coming.

"Surely Freud," he said, "there is a world of difference between stories, which at their best convey deep truth about our strange kind, and gossip, to which truth, when present at all, is incidental. You can't be seriously proposing that there is the slightest affinity between the two, gossip and art?"

He then brought up my frequent questions about the reti-cences and silences in his stories. "I'll give you an illustration of the difference. You recall," said he, "our discussion regarding Kate Croy's wretched papa and Milly Theale's unspecified illness in Wings of the Dove?" *I certainly recalled those questions. All we learn is that "papa has done something wicked," and that poor Milly has a mysterious wasting disease, being treated by the London specialist (in what?), Sir Luke Strett. It may be con-sumption but is never identified. "And you, I take it," he went on, "would have me explain old man Croy's wickedness down to the last looted sixpence! And Milly's disease to the last deviation in temperature on a hospital chart! You would leave nothing to the imagination. Stories are not clinical reports."*

"You see," he continued, "I take great pains—for aesthetic reasons—to avoid the trivial details without which gossip would be a wisp of smoke. Of course, such philistine readers as my brother William would prefer that I drop all such delicate bypasses as 'deep disorder of the blood' and describe an illness with all the detail of a medical analysis."

"A palpable hit!" I replied, echoing one of Mr. James's favorite allusions to the play Hamlet.

He paused, then continued: "Fiction! A misunderstood term. Let us speak, my dear herr doctor, of your own case histories, the history of Dora for instance. It can hardly escape the close reader's notice that you and she disagreed so intensely about her problem that she quit the treatment. You said it was one thing, she another. You impose your theory in defiance of her own sense of the case. Isn't your construction, which you pressed upon her, a fiction?"

I disputed the term "fiction."

"Come now, Freud," he said. "You are too shrewd not to see what I am saying—namely, that your psychoanalysis, with its mechanical dynamics of the structure and pressures and gauges of consciousness, aspires to science but is no less a form of storytelling than my own."

"It is empirical, Mr. James," I protested. "Based on carefully sifted clinical evidence."

"Oh, stuff and nonsense, Freud," he said in an energetic but friendly tone. "You are a storyteller and a good one. Your ingenious reconstruction of the psychic life of Leonardo proves it. Admit."

I said that the idea is inadmissible.

"Well, you claim, don't you, that the 'unconscious' is a dynamic cauldron of undifferentiated energy that drives us

whether we know it or not. So you are engaged in a conjuring process, imposing a pattern that satisfies one's human thirst for a story. In fact, my friend, both of us are magicians, if you will, seeking with our spells and incantations, our voodoo and rain dances and shaking of our rattles, to move the world. What else might your patient Anna O. have meant when she spoke of the 'talking cure'? It is thaumaturgy, like the royal touch. All that is needed is that the subject believe in it!"

I have abbreviated a monologue that continued with animation, for some twenty-five minutes, consuming half our penultimate session. I wondered at times who was the analyst and who the analysand! Mr. James has never been so effusive, but his resistances were never more evident, or for that matter more brilliant. Of course, he is wrong, quite wrong! I emphatically deny the subjectivity and, as he calls it, "magic" of psychoanalysis!

When Horace was shown into the familiar parlor on Mermaid Street, the word that sprang to mind was formidable, as it applied to the master of the house. The Archdeacon, whom he had last seen roaring at his dinner table, towered well over six feet and bore himself with a royal air, although Horace noticed that he walked with a slight limp. In the light of day his sharp-featured face with its long nose and thick eyebrows seemed even swarthier than it had by candlelight, as if he had just returned from months in the tropical sun. The thick, fashionably styled shock of graying hair looked like a stage periwig and, if one imagined the little black cap, brought to mind the term "hanging judge."

"Uncle," Agnes said, "you have met Mr. Briscoe, of course, Mr. James's young friend, who was here for dinner the other evening."

"Even so, Agnes," he said, crushing Horace's hand in his grip. Horace gritted his teeth and tried not to cry out.

"It would appear, Mr. Briscoe," Fengallon boomed, in what

their visitor had come to think of as his pulpit voice, "that I am now exposed to obloquy as a village gossip. Having myself been the victim of vile rumor I am eager to get to the bottom of the affair."

He waved before Horace's nose a retraction notice that had appeared that morning in the Rye *Register,* in response to the visit to the editor's office, slapping the newsprint with the back of his hand as if to condemn and punish it:

CORRECTION

The editors of The Register *wish to make it known that yesterday's item regarding Dr. Sigmund Freud's visit to Lamb House was in error.*

The visit, we are informed, is entirely social and any implication that Dr. Freud's host, Mr. Henry James, the noted novelist, is ill or under Dr. Freud's medical care is emphatically denied. The Register *relied, regrettably, on the information of a distinguished personage which proved to be misleading, though no doubt unintentionally so.*

The ink had hardly dried on the *Register* when a servant from the Fengallon household had knocked at Lamb House and delivered a note addressed to Horace and marked URGENT.

Horace [Agnes had written there], *Uncle is jolly upset by the item in this morning's paper implying that he is responsible for misinforming the editors about Dr. Freud's visit. He formed a favorable impression at dinner the other night and would like to speak to you privately. Please come here as soon as you can. I mean, immediately. Agnes.*

Horace feared, with reason, that he was becoming ever more imbroiled in the affair. Was it disloyal, he asked himself, to answer the summons without telling Uncle Henry? The double agent's role was repulsive, but Agnes still haunted his dreams and paralyzed his will. Even a supervised visit was not to be dismissed and after a brisk walk in the garden he presented himself at the house on Mermaid Street.

"Sir?" Horace answered distractedly, responding to the Archdeacon's comments. "May I help, sir?"

"Agnes, you may leave us for a few minutes," the Archdeacon said. She glanced nervously at Horace and turned toward the door. "Shall I ask Stoner to bring coffee?" she asked.

"Yes, but give Mr. Briscoe and me ten minutes, my dear." The door closed.

"Now, sir, I ask you straight out, as one gentleman to another. Is it not true, notwithstanding this retraction, that Freud is analysing Mr. James? And doesn't that presuppose mental imbalance? You know how word of such a thing flies about a small town. It is common knowledge that every day, in the early afternoon, the two of them may be seen through the bay window overlooking West Street—consulting, I believe the term is. Mr. James is reported to repose on a settee, whilst Freud, with a notebook on his knee, sits just behind him asking questions and taking notes, as is the practice in Vienna. My information is, I believe, reliable. Do you deny it?"

Horace was stunned that the privacy of Lamb House had been so flagrantly compromised, and he hardly knew what to say. The information was "reliable," all right, although the inference the Archdeacon drew from it was altogether wrong. To deny it was to lie; to confirm it an act of disloyalty. He hedged—artlessly.

"Who says all this?" Horace asked. "Conversation is conversation—to say nothing of mere talk and rumor. Cannot these two giants of the mind converse together without being spied upon? It is true that they have been talking in the Garden Room after lunch every day. But I am not there; nor is anyone else other than the eavesdropper who makes these charges. Who is he?" he repeated.

"Never mind who says it; and 'eavesdropping' is not the word. Nothing has been overheard. Do you deny that Freud is treating Mr. James, Briscoe?"

Horace was silent and trying desperately to think what to say.

"Ah! *Tacere consentire!* I thought so!"

"Wait a moment, sir. Sometimes silence is merely silence. Wasn't that Thomas More's position when he refused either to take the oath of supremacy to King Henry VIII or deny it?" Horace's words struck him immediately as sophistry, but it was such as might beguile a clergyman.

"You are an inventive young man," Fengallon laughed, "and your history is sound. But you still haven't answered my question. Your silence forces me to assume that the answer is yes."

"Did I understand you to say, sir, that you yourself had been a victim of gossip?"

"I did say so, but that is old history. It doesn't concern us here and now."

Horace pressed—anything but direct engagement with the dreaded question. "May I ask what you refer to?"

As Horace knew, even at his age, the urge to confide is often overpowering, especially if a grievance is involved. He could see that Fengallon was measuring how much of his "ancient history" he might repeat. Fengallon sighed. His eyes flashed angrily at the sore memory.

"You are complicating matters damnably, Briscoe. But sit you down and I shall tell you a bit . . . but only because it seems Agnes is keen on you."

"The feeling is reciprocated," Horace said, embarrassed by his pompous words. But wasn't that the way one talked to a high dignitary of the church?

"Don't assume, by the way, that I have abandoned my inquiry . . ."

They sat opposite and Fengallon sighed again, as if he had told the story too often. "Twenty years ago, I was tried by a canon court. You are a literary chap? You have read Tony Trollope's *The Warden?* Yes? Then you are familiar with English ecclesiastical politics. My accusers swore that I had made indecent advances to a cathedral choir mistress. *Damnable lies!* I denied then, I deny still, on my word as a gentleman. But the rumor mills ground away and my denials were taken as affirmations—you know how that happens. Once an accusation is launched, and the slander put in circulation, the victim of it may deny it again and again but the more he denies it the more he is assumed to be lying. *Methinks the gentleman doth protest too much!* A mischievous line! The court reached no verdict. The key case against me was the perjured witness of the 'lady' in question, who was insanely jealous of my late wife. It would be unchivalrous to elaborate, but you are familiar with the fate of young Joseph at Pharaoh's court? How the overseer's wife tried to seduce him and he ran from her, leaving a telltale rag of his robe behind? My accuser had the indecency to claim she could produce an item of intimate clothing to prove her point. The prosecutor before the canon court, a foul-minded prig named Letoile, pretended to believe her and wrote a lurid report, then slipped savory details to the press. It then seemed to me in the best interest of the church and the diocese to make a quiet exit. The record was sealed. And that, sir, is the sum and substance of it, the ancient history. The papers made much of it, even the normally reticent Old Lady, as I was reminded when the *Register* contradicted my story this morning.

"Any but the senile old men on that court would have dismissed the perjured charges summarily, with prejudice. But when they hesitated I decided that my usefulness at Wells was at an end. And there you have it, except. *Except! . . .* "

"Except?" Horace echoed eagerly; it was quite a tale.

"*Except* that I have never felt the slightest doubt that my well known differences with the Puseyites in Oxford, and their contemptible parrots, acolytes and lackeys, were behind the whole affair. They hoped to bring me down and they succeeded. I strive for Christian forgiveness, but so far without notable success! Now let us summon Agnes and our elevenses and see how we stand on the matter of Dr. Freud's business in Rye."

Horace sensed that he had gained a friendly footing with the Archdeacon—and, remarkably, it seemed that his brazen solicitation of Fengallon's "story" had done it. He pressed his new-won advantage.

"Do you mind telling me, sir, how it happened that Agnes is here, while her parents remain in Kenya? I don't mean to pry but you are aware that her presence here is my great good fortune, that I have high regard for your niece."

Fengallon glared as if at an impertinence, but his expression softened.

"You are an inquisitive young man, Briscoe. We English are unaccustomed to your tireless American curiosity. You should probably be a journalist. Still, I see . . ." He checked himself, as if wondering how much to say.

"I see no harm in telling you the bare facts. There is little, er, that is, nothing to conceal. You see, my wife died ten years ago, poor thing. I was desperately lonely. Agnes was passing then from childhood and the educational advantages in Kenya for a young woman are few. Moreover . . ." Fengallon paused again to measure his disclosures. "Moreover," he continued, "a certain, shall we say, tension had arisen in my brother's household in Nairobi. I shall say no more of that, save that Agnes's mother was angry, distraught—she is by nature an excitable little woman, given to extreme neurasthenia. I warned my brother of that before he married her. It was plain to see."

Horace marveled how much people will say when they resolve to say little.

"At all events, it seemed convenient both here and there for Agnes to come to me for her schooling. I could well afford it, I relished her companionship and, frankly, she needed to get away from that . . . that unwholesome family atmosphere.

"But my dear Briscoe, you tempt me to speak of family matters that should be kept under the seal of discretion. Private family matters. Very private! I can't imagine why I have told you this much—or for that matter why I told you so much about my ecclesiastical ordeal; but there you are. Suffice it to say that Agnes is here and her unhappy parents are there, and will be there for some time to come."

"I hadn't meant to pry, sir. But you see, my regard for Agnes . . ."

"Regard! A weak word, sir for what I detect is a strong feeling! Regard!" The Archdeacon repeated the word scornfully, then laughed loudly; it seemed to Horace that there was something strange in the laugh, something (what was the word?) . . . *carnal?* He remembered hearing it through the window of the dining room that night when he—he—had 'eavesdropped' and thinking that it resembled the braying of a donkey, said to be a very lascivious animal.

Just then, Agnes knocked and entered the room, followed by the maid carrying the coffee service.

Horace climbed West Street an hour later in a state of confusion, feeling that he had been less than loyal. But was it, after all, such a grave matter, this gathering comedy of errors? Under the Archdeacon's renewed questioning, he had admitted that Freud and James were consulting "systematically" every day. He had avoided the word "psychoanalysis."

"Absolutely nothing pathological is involved. The purpose is literary," he had insisted. "So far as I know, they are simply matching wits. The contest started the moment Dr. Freud entered Lamb House two weeks ago and it goes on. They were talking one day and Freud jumped at a chance to test his theories on a distinguished writer, face to face. That's all—the truth and the whole truth."

The Archdeacon had arched his eyebrows but otherwise had shown no strong reaction and there the matter of the errant Rye *Register* report had been left. Fengallon had neither admitted nor denied that he was the source of the story, although that seemed to be taken for granted. As Horace was leaving, Fengallon fired a parting shot.

"My dear Briscoe," he had said, "beware of journalism, at least of the Grub Street variety." Horace said he had no journalistic ambitions.

"Do you recall, Briscoe, what Sir Walter Scott once said to a young friend who was thinking of a newspaper career? 'I would rather sell gin to poor people and poison them that way!'"

"He must have had a grudge against the press," Horace said, "to say something that extreme." They both laughed at Scott's words and Horace said his goodbyes, bending sedately to kiss Agnes's hand under her uncle's vigilant eye.

As Horace mounted the staircase at Lamb House, a few moments later, he met Uncle Henry slowly descending with Max under one arm and the little dog's leash in the other hand.

"May I join you for a walk?" Horace asked. "I have a confession."

"Of course. I gather you were at the Fengallons' for elevenses. You are going to tell me you've asked for her hand."

"Good God, no, Mr. James! But I did have quite a talk with her uncle. It seems that everyone in Rye knows that you and Dr. Freud have been having 'consultations' in the Garden Room. Don't ask me how they know. It's astonishing how word travels here. I could hardly deny it, but I assured him that it is 'literary' and nothing else."

"Fengallon is a meddling, prurient ass!" James said. Uncle Henry's feelings about the Archdeacon had not been tempered by the recent dinner party.

"I am not sure that I believe that any longer, Uncle Henry. He and I discussed the report in the *Register,* and gossip generally. He said that he is sensitive to 'villainous gossip'—his words—because he has been a victim of it. So help me, that is what he said. He told me quite a story."

"Gossip! His disgrace is common knowledge."

"He says not. He tells a very different version of the story. He says that the episode at Wells that led to his resignation— not deprivation—was trumped up by a jealous woman, a seductress, who hated his wife and played the same role to him that Potiphar's wife played to young Joseph . . ."

"Now I have heard everything. Can you be so gullible, Horace?"

"I hardly knew whether or not to believe him, but in spite of myself I found his story credible. He swore it as a gentleman."

"As the Duke of Wellington said to a woman who addressed him on the streets of London as 'Mr. Smith,' 'Madam, if you believe that, you will believe anything.' Your defenses are down, Horace. Agnes's uncle can do no wrong, speak no fiction, merely because he is her uncle. *Cherchez la femme!*"

"No, no. We may be as mistaken about him as he was about your supposed 'mental disturbance.'"

"Well, what a queerness if so, if you are not merely gulled. It makes me think of writing a little tale—not the first by any means—about the unreliability of common report. After all, as I was insisting to Freud just the other day, the affinities between fact and fiction are substantial; the membrane that divides the one from the other is entirely porous. Who ever knows these days what perceptions or pictures of the social scene to believe?"

*

Freud annotated the final session of the "short-term analysis" the next day.

I have been here now for two weeks, far longer than I planned to stay and now long enough. I have informed Mr. James, with thanks for his hospitality, of my intention to leave soon. I am overdue in Manchester and my brothers will be impatient. Naturally, then, our session today had valedictory overtones. But it was friendly, as a certain strange affection has taken root—two different wayfarers in quest of the mysteries of consciousness.

That affection is ill-advised, clinically, as it will doubtless impair my detachment. But I have abandoned hope of reaching far into Mr. James's unconscious. We have struck glancing blows. I leave the reasons, complex as they doubtless are, for further consideration when and if I attempt a case history—obviously not while Mr. James is still living, given his sensitivity to the issue of privacy. He would easily be identified, however disguised. "Let me paint him an inch thick" . . . Meanwhile, the following notes will concern themselves with our final session. Mr. James had stretched himself on the sofa and I was, as usual, perched with my notebook in the bay window with its pleasing prospect down West Street, where sun and clouds raced each other and I was fascinated by the play of light and shadow.

James: Well, herr doctor. What are your conclusions?

Freud: My conclusion is that when one probes the unconscious of a great imaginative artist the powers of psychoanalysis are diminished. Or as I would put it, before the problem of the creative artist analysis must, alas, lay down its arms. Have I said that before? Yes, I believe I have.

James: A strangely martial metaphor, laying down arms. What do you mean? Is analysis, then, a military campaign, a form of mental combat?

I asked if he really wanted to know and he said he did.

Freud: Very well, in my Three Essays on the Theory of Sexuality, *I concluded scientifically that individual psychosexual development recapitulates the development of the species, as Darwin believed the physical does. Sexuality evolves, from the embryonic stage of mono-sexuality, through what I call polymorphous (undifferentiated) perversity, anal and oral, so obvious in the infant, then through latency and adolescence to the mature stage that I designate "genital." But since you, Mr. James, have resolutely declined to engage with me in the analytic work, I can't place you in that framework. Before our consultation began, I would have speculated that there is some repressed orality in your attachment to Dr. Fletcher's digestive theories, as well as some anality in the obsessive revision of your works for the* New York Edition. *I would also have hypothesized that your celibacy indicates some underdevelopment, perhaps a repressed homoeroticism. You must excuse the crudity of the nomenclature. I name it; I do not apply it. You will, however, see what formidable arms I have had to lay down.*

There was the usual silence. He seemed to mull my comment. He cleared his throat several times—nervous resistance?—but displayed no such indignation as marked our initial encounter.

James: Don't you think, Freud, that the artist must contain, even supersede and transcend those ordinary but, after all, conventional binary distinctions? For instance, Shakespeare in the sonnets, with their erotic ambiguity—is that the right term for words of affection aimed at both sexes?—directed both to the mistress with wiry hair and the fair youth, the beloved creature from whom 'increase' is desired?

Freud: I have never pretended that my science is well fitted to the infinite subtleties of high artistic creativity. That is just what I mean by laying down my arms: a confession of modesty, of less than certainty. I have no idea what mix of literary convention and life experience went into the sonnets, though we may of course speculate. We do know, I believe, that Mrs. Shakespeare was some years his senior and may have seduced him in his youth.

James: That is true, I believe; but I fail to grasp your zeal to reduce personal complexity to "scientific" formulations. You certainly did it in the little sketch of Leonardo you showed me. I was hard put to see the modesty in its pages. Why do you regard this reductive technique as imperative?

Freud: You see that I am admitting limits that I wouldn't admit to a less remarkable patient. As we agreed the other day, that ordinary patient needs to believe that when the witch doctor rattles his wand, the gods respond. But with all its limitations I claim one advantage for psychological science. Great artists such as yourself are necessarily rare, mutants of our species; and we relish your prodigies of insight. You recall how I stand in awe of your divining the sexuality of children in your story "The Turn of the Screw," even though conventional society clings to the myth of childish innocence. All the more, then, I insist that such prodigies of insight come along all too seldom and require high intelligence for the grasping; and insofar as we can devise an objective science of the psyche and a method with it, we can greatly extend the benefits of self-understanding. Competent analysts will be far more numerous than artists; and with proper clinical training can perform useful service. That is my claim, Herr James, and I believe it justifies the zeal with which the psychoanalytic movement pursues science.

James: I see your point; but the very earthiness of your theory—by which I mean its single-minded preoccupation with sexuality—suggests that you take a secret pleasure in human irrationality, our lack of control over our impulses. One might even call it gloating.

Freud: No; we draw no such conclusions; and I do not gloat over human susceptibilities. But unlike yourself, most men and women, even when intelligent, lack the artist's uncanny powers. They have no mirrors for self-recognition, save literary sources which they imperfectly understand. Accordingly, in their lives the ego, as I have put it, is not master in its own house . . .

James [with a tone of sadness]: My dear doctor, your optimism about human reconstruction surpasses my own. My expectations are modest. I believe our sort are inveterately prone to badness, however that tragic strain originated. Some call it the Fall; others think it is chemical or neurological, as you seem to do.

Freud: Very well, but you do see that your resignation is fundamentally theological, deterministic, and if I may say so, primitive?

James: I prefer to call it realistic. Why not realistic?

Freud: Because, Mr. James, the term "realistic" begs the question. What is the real? Is it fixed or malleable? What if, through the advance of mental science, we could write upon a new slate? Reorder society and its powerful actors, so that they perceive with greater consciousness their hidden impulses?

James: Perhaps you shall do so, Freud, and inasmuch as your purposes are rational and benevolent I wish you good luck. But the very idea—the prospect of a tabula rasa *of human personality, upon which God knows what may be inscribed, by God knows whom, for God knows what end—terrifies me. I am an old man. I shall cling to the Old Adam and try to make the best of it.*

Freud: Then we are at an impasse, and perhaps we may agree to leave it at that—you with your fine and subtle old art, I with my crude new science. After all, we have discovered some few convergences. I have always acknowledged that the shadowy recesses of the human consciousness were visited by men of creative insight long before clinical science stumbled upon them.

With that armistice, our final session came to a friendly and philosophical but inconclusive end. I thought that there would be a revelation, an epiphany at the end. But alas, no.

* * *

The end of Freud's Lamb House sojourn was, if anything, even more "bizarre" than anyone expected. It was a dim, windy day; the English weather was being very much itself. Cordial and courtly goodbyes were being said in the oak parlor. Horace lingered upstairs, lying low since the previous evening, wondering when the other storm would break. As fate would have it the cloudburst came as Freud's cab was expected. The jingle of harness and the sound of hooves pausing and clattering on the cobblestones seemed to announce that conveyance to the station. But when Henry James peered out, he was astonished to see the towering figure of Archdeacon Fengallon, in frock coat and gaiters, unfolding his frame from a carriage. A thunderous knock sounded; and to Horace, lurking just outside his attic room, it sounded like the crack of doom.

"Fengallon!" he heard James cry, as the master of Lamb House quickly retreated from the window. "Smith," James called to the butler, "answer the door and tell the reverend gentleman that Mr. James is not at home just now, as he is saying his goodbyes to Dr. Freud."

Smith could be heard repeating the words at the open door in his usual slurred syllables. From his perch upstairs Horace heard the Archdeacon shout. "I insist, indeed, this has very much to do with Mr. James's other guest." Oh, God, Horace thought; my goose is cooked now.

"One moment, your reverence," Smith said, closing the door and bearing the crested visiting card, he lurched into the parlor. "He insists, Mr. James. He is very determined. The young lady is with him, but she is still in the carriage."

"Oh dear," James sighed. "I suppose there is no avoiding this. But I shall dispatch him in short order."

James and Freud took seats, as if they had been waiting for just such a visitor. They rose as the agitated archdeacon strode into the room. "The Archdeacon Fengallon," Smith announced with an air of formality.

"Will you have a seat, sir?" James asked, rising as if to suggest that he would prefer a standing interview. "Our time, alas, is short. Dr. Freud's train departs in little more than an hour."

"Indeed I shall not sit down," Fengallon said brusquely. "I have come to discuss with you, Mr. James, the behavior of Mr. Briscoe, whom you are harboring."

"Horace? Harboring? What behavior do you mean?" James gasped.

"I mean, sir, that my house parlor maid late last evening discovered your guest and my niece in a most compromising situation in the gazebo at the bottom of my garden. What do you say, sir, of harboring a seducer, a veritable Casanova, under your roof? What? What?"

James stared. "Horace, a seducer?" he repeated.

Horace, listening to the exchange from the top of the stairs, thought of the proceedings below as a death sentence, as when an English judge places the little black cap on his periwig. It was true that at Agnes's invitation he had slipped into the garden and met her there at a late hour. It was true also that he and Agnes had allowed their impulses to gain the upper hand and the rest was . . . well, it simply was what it was—a folly, an impulsive moment. As for the question of who had "seduced" whom, the answer was far from clear in Horace's memory; the steps down the primrose path were simultaneous, mutual, and no less than spontaneous. But of course he could not say that; it would be ungentlemanly to deny responsibility. He would have to assume all the blame.

"Smith," James called to the butler, who was standing with his back braced against the wall just outside the parlor, "do please ask Mr. Briscoe to join us."

Horace was already creeping down the stairs, slowly descending to face the music which now suggested a highland reel of the most hectic sort. But when he reached the double doorway, Fengallon had turned his fury on Freud.

"As for you, doctor," he was saying, his voice raised to sermon level, "I may say, sir, that I am altogether inclined to attribute this mischief to you. You come among decent and quiet folk with your libertine theories. And for what purpose, pray, unless to subvert the morals of a peaceful town and to corrupt youth with your smutty theories? No wonder Mr. Briscoe abandoned all restraint after two weeks under your influence!"

Horace froze. This would not do. Uncle Henry, raising a propitiatory hand, said, "Please . . ." Freud approached the archdeacon and stood glaring up into his face.

"Don't suppose, sir, that you can with impunity sermonize and bully. I have your like in Vienna faced down, with your hypocritical moralism. It is a case of infantile regression, this distemper of yours. You have yet to come to terms with the tyranny of the father projection."

The Archdeacon was beginning to sputter.

"*Gentlemen,*" James pleaded.

"How is it," Freud continued, "that you pretend indignation over the sensual play of these . . . these children, when you yourself have been cashiered on charges of exploiting your own sacerdotal authority?"

"So you, Freud," Fengallon roared, "are the source of those slanders." And before anyone else could move to stop him, he seized Freud in a choke hold. As Freud struggled to break Fengallon's powerful grip, gasping for breath, James cried out again, "Please, gentlemen, do desist . . ." He staggered to a chair and sat down, and Smith began to fan him with a magazine. Horace, who had been watching from the doorway, ran into the room. "Stop it, both of you," he shouted. "Remember Uncle Henry's angina."

The combatants stopped abruptly. Freud dashed into the hallway and after some rummaging in his valise produced a stethoscope. He held it against James's chest. "Breathe, Herr

James," he said, a look of concentration on his sweating face. "Ah, good. Your pulse is perfectly normal; you are merely out of breath." Fengallon, still flushed and puffing, stood watching and Horace thought he seemed embarrassed at his loss of temper.

"Are you sure he is all right?" the Archdeacon asked.

"Ja, he is fine—no thanks to you!"

Moments later, the sound of Freud's cab could be heard. To Horace, it was the sound of a deliverance.

Dear Edith [Henry James wrote in the last of his letters about the visit to Mrs. Wharton],

The sojourn here of the Viennese sage came to an explosive end today. We saw him off on the 1:30 train to Ashford and London, whence he will go on to Manchester to visit his half brothers and their families. Noakes & I saluted him from the platform of our elegant little Palladian depot as the train puffed out. But I say "explosive" because his departure was preceded by a final stormy and titanic struggle—literally—with my Mermaid Street neighbor, the egregious Archdeacon Fengallon. You already know of our earlier encounter at his dinner table. Today in the late morning he came bristling up to Lamb House, armed at all points, cap-a-pie, as Freud was waiting tranquilly in the foyer for his carriage. He was all in a huff because Horace had been spotted last evening by some hysterical parlor maid in an embrace in the summer house with his niece Agnes. The parlor maid screamed and brought him racing out of the house. Just what the youngsters were actually doing (apart from collaborating in an effort to defeat the evening chill) I do not know & don't especially want to know. I suspect Fengallon of exploiting this incident as a pretext for a final assault on Freud; but however motivated, he was outraged, or pretended to be. He raged into the parlor hard on the heels of his carte de visite, accusing poor Horace of "seducing" his niece. Horace was bewildered, since not many hours earlier he and the Archdeacon had had a very tranquil and civil interview!

One suspects that Miss Fengallon was as eager for this rendezvous in the summer house as Horace was, having whispered
the suggestion to him as he was leaving their house, & as I have
told you he is thoroughly smitten. But even as the accused
Lothario had descended the stairs, & entered the room,
Fengallon abruptly transferred his wrath to Freud, who stands at
least a head shorter than he. He accused Freud of subverting the
morals of Rye as well as the youth, intimating that he had
cheered on Horace's attempt to "seduce" Agnes. They exchanged
ripe insults. Then, Fengallon suddenly attacked Freud, & so
appalling was the spectacle that it brought on my breathlessness.
Your poor old Rye-bird grew dizzy & had to be ministered to by
both the antagonists. Tempers cooled rapidly then, so at least my
condition was useful. Fengallon seemed abashed—a novel posture for him!—to have resorted to a physical attack on a smaller
man & apologized at length to me and even to Freud. I suspect
that there is something in his relationship with his lovely niece
that brings out the beast in him. I tested that theory with Freud
as we drove down to the station—without Horace, I needn't say.
I could hardly carry the accused youth away under the very eye
of Fengallon, who was still glaring when we left for the station.
Freud looked at me with something like astonishment.

"Ja," he said. "I share your surmise. There is something dam-
aging in his care of the girl, but remediable. You may as well
know that when Briscoe took me to visit I recommended to her
the name of a colleague in London . . ." I gaped at this; one hardly knows what goes on under one's own roof—or others.

You may, my dear Edith, view all this as a misfortune. But I
needn't remind you, the wisest of women, of the ever-surprising
uses of adversity. The jewel in the crown of this venomous toad
is that, as the rage subsided, the combatants succeeded in clear-
ing up an apparent double misunderstanding. It was Fengallon's
notion, you see, that Freud had been spreading the story that he,
Fengallon, had been deposed as a sensualist as Archdeacon of

Wells. No suspicion, of course, could be more preposterous! Fengallon denied it to Horace so strenuously as to persuade Horace that he is traduced. He blames the episode on his ecclesiastical enemies. Thus we were all caught up in a symmetrical comedy of errors, Fengallon believing that I was under Freud's cure for some species of lunacy, whilst I was depicting him, unjustly I am now prepared to admit, as a disgrace to his collar. All this we managed to establish and clarify before Freud's departure.

If I myself weren't in the midst of it, & if I had heard such a tale related in bare-bones outline, I should almost certainly have flown to my notebook with the seedling of a small comedy, although the theme has declared itself more clearly than the plot. Even living as you and I do every day in a world of artifice, and burning our incense at the altar of the muses of truth and beauty, we forget the unreliability of common report & the so-called "news" & how credulously it comes to be accepted not merely by the multitude but by the rational and lettered. How often, as I think of it, did this idea fire the imagination of Shakespeare!— to think only of poor, deluded Othello and his hotheaded leap to horrible imaginings. And all those mistaken identities! As Othello, so Fengallon! At first glance, the defect of my milder and funnier story is that it may so easily veer into banality. It needs a gripping plot, to undergo the transmutation from mere idea to tale. In a sense this propensity to believe nonsense has been the main fodder upon which Freud and I have chewed these past days. Freud will concede the superiority of intuition, as it is found in the artist. Yet he pursues, he quite pants after, the fool's gold of "scientific" certainty regarding our mortal striving. I told you earlier, I believe, of my quite ruthless little fable about poor Fenimore's dresses; whether Freud believed the story I do not know.

As if to confirm the oddity of the encounter, Freud did confide to me a wild and hurried speculation before he left. "From what little our young Briscoe has said of Miss Fengallon's for-wardness, as I believe you call it, I would guess that she has been, let us say, 'tampered with' at some stage in her early develop-ment, very possibly by that aggressive and vociferous uncle, the holy man, although I naturally shrink from reaching such a con-clusion without hearing her story from the analytic couch. I have learned by hard experience that even when seductive overtures are complained of we may be dealing with the Oedipal residue, rather than with history. And happily the young lady is no hys-teric and shows no outward sign of damage." When Freud said this, much as I loathe the Archdeacon, I clapped my hands to my ears . "Nay, herr doctor," I cried, "no more of this—no more."

But to go on: Freud, I needn't say, did not convert me to his "science," but I found him surprisingly deferential to—no, respectful of—the poetic. He concedes that we storytellers do sometimes intuit what he aspires to reduce to a systematic hydraulics of the consciousness, replete with valves & vents, taps & gauges, pipes & conduits. We scribblers do not deal in outright lunacy; however unhinged some of our specimens are, they com-monly fall short of dementia, if only because their actions & thoughts must be understood by the reader. Our purposes are not clinical. Still, Freud & I met as worthy foemen on the jousting ground of literature. Freud, for instance, taking a psychoanalytic view of Hamlet, makes the Prince of Denmark out to be a psy-choneurotic who never resolved his "Oedipal" wish to sleep with his mother, Gertrude, hence his towering disgust at her "damned incest" with Claudius. Were there not echoes of this in what he said to me of the Fengallons? I myself hold his view to be unten-able, at least in the case of the Prince of Denmark, since it is clear that Hamlet's compunctions are theological, when they are not mere blind loyalty to his royal father. I will admit that Freud is on firmer ground in his reading of "Oedipus Rex" itself, where the Sophoclean text explicitly echoes the playwright's grasp of that primal desire. The other day, as we were discussing the *issue, Freud plucked from my shelves a copy of the play & read aloud—in the Greek, mind you—the remarkable words of Jocasta to Oedipus, spoken of course before he realizes the horrific truth —*

> Nor need this mother-marrying frighten you.
> Many a man has dreamt as much. Such things
> Must be forgotten if life is to be endured . . .

"You have something definite, herr doctor," I said, "although it seems to me that you advocate remembering, not forgetting"; & we left the great matter there. Meanwhile, the happier outcome of the bizarre curtain on the scene was that Fengallon, once appeased, was persuaded to think sufficiently well of young Briscoe to consent to his courtship of his niece, which continues day and night, to Horace's distraction. I worry that his projected thesis lies dormant, begging for attention. At least their romance no longer need be furtively pursued, in darkness, in the summer house! Who knows but that it may lead to a match, yet another variation on my so-called "international theme." And this under the very roof of your mild, devoted and ever dedicated, Henry James.

4

BALTIMORE, LATE DECEMBER 1941

W hen Horace Briscoe gave his incautious interview to the eager young reporter from the *Sun*, his former student, he had no idea how optimistic it was—optimistic, in his assumption that the mystery would soon be solved and laid before the literary and psychiatric worlds. He would examine and authenticate the fragmentary case history of "Mr. J," presumably by Sigmund Freud, and humanity would be one fascinating document the richer. One small plus in a world now darkened by Nazi gangsterism and book-burning.

The initial word from London's Maresfield Gardens, where Freud had alighted after his escape from Vienna, was encouraging. Masses of personal papers awaited arranging, including the "fragment" of the Henry James case history. It might indeed be fragmentary, but Freud had the habit of attaching that qualification to practically all his case histories, as if they were provisional. Once translated, the document would be sped on its way by special airmail to Horace's desk, as he was easily the best qualified to verify it, not only as an authority on James but as an eyewitness to the meeting he fondly called "lions at Lamb House."

Now, however, days had stretched into weeks. Terse notes on flimsy airmail paper informed him that "complications" had developed but soon would be resolved.

What could be going on in London? One night Horace complained sharply to his wife Agnes (née Fengallon) that he smelled "monkey business" in London. "All Freudians are paranoid," he declared with irritation at the dinner table. "You can take that as axiomatic, Agnes. I suppose they got it honest from the old man."

"Well, dear," Agnes said, "you may yet have to go to London and see what can be done on the scene, war or no war. I could visit cousin Mary in Rye."

"I can't imagine how we could do that in wartime conditions, and I don't want to spook the keepers of the flame. You know how cautious the original inner circle is—The Committee, as they call themselves. Not so much Anna as the others: Marie Bonaparte, Bill Bullitt, Ernest Jones. Of course, they went through fire to get the poor old sage out of the clutches of the Nazis. If he'd died in Vienna, God knows what those thugs might have done. Displayed his head on a pike, maybe, as a grim warning against 'Jewish science'?"

Horace stared at his half-empty wine glass.

"Don't be gruesome, dearest."

It had been two months since the morning *Sun* had broken the story of the "lost" case history, and it had echoed quickly around the not inconsiderable worlds of Freudians and James scholars, who'd had no idea that the two men had ever met, let alone that Freud might have analyzed Henry James. Horace, who had been there all that late summer of 1908, had published contemporary excerpts from his diary and a long account of the meeting as he had watched it from the outside. But they had appeared in the back pages of the *Sewanee Review* and other literary journals at the time of Freud's death and had been noted only by Edmund Wilson, who'd written a brief piece for the *New Yorker*. Now the story had been amplified by one of Alistair Cooke's witty dispatches to the Manchester *Guardian*. Horace, sitting in his office at Hopkins and staring out the window at the snow and slush, was thinking for a change about something entirely different—a symposium paper on Henry James's notebooks he was to give in

Chapel Hill three months later and had not yet written. The phone rang.

"London here," the operator's voice said over the static. "Professor Briscoe?"

"Speaking."

"Go ahead, London."

"Professor Briscoe?" It was the voice of Anna Freud, a soprano ringer for her father's. "I am embarrassed that I have not yet managed to cut this Gordian knot . . . this damnable matter of the James case history. I suppose the cat is well out of the bag now. I read Alistair Cooke's front page story in *The Guardian*."

"I don't understand," Horace said.

"I still need authentication. I shall send it along, but you must promise here and now that certain of my father's asides about psychoanalysis—not especially pertinent to the case history—will remain *entre nous,* at least until I release them."

"Is that the complication? How can certain parts remain secret if the document is to be in the public realm?"

"Oh, but when I say *entre nous,* I mean it, literally. You must give me your solemn word. Some of the flock believe that publicity would be disastrous."

"Saints above," Horace said. "What on earth could your father have written? Everything that can be said about Henry James has been said."

"That's not really the point. It would appear that in his confrontation with Mr. James my father came very near repudiating psychoanalysis."

"Surely not, Miss Freud. He left Lamb House, as I recall, in a very jolly mood."

"Repudiating scientific psychology, *tout court,*" Anna Freud elaborated. Horace sensed that it would be easy to say the wrong thing and spook the inner circle into hiding the document, or even destroying it. Anna Freud's next remark confirmed his fears:

". . . There is even a disposition here to burn it. To appease *them* (Horace noted that the faceless and impersonal 'them' had not been named, but he could guess who they were). We have for the time being placed the manuscript in the vault at Barclay's and may yet have to move this and much else to New York because of this horrible war. You will be getting a numbered copy and will be on your honor to return it."

"If that's the price of seeing it, I shall be glad to pay it. But you do see, Miss Freud, that it would be a great scandal if it were known that the Freud executors are bowdlerizing or destroying anything of your father's. Let the Nazis burn books . . ."

"I see your point, Professor Briscoe, and I myself have no such intention—other than honoring my father's explicit directives. But you have no idea how hard it is to restrain the true believers."

"Believe me, I do. They're everywhere. You should attend a board meeting of the Modern Language Association."

"I must ring off now. But remember, you promised."

"Promise," Horace shouted into the crackling receiver, and the line clicked at the other end. That night be slept fitfully, wondering what Freud could have written that had caused this circling of the wagons. Repudiation of what, precisely? His own theory? Wasn't that a prophet's prerogative? There was always the possibility, of course, that this "case history" was a forgery or a bad joke. He would detect its fraudulence soon enough. But that minor worry—Anna Freud herself seemed to have no doubts and it was in Freud's own hand—did not help him sleep.

Another tantalizing wait began, punctuated by a nightmare in which Horace saw the "fragment of a case history of Mr. HJ" floating down somewhere over the mid-Atlantic from a cloudy sky like confetti in a ticker-tape parade and being devoured leaf by leaf by large fish. But finally a registered envelope was delivered to his door in Roland Park, a type-script of about a dozen pages and clipped to it several Photostatted pages from the original holograph. Horace recognized the handwriting. He dropped into a chair and began to read eagerly . . .

FRAGMENT OF AN ANALYSIS OF A LITERARY ARTIST

Prefatory Remarks:

Those who have read my monographs on the great artists of the past—for instance, Leonardo and Michelangelo—will be aware of my abiding interest in the psyches of leading creative spirits. When during the self-analysis that preceded my *Traumdeutung* I began to understand the universality of the infant's attachment to the mother as a love-object, and the consequent jealousy on the part of the male child against the father, I named it without hesitation after the hero of Greek legend whose interpreter was the incomparable Sophocles. That was a representative tribute to my exalted view of the intuitive insight of the artist.

For some years, I had been interested in the speculative psychological and philosophical writings of a certain philosopher whom I shall call The Doctor. It may therefore be imagined with what enthusiasm I received a letter from him in the spring of the year 1908. He was to be among those invited to assemble the following year at Clark University for my American visit and lectures, when we first made personal acquaintance in walks about the college precincts. I shall always recall the gallantry with which, suffering as he did from a dangerous heart ailment that was to kill him within two years, he faced the prospect of death. As we were walking one day he became so painfully short of breath that he stopped to lean for support against a sapling. This courageous

Doctor had learned, the year before, of an impending journey of mine to England. It happened that his younger brother had long been resident in an ancient town on the Sussex coast. My correspondent had taken a keen brotherly interest in the literary labors of his brother, whom I shall call The Writer (not untouched on his part by sibling rivalry), and had become quite worried about him on two accounts. The Doctor reported that his younger brother the Writer was revising much of his earlier fiction to conform to a so-called "late manner" (which the Doctor disliked). He feared that this recasting of earlier work heralded the onset of a paralyzing obsessive neurosis. (I use my terminology, not his.) Also, having inherited with others in the family a susceptibility to digestive problems, the writer had also of late become the acolyte of a certain Dr. Fletcher, who posited that the mastication of food to a very fine pulp was the sovereign remedy for costiveness, or "repletion" as the Writer called it. This devotion not only revealed a credulous ignorance of the physiology of the stomach and intestines, known to any competent physician who ever attended a gross-anatomy lab, but also, like the textual revisions, might betray a certain neurotic obsession, with anal features.

Having grown quite alarmed about these problems, the Doctor begged to arrange a visit with his brother during my visit to England in the late summer. He expressed the hope that I might not only make the writer's acquaintance but observe and report on the severity of these disorders—if, indeed, they were disorders rather than harmless eccentricities or issues of craftsmanship. I welcomed the Doctor's overture less for medical reasons than because it promised to place me in the company of a literary giant, some of whose work I had already read with pleasure, with whatever opportunity that exposure might offer to observe genius at close range. If the present case history should chance to fall into unauthorized hands, I realize that questions may be asked about the violation of medical privacy since it might appear from the foregoing that I consented to visit the Writer on a false pretext, intending to act as a spy for his brother. It is embarrassing to admit that indeed I was willing to lend myself to a mild deception. It is no disgrace to admit this, perhaps, now that both gentlemen are long dead and many years have passed—so many that the notes I kept on our conversations, spread before me as I write in the year 1931, are yellowed with age and in some passages difficult to decipher, although at the time I was trying to write in fairly finished form.

At all events, it came about that I arrived by train from London in late August at the Writer's house in the village of R—, and was escorted to his pleasant hilltop seat by his valet and by an engaging young American scholar who was resident with him by special arrangement (a favor to his nephew, the son of the aforesaid Doctor). The young man was studying Mr. J's writings on art and artists. I will record confidentially here that I could not resist the initial suspicion of an abnormal sexual attraction between Mr. J and the comely, bright young American. For reasons to be explained, I was shortly compelled to abandon that suspicion.

I was cordially received at LH by my host, a stately, carefully dressed, portly, balding and clean-shaven man whose countenance and manners (as his young female secretary, Miss TB, remarked to me) could be that of a veteran English sea captain. Or, as I thought, that of a so-called captain of industry of the American sort, or even a banker, were it not for the penetrating stare of his intelligent, deep-seeing eyes: the eyes of a creator, of what I would call a visionary of consciousness. One assumed, *a priori,* the usual quantum of repression in so rich an unconscious. Yet his preternatural alertness, together with my sense of his peripheral notice, warned me against undue presumption.

My visit had been scheduled as the usual "Thursday-to-Sunday" weekend, so popular in the British isles, at least among those classes who own or visit country houses. All roads lead to and from "town," as the English of those ranks call London; and it sometimes seemed that those roads were designed to connect the capital with country houses, and little thatched villages with ancient manors! As the first two days of my visit passed we discovered, my host and I, rather unexpected interest in one another's company and views, and we both felt that the scheduled three-day visit might be too short for satisfaction. An extension of indefinite length was agreed to. The Writer had many friends, including the eminent American writer Mrs. W, whom he frequently mentioned and regularly corresponded with. But it was clear all the same that he was a lonely man, starved for intimacy (a deficit to which I shall return) with a deeply realistic, bleak view of the world we live in and its habits. The great catastrophe of 1914-1918 had not then broken upon Europe, with the calamitous meddling of the American professor-president Wilson whose warped and moralistic personality so interested Mr. Bullitt and myself. But portents were already clear to one so visionary as my host. He was even then fond of saying that life turns what he called a "Gorgon stare, a cold Medusa's face" to us poor struggling humans—"on many days, though not all" he usually added. I took that as a symptom of depression, but also saw that it tallied with my own sense of civilization and its discontents. Almost at the outset of our visit, the Writer evidenced an interest in the science of psychoanalysis, as if he planned to make use of it in some story. When I casually mentioned the possibility of a short-term analysis he readily agreed. And so my planned visit was prolonged for that purpose as well as others more social; and it provided the raw material for the fragment of a case history that follows.

The Clinical Picture

The setting of our analytic sessions was far from ideal. It was a large and lofty, detached chamber known as the Garden Room, designed by an early owner of the house as a banqueting hall. At one end, a pleasant bay window afforded a view down the narrow cobbled street of the ancient town. The room was ordinarily the Writer's workplace during the summer months, where he dictated his work to a young woman, his secretary. I could not avoid the feeling that the locale gave him a certain advantage in the struggle, the *agon*, that invariably appears in the analytic situation: that is, when the analyst suggests unacceptable theories about the patient's repressed conflicts. The Writer proved to be a stubborn and resourceful foe in this struggle. In more than a week of daily hour sittings, all interesting and some revelatory, I seldom felt that even my most aggressive probing broke through the crusts of resistance. For example, I urged Mr. J to record and report his dreams. But he insisted that he had no dreams to speak of (with the exception noted below). He offered the counter theory that his dream-work consists of writing stories. Of course, there was some plausibility in that. I have suggested that daydreaming, familiar to even the most uncreative, affords an entrée into the unconscious. I did insist that *of course* he dreamt, but merely failed to recall his dreams. I noted, as I do in my *Traumdeutung,* that even important dreams often make use of trivial residues. Finally I suggested that dream amnesia may in itself be significant—an idea to which he was also resistant. In short, he was defended at every point of the psychic compass.

Patently, the situation of an unmarried man then in his mid-sixties, whose most intense friendships seemed to be with young men, would suggest repressed, even conscious, homoerotic yearnings. But hint at these as I might, it was difficult to coax from my analysand any revelation of his associations or phantasies. I thought we might get somewhere when I asked him one day about his associations with the sculptures of his young friend, the Roman artist Henrik Andersen, of whom he speaks in lavishly romantic terms. I asked him, in particular, about Andersen's terra cotta bust of the young Count Bevilacqua, which is conspicuously displayed in his bedchamber. "He is the first object my eyes greet in the morning and the last at night," he said. But when I asked him what associations the bust aroused he demurred. "A matter of esthetics merely," he said, though that cannot really be true. At a lively dinner party we attended during my time in R—, there arose an animated discussion of Oscar Wilde and the Wilde scandal. It seemed a natural opening and I listened closely to what the Writer contributed to the discussion. But this too proved to be evasive. All he would say was "poor Oscar, poor Oscar," and when challenged to explain he gave a manifestly strange answer: It was not Wilde's erotic entanglement with the treacherous son of the brutal Marquis of Queensberry he had in mind, he said, but Wilde's Irish "raffishness" and his public posturing.

As might be inferred from that disingenuous exchange, his associations were so heavily guarded as to raise a suspicion of projection, as if he feared in himself some impulse to which Wilde had yielded. But perhaps it was remarkable that he would disclose the revealing chain of associations, Andersen-Bevilacqua-Wilde. We did get one day into the substance of Shakespeare's sonnets and Mr. J was prepared to grant that the great creative sensibility was bisexual and that there was nothing remarkable about that. *"Nothing, nothing, nothing, herr doctor!"* he exclaimed with telltale affect.

Of more definite interest, in the clinical setting, was his fantasy regarding his friend a Miss CFW, an American lady writer of prominence, the niece or grandniece of the novelist Fenimore Cooper. This woman took her life in Venice some fifteen years before I visited Mr. J. With some reluctance, Mr. J related a story of balked intimacy (as one might call it) that began with professional association in the craft of writing and led on to what he described as a "warm friendship." He began to suspect deeper complications when they shared a house in Florence for several months, where each occupied a separate bedchamber. He mentioned that Miss W was troubled by chronic deafness (often, in psychoanalytic terms, a sign of suppressed impatience with tutelary advice which one "doesn't wish to hear"—although to be sure it may be organic.) She used an ear trumpet and he professed surprise when I told him that the ear trumpet might well be a displaced genital device, involving as it does the insertion of a "shaft" into the aural orifice. But Mr. J in his recital of these details suggested to me deep innocence of such symbolic or symptomatic complexities. He felt, he said, that "there was a page to be turned, a corner to be rounded," in their relationship, which was

never successfully negotiated. He had been very solicitous of her health. In his guarded account, it was not
before she made a distinct attempt to seduce him that he
was brought to confront her view of the friendship; and
at that point he in effect took flight. It was not very long
afterward that Miss CFW, in an act that came to him as
a brutal shock, leapt or fell (he insisted on that alternative possibility) from the window of her palazzo in
Venice and died within hours. She had been very ill, and
my analysand wished to believe it possible that she fell
by accident. In telling me all this he showed unusual
emotion. I naturally asked whether he might at some
point have thought of marrying Miss CFW, and he
responded that at the height of their friendship he was
no longer of marriageable age, and had been for many
years "wed to his craft." This was patent evasion; he was
no older then than my own father was when, as a widower, he married my mother. I explained that I was not
referring to marriage institutionally or socially so much
as to the basic marital relationship. He declined to
respond specifically to this query but, in effect, did a
volte-face and began to intimate that certain things he
had previously said about the relationship with Miss W
(for instance, the bizarre attempt to "bury" her dresses
in the Venetian lagoon after her death) were fictive. Or
rather—his tune began here to modulate—that the
memory of the friendship had now become so surcharged and blended with his storytelling compulsion as
to be unreliable. (This was as close as he came to a confession that he was spinning a fable; and it left me in a
state of uncertainty.) I did not say to him that in the psychoanalytic process fabrication and fantasy are often as
significant as "truth," so called, provided that the
patient is willing to identify fabrication and probe his

motives for committing it. I merely said that fabrications of autobiographical myth, as I have good reason to believe, are quite usual. I concluded that the Writer's sexual "reality" had been so chastened by denial and sublimation as to be inaccessible to the analyst and possibly to him as well. That suspicion was confirmed one day when he began to speak of an injury—an "obscure hurt" as he termed it, with typical abstraction—he had sustained in early youth, while serving as part of a fire brigade. It sounded to me like an ordinary internal rupture, but he refused to specify and turned aside my suggestion that colleagues of mine in Vienna would be well suited to conduct a clinical examination when he passed that way, and there we were forced to leave it. But it was clear to me that this "hurt" is somehow related to his thwarted sexuality—if it is thwarted.

The Writer's First Dream

Toward the close of one of our later sessions, Mr. J mentioned that he had had a vivid dream the night before and, as instructed, had made notes so as not to let it slip his memory. This was the manifest content: *He was at Lourdes, where the celebrated miracles of healing occur, standing with other pilgrims near the vast pile of crutches, walking canes and sticks cast aside by those who had undergone miraculous cures. He was surprised to find himself there, inasmuch as his spiritual views, while not doctrinaire, were naturalistic. He felt a keen pain in his right hand. When he brought it up to eye level, which required some effort, he was aghast to find that two fingers had been severed from the hand at the second knuckle. He then realized that he had come to Lourdes in search of a "cure," a restoration of the missing digits. He heard a skeptical and mocking voice, which he identified with*

Anatole France, saying "What, no artificial legs?" France supposedly had said this about the Lourdes miracles. But the Writer felt it to be misleading, for among the discarded canes and crutches he could distinctly see a peg leg which he instantly identified as that of his own father! He felt that if he could grasp it, it would have a talismanic power and by some miracle it would ease the pain in his hand and restore the missing fingers. But before he could lay hand on it, a bearded man, years younger than he, snatched the prosthesis from his outstretched hand and, fastening it to his own stump, raced away as fast as one so handicapped could move and vanished into the crowd . . .

<u>Analysis:</u> As is now well known, psychoanalysis divides dreams into two levels, the manifest and the latent. It is the latter, often difficult to tease out, that is the more important. I long ago concluded, as I say in my book on dream interpretation, that there are no trivial dreams; that even the most inconsequential-seeming dreams may call up buried or, as I call them, screen memories of significance in the psyche of the dreamer. To a master artist such as my analysand, the distinction did not have to be labored. But he professed himself mystified by the manifest content—until I reminded him that the feeling of pain, and also the missing fingers, stood for a sense of danger to his craftsmanship. It might have to do with the hostility of certain critics, or the unsatisfying sale of his monumental revision, then in progress, of his body of work. I reminded him also that he had told me the day before that his father had lost a leg and had such a prosthesis. It was likely that the "bearded stranger" who snatched the peg leg from his hand may have been (like other unidentifiable figures in dreams) a double or alternative aspect of himself, at an earlier age and not yet

impaired as he felt himself to be. Because I did not wish to alert his defenses, I refrained from pressing upon him what seemed to me so very obvious in the latent meaning of the dream. That is, that the missing leg was most probably a veiled image of his *membrus virile:* in short, the dream was a significant little drama of impotence, with some intimation that his younger self might well have made better use of the missing "leg"!

Beyond that, the "religious" or spiritual element in the dream—the miraculous cure promised to paralytics by ancient superstition—arose from a comic episode. At about that stage of my visit, the local newspaper printed an item of gossip in which my presence at LH was ascribed to the Writer's need for a "cure" of an unspecified mental disorder. This absurdity, springing from the popular delusion that psychoanalytic science is *primarily* a form of therapy rather than a means of bringing the unconscious to light, enraged him. Nothing would do but that we must both of us march down to the office of the editor and lodge a formal protest. The *démarche* did produce a retraction, but in the course of it we learned that the source of the gossip about my visit in R— was a somewhat disreputable Anglican clergyman, whose niece, as it happened, was a friend of the Writer's other lodger. The episode would be of only marginal pertinence to this history but for a bizarre development, later to be related . . .

The Second Dream

As we were working on my analysand's intriguing dream of Lourdes, I observed that, notwithstanding his demurrer, he was a formidable dreamer. "If you aren't remembering your dreams, perhaps, before our sessions end, some earlier dream will come to mind," I said. "Dreams do tend to vanish in a twinkling, but sometimes they are too vivid to be forgotten altogether."

"Really, no effort is required," he said, to my surprise. "The great dream of my life—or is it more properly a nightmare?—was much too vivid to be forgotten, as you say. And it has occurred in variant forms more than once."

He related the following:

He was in Paris as a small boy during the Second Empire, visiting the Louvre. In the great Galerie d'Apollon one day he experienced a vision not only of beauty and art and supreme design but of history, fame and power, "the world raised to the noblest and richest expression," as he put it. Then, years later, he suddenly awoke one morning from a dream, or nightmare, in which he was pursuing some dim figure down a huge, high salon (which he recognized as that same Galerie D'Apollon, with its cove ceiling and polished parquet floor), a figure from which he had previously been trying to defend himself by pushing against a closed door. On an impulse, he realized that the figure found him more appalling than he it. He rounded upon it, pushed the door outward, and turned the tables, chasing and routing this "visitant," who disappeared into the distance while a great storm of thunder and lightning raged and glimmered through the windows. "An immense hallucination," Mr. HJ called it as I listened, spellbound, to his narrative.

Analysis: It was clear that the dream/hallucination was of a classic type, independent of its personal setting and significance for the Writer. I observed that the "hideous presence" whom he had put to flight was no other than a double, or *doppelganger*, of the sort often encountered in Gothic literature. Usually, a double is simply a projection of the ego, an alternative self, which appears in the dream-work as well as in certain hypnagogic states. In its primitive meaning, it represents a sort of talisman against death, against the extinction of the familiar self; and that is why, for instance, the ancient Egyptians crafted for the mummified Pharaohs those priceless death-masks of gold and precious stones—of a material which, unlike mortal flesh, would be proof against the wear of time, even millennia. In his case, a primitive narcissistic purpose could hardly be doubted. I speculated that had he been overtaken or "caught" by this dim figure, this alter-ego, the danger would have been the extinction of his creative powers. The fact that in the dream he put this threatening presence to flight indicated a triumphant conquest of lurking doubts about his creative powers.

"Remarkable!" he cried. "That is quite the feeling I had about it." For one of the few times in all our sessions, he registered emphatic assent to one of my interpretations, which he usually greeted with teasing, raillery and mockery.

". . . So much was it my feeling that I am working my way toward a story, a sort of parable, based on that experience. And bringing in the missing digits of the Lourdes dream, by the way." He was as good as his word. The next year he sent me a copy of his wonderful story "The Jolly Corner," in which an alias of the writer (called Spencer Brydon in the tale) pursues just such a *doppelganger* through the deserted rooms of his old childhood house in New York City, confronting him and realizing with horror that the double represents what he might have become had he rejected Europe and the life of art and stayed at home to become a New York millionaire of what is called "the gilded age." And to be sure, the haunting figure in the tale is missing the same fingers! (I acknowledge here the likelihood that my mentioning this famous story may well give away the identity of the famous analysand, but what matter now? By the time these words are read, we shall both be dead and gone.)

Conclusions: Looking back after almost a quarter century on my encounter with the Writer, the supreme impression is a sense of the *strangeness,* the otherness, of the great creative mind. He and I were fated to differ on the very possibility of a science of the unconscious and the neuroses. He rejected it out of hand, not because he was hostile to science or the scientific method as such but because he regarded it as unfit to compass the subtle multiplicity of human impulses. According to my yellowing process notes from that visit in 1908, our fundamental difference usually came to a head in sharp if amiable exchanges regarding great works of literature. For instance, there was the exchange we had one day about the Writer's own late novel (*TWotD*) about a wealthy American girl who is gradually dying at Venice and who becomes aware that she is preyed upon by solicitous friends, including a young journalist from London who professes to be her lover. Wishing to provoke, I called attention to a scene in which one of the central characters learns from her sister that "papa has done something wicked." In the Writer's most cryptic manner, this "wickedness" is unspecified. I told him that such teasing inexplicitness will soon be outmoded, even in works of literature; or at least will strike the reader or playgoer as absurd. (Of course, I don't really believe that, and did not at the time, but maintained it *arguendo* to get his attention.)

"It was excusable," I said, "when Sophocles and

Shakespeare engaged in such mystifications. For instance, the plague in Thebes. What was it really? All they knew were the terrible symptoms and they thought they knew what 'caused' it. They ascribed it to Fate, and to the divinities who manipulate human fortunes. Embedded in the Oedipus myth, as we know now, is a primitive fertility rite. They had absolutely no clinical information about disease, evil or madness."

"What are you suggesting?" the Writer demanded.

"We live," I responded, "in an age of science, of exact knowledge. Disease and disorder, whether of body or mind, need no longer be a matter of conjecture and mystery. Nor morality either. I shall see to that!"

"See to what, Dr. Freud?"

"To morality, to rational behavior! That where impulse is, be it wicked or charitable, it shall be understood by both saints and sinners, so called. Ego and conscious choice will control libido!"

The Writer made a dismissive puffing sound. "You speak," he said, "as if literature will soon be dispensable. I suppose that if you had been writing my novel you would have added a footnote explaining that Mr. Croy's 'wickedness' was a sort of error, the result of a misfiring of the brain, rather than something rooted in nature. You would leave nothing to the imagination, no work for storytelling to do. But my dear doctor, imagination is all. A novel is not a medical treatise." Once, speaking in an essay of Shakespeare's *Richard III*, I made a related point: that the wicked king's speeches invite us to flesh out his interior thoughts; and that if the dramatist had done this work for us the dramatic illusion would be compromised. On a similar occasion, we engaged in a friendly struggle over *Hamlet,* which the Writer resolutely viewed as theological drama.

"It hardly matters," he argued, "whether or not the audience happens to share Hamlet's theology. It clearly is there. What else, pray, is Hamlet's dilemma rooted in when he speculates on the danger that his father's ghost may be a 'goblin damned,' sent to tempt him to mortal sin? Or later in the play when he canvasses the prospect of killing the now patently guilty Claudius at his prayers and rejects the opportunity because he would send his uncle straight to heaven? What could be clearer?"

I found the argument formidable. Yet Hamlet's religious compunctions patently, in my view, are neurotic echoes of the unresolved Oedipal conflict, so evident in his attitude toward his mother. I told the Writer I could not agree; and we left the argument there.

I suspect that had I direct analytical access to Sophocles or Shakespeare—or my near contemporary, Fyodor Dostoyevsky, whose *Brothers Karamazov* seems to me the summit of the modern novel—the debate would go much as it did with the Writer. All such creators are serenely confident that their intuitive powers are superior to any conceivable analytical system, including scientific psychology; that it precedes and subsumes such systems. And I must admit that strong evidence for this view is the Writer's prodigious anticipation of our discovery of childhood sexuality in his "horrific little Christmas fable" "TTotS", which he and I discussed at length. In fact, I was bursting to tell him this and did so very soon after arriving at his house!

Apocalypse (*later and most secret!*): Why then is it—and here I embark on arcana that absolutely must, to the end of the psychoanalytic era, be veiled from simpler minds and shared only with those adventurous enough to grasp what I am saying—that I do not renounce the competition? Give in, finally, to the superiority of the sacred monster of creativity? In the first place, that order of intuitive discernment is exceedingly rare. As indeed I explained to the Writer, the justification for a scientific quest into the unconscious is that the great multitude are not so lavishly endowed, even when otherwise intelligent, and require instruction such as I feel qualified to give—to say nothing of the relief from their anguish and obsessive behavior that the psychoanalytic therapy occasionally grants. My *Traumdeutung* should long serve as a handbook of dream interpretation for the uninspired and unimaginative workaday analyst, as certain of my secondary writings also will do.

I have been often accused of messianic ambition, of aspiring to found a secular church with all the marks of an orthodoxy—messiah, pope, apostles, dogma, anathemata, heresies, etc. etc., the whole panoply. To this I cannot plead guilty. The psychoanalytic movement is most certainly *not* a religion or faith, nor can it be adulterated with spiritualistic alloy (the problem with Jung) but it must have coherence; and the petrine fundamental, so to say, is the sexual root of the neuroses. Any deviation from this principle, call it "dogma" or not as you like, is not psychoanalysis properly speaking and cannot be so described. That, as I note above, was the basis of my quarrel with Carl Jung. He began to drag deviant religious, mystical and mythic elements into the interpretation of dreams. From that point we were doomed to go our separate ways, for he clearly was projecting his own "numinosity" on me.

The risk, as our movement spreads and prospers, as it is now doing, is that rigidities and sterilities will creep into it as they do into any orthodoxy. On the one hand will be the grand heretics, like Jung and Adler, who permit their imaginations to run amok; on the other hand, there are the multitude of the intellectually second and third rate whose inflexibility tends to have an ossifying effect on doctrine. The day may indeed be foreseen, if it is not upon us, when the true believers in psychoanalysis will become as unshakably rigid in their dogmatic slumbers as the monks of medieval Christendom; and anathema will be hurled at any deviant, however inventive or original. And I shall not be available forever for a consiliar role.

I am reminded here of Dostoyevsky's powerful fable of the Grand Inquisitor in *The Brothers Karamazov,* who lacerates his silent and forbearing prisoner, the Christ figure, for daring to assume that the generality of mankind are capable of imitating the lilies of the field and pursuing true freedom of the spirit. The Grand Inquisitor's loving cynicism is represented, by the skeptical Ivan Karamazov, as the inevitable posture of all guardians of a world-historical faith. Yes! It is true enough: bread before freedom! Thus I must often assume the burden of the Grand Inquisitor myself, recognizing that our science falters at the boundary of the deeper human mysteries, but withholding this dangerous admission from the unwashed rank and file. It could well send them flocking after Jung! Their food and drink, their manna and addiction is and must be . . . science! It is the sacred ark of the covenant. This would seem the unavoidable price of safeguarding the arcana of psychoanalysis. After all, my primary objective has been the enhancement of consciousness, which is to say, freedom and rationality. In this I am, I fancy, a considerable cut above the Grand Inquisitor and his cynicism! To such perilous reflections does my fond recollection of the Writer and his genius drive me after all these years.

When I left him I was not to see him again, and within less than a decade he was dead. As I feared, however, it was dangerous to keep the charmed company of a supreme storyteller. His intuitive power lit up the landscape of the psyche with a brilliance no clinician, however skilled, can hope to rival. There were indeed moments in his company when I was tempted to lay the sword of psychoanaltic science at his feet and apprentice myself to poetry. But the hour is late and I am old and weary. I must reflect more on his influence when I am rested . . .

* * *

There, the tantalizing "fragment of a case history" broke off—"as if," Horace Briscoe penciled at the bottom of the last page, "Freud gaped into this void of psychoanalytic agnosticism and found it too deep and dreadful to revisit."

When he finished reading the typescript Anna Freud had sent, Horace sat for some time in the fading light of his upstairs study, thinking back to that adventurous summer of 1908 in Rye. His thoughts gravitated toward what was for him much the most important memory of his introduction to Rye, Lamb House, Freud and the science of psychoanalysis—winning Agnes Fengallon's hand, his wife now of more than thirty years and one of the sanest people he knew. He remembered how he first saw her in the churchyard at Saint Mary's and her enchanting voice when she marched up to him and said she could see he was American and asked why he was staring at her. He glanced at her picture as she was then; it still stood in the place of honor on his desk. He felt a familiar surge of affection. Then, as if by coincidence, he heard the front door close and her light familiar footsteps on the staircase. In her capacity as a docent at the Baltimore Museum of Art, she had been helping to arrange a big show of its extensive Matisse holdings—part of the munificent gift of the Cone sisters, friends of Gertrude Stein. He called down to her from his study, "Good day, dear?"

"It was a good day, Horace. Anything new?" she called, aware that he had been wrestling with the Freud document—and his literary conscience. He beamed down at her over the bannister; she returned his smile, but she could see at a glance that he was still worried.

"It's pretty routine on Uncle Henry, but apparently by 1931 when Freud drafted this damned thing he was thinking heretical thoughts. No wonder the London keepers of the flame are disturbed."

Agnes continued to climb the stairs. "Horace, why don't we go into the little sitting room if you want to talk?" They opened a door opposite the first landing and sat down.

"Weren't Freud's heresies, as you call them, already a matter of public record by the Thirties?"

"They were, but they were far less explicit than they are here." He handed her the sheaf of photocopied paper. "You'll see. The bombshell is a sort of appendix where he casts himself in the role of Dostoyevsky's Grand Inquisitor and prophesies that after he's dead psychoanalysis could drift into some sort of mysticism or literalism. Like his feud with Jung, you know."

"So that's why Anna Freud is hesitant. I can sympathize," Agnes said. "After all, I owe the old prophet a lot."

"How could I forget that, Agnes? Don't you remember that I went along with you to the office of that analyst in London he recommended—his former student, Dr. Eliot—when you saw him the first time? I had to sit for an hour in the waiting room with all sorts of odd people. Quite a zoo."

"Don't joke about it, Horace. It was a turning point for me. Of course I had to convince Uncle that I was making those weekly trips to London for ballet. I would leave on the early train with my slippers and leotard. He never suspected."

"Yes, it all comes back . . ."

"I was a hardheaded girl and I resisted Eliot's efforts," Agnes continued. "But he finally helped me reach back to those bad times in Nairobi I'd tried to forget—Papa and Mama screaming at each other. It was hard. Even more horrible for me, when I realized that I hated Mama, absolutely despised her. I thought she had forced Papa to send me away to England. I was humiliated by those feelings; it was a bitter pill. But Eliot said, 'Don't apologize, Miss Fengallon. Feelings are feelings. You're just facing them for the first time, really.' He helped me see that I had transferred my thwarted love for Papa to Uncle. That I couldn't get enough affection from Uncle, or any other man—Father Morris, the rector at St. Mary's, or you, Horace, when you showed up in the church yard that day. Gradually, he worked me toward the big question . . . But I'm not telling you anything you don't already recall. We discussed before we married."

"Yes, of course. Eliot's big question, as you call it, was whether your Uncle Fengallon had ever been 'overfamiliar.'"

"That was a bad day. I boiled over like an overheated kettle. Eliot just sat there like a Buddha while I called him every nasty name I could think of, said things like, 'How dare you insinuate such a thing? My uncle is an archdeacon! A Christian gentleman!' I raged and raged and finally got so wrought up that I began crying—hysterically. It's a wonder I went back."

"But you did go back, Agnes. When you cooled down you could see that your uncle had been 'overfamiliar' . . . in a way."

"But not sexually, never that way, Horace. But who can draw a clear line in those matters? Eliot explained Freud's discoveries about female fantasies. He made it sound so . . . well, so ordinary. I remember asking him, 'Do you mean, Dr. Eliot, that my case is pretty routine?' And he said that as in most manageable cases it was—quite ordinary. Then the dear man asked me if I was disappointed. And I had to laugh.

'Disappointed?' I said. That was when I blurted it out—'How could I be disappointed? I'm cured.' I think Eliot was startled. But I really was. My worry and confusion lifted suddenly, like a spring cloud."

"Not that Freud himself would have used the word 'cured,' my dear," Horace commented. "He considered psychoanalysis an ongoing process."

"No, 'cured' was my word. I was probably naïve. But that was the day I made up my mind to become Mrs. Horace Briscoe, not a whore."

"What?"

"I'm only teasing, Horace. Don't look so startled. But I couldn't wait to get back home to Rye and tell you."

"Thank God for Freud and Eliot; it was a great day for me too."

Agnes glanced at her watch. "Oh my goodness, from the sublime to the ridiculous! Duty calls. I need to see about our dinner."

Horace's exchange of letters with Anna Freud followed, along with Anna Freud's struggle with the keepers of her father's flame who pressed her to destroy the "lost" case history; they urged her to protect true believers against the master's "senile heresy," as one of them called it. After his worried letters to Anna Freud, Horace told Agnes that he would "sleep on it" before deciding to try to stop the "vandals," as he had come to call the psychoanalytical "committee." He had been careful to thank Anna Freud for enclosing, in one of her notes, a copy of a letter of uncertain date, probably late 1908, from her father to William James. She had written: *This will interest you, Dr. Briscoe, especially the last paragraph. The letter is in my father's hand but we have been unable to trace the missing pages or indeed to be sure that the letter was ever mailed."*

". . . look forward to seeing you next year in Worcester, when I shall tell you more, but I am certainly obliged to you, Dr. James, for arranging the visit to Rye. As you may have heard, it grew from a country weekend to more than two weeks. I had ten formal analytic sessions with your brother in which we explored issues both general and personal. On the personal side, I concluded that your brother, while eccentric (as who isn't?) and wary of medicine, is a balanced man with no marked obsessional neuroses such as you had feared. So far as I could discover, he is writing his extensive New York Edition revisions for the most prosaic of reasons: He wishes to leave behind a literary monument, and he hopes to make some money. I found him unwavering, however, on the subject of 'Fletcherizing' his food. And in our general discussions of the great issues of art vs. science, we came to a respectful impasse.

"By the way, one of the pleasures of my visit was to make the acquaintance of your son's young friend, Horace Briscoe. He is a remarkably friendly, informative and perceptive companion and I am hoping to visit him in Baltimore next summer. He has promised to show me around Washington . . ."

Horace struggled to recall when he had invited Freud to Baltimore, but admitted to himself that looking back he was relieved that Freud's crowded schedule during his visit to Clark University the following summer, along with routine tourism and his journey into the wilderness of upstate New York to visit an important American disciple, left no time for a visit to Baltimore.

Horace continued to wrestle with his conscience over the case history. He wondered how many documents of vital importance had perished, over the centuries, from malice, shame or neglect when they might have illuminated the course of human history or some shady corner of it; and he did, following his discussion with Agnes, sleep on the dilemma for three nights. It was after the third night that he summoned

Winton Towson to a luncheon rendezvous at one of his favorite restaurants. The upshot was explosive.

From the Baltimore *Sun*, April 16, 1942:

SUN REPORTER WINS AWARD

Winton Towson, 30, former literary editor of *The Sun*, has won the 1941 Pulitzer Prize for reporting, it was announced today at Columbia University. Towson, now a U. S. Army captain stationed at the War Department in Washington, will receive his award in absentia.

The award, established under the will of the late Joseph Pulitzer and administered by the Columbia trustees, went to Towson for a series of *Sunpaper* articles in which he disclosed a plan to destroy a valuable "lost case history" of the writer Henry James, written by Sigmund Freud, the founder of psychoanalysis. Freud died in September 1939.

In a three-part series whose repercussions were felt all over the world, even in wartime, Towson revealed that Freudian circles in London, where Freud was driven into exile in 1938 following the Nazi annexation of Austria, were so upset by Freud's skeptical remarks in the case history that they had planned to suppress or destroy it. The revelation of their plan caused an uproar last winter and it is believed that Towson's reporting halted what the New York *Times* called "an appalling act of historical and literary vandalism, worthy of the Gestapo."

In their citation, the Pulitzer judges wrote: "It is very rare that a newspaper reporter plays a role in the preservation of history, but that accolade must go to Mr. Towson, whose *Sunpapers* series on the 'lost case history' of Henry James is both gripping and stylish." Anna

Freud, daughter of the late psychologist, commented by phone from her home in London: "I am glad of the news. Mr. Towson's reporting saved the Freud archive from a serious error of judgment."

The "lost" case history was discovered among Freud's unpublished papers at his death. From internal evidence, it was established by a noted Johns Hopkins authority on James, Prof. Horace Briscoe, that the "case history" was based on notes Freud made in 1908 when he spent some two weeks at Lamb House, Rye, Sussex, and actually written some time in 1931, then set aside in an uncompleted state. A copy was sent from London, as Towson had previously reported, for authentication by Briscoe, an internationally recognized authority on Henry James. James died in 1916.

Towson's articles reported that Freud had worried aloud, at the conclusion of the James "case history," that his successors might turn the science of psychoanalysis, of which he was the founder, into a "rigid" and "dogmatic" system. After musing on the competing roles of psychology and literature in the understanding of the human mind, Freud compared himself to the "Grand Inquisitor" of a famous Russian novel by Dostoyevsky, who doubts the capacity of the ordinary faithful to place matters of the spirit before material needs. "He seems to be implying," Towson wrote, "that the human mind is too complicated to be fully understood by any scientific system. He doubted that the psychoanalytic faithful could be trusted with such thoughts. It was that apparently heretical concession, based on his discussions with Henry James, that disturbed the caretakers of psychoanalytic orthodoxy."

Professor Briscoe, reached yesterday, said that he was delighted that Towson, a former student of his at

Hopkins, had been recognized for his "wonderful series. He is as resourceful a journalist as he was a student," Briscoe said. "Where he got all that information is more than I can guess." The professor declined to speculate on Towson's source or sources. In a controversial footnote to his articles Towson explained that he was not at liberty to say how he came by a copy of the endangered case study.

Dr. Briscoe, 57, who has written extensively about the American expatriate novelist, recently published his fifth book on James, a study entitled *Figures Reconfigured: Henry James's Late Themes.*

"I was there when it happened," Briscoe said of the meeting of Freud and James, which took place during the two-week period in late August, 1908. He described to the *Sun* how, as a graduate student writing a doctoral thesis on James, he had been invited to stay at Lamb House, James's residence in the ancient seaside town, through much of the summer and autumn of that year. He lived in attic servants' quarters and studied James's comic stories of art and artists.

Asked to comment on the case history, Dr. Briscoe said: "I don't think the 'short-term analysis,' as Freud called it, satisfied either of them. They weren't really on the same wave length. They got to be on cordial terms but they argued a great deal—in a friendly way. It would appear from what Freud wrote in 1931 that he felt Henry James had had the better of their arguments. I gather that's what troubles the orthodox Freudians. I haven't discussed the matter with them, but you see, their main point of difference, always polite, was over the efficacy of a 'science' of the human personality. Henry James doubted that such a science was possible— a doubt I cited in my first book, *Henry James's Comedy of the Arts.* As readers of Freud know, he admired writers and felt that they had been trailblazers for psychology in exploring the mysteries and quirks of the human mind. After Freud left Rye, Mr. James told me—I recorded his exact words in the journal I was keeping: 'I do concede, Horace, that Freud made a point when he said that if a psychological science could be devised and if people of ordinary talents could be trained as analysts, it would be useful to humanity since it would greatly expand the circle of human self-knowledge. But, my boy, those are very big ifs."

Dr. Briscoe went on to say that in 1908, when the meeting occurred, psychoanalysis was new on the European scene and just gaining an intellectual foothold. Freud's writings about infantile sexuality had shocked psychological circles here and abroad.

"When they realized Freud was in Rye, the village gossips jumped to conclusions," the literary scholar laughed. "They thought he was treating Henry James for mental illness. It was laughable, because no saner man than James ever lived. Freud was paying a mainly social visit and jumped at the chance to psychoanalyze a living writer. He was intensely interested in artists and regarded them as his most important precursors. But I think he found Henry James a harder nut to crack than he'd expected. Mr. James told me that he found the experience entertaining—it appealed to his sense of fun."

Professor Briscoe plans to write what he called "a long article or a short book" on the episode. "Mine will be a sort of detective tale—a form Henry James admired and liked to read but never wrote. But it's Winton Towson's story," he said. "I don't want to poach."

Horace read the *Sun*'s story again with satisfaction that

evening when he and Agnes settled down with a drink. He chuckled over his little joke about "a harder nut to crack," which had gone right over the head of the *Sun* reporter.

"You can't guess where Towson got his information?" Agnes laughed. "Who do you think you're fooling?"

"Nobody, probably, since as you know I don't need to 'guess.' But I defy anyone to top what I said for ambiguity. You remember when Bullitt, Jones and Marie Bonaparte were trying to rescue Freud from the clutches of the Nazis. The Gestapo insisted that before leaving Vienna he had to sign a statement certifying that he had been well treated. Freud then asked if he could add a sentence and wrote, 'I can recommend the Gestapo to anyone.' Those idiot thugs thought it was a compliment!"

"You're a clever man, Horace," Agnes said. "Maybe as clever as your hero Mr. James."

"You know, Agnes," he said thoughtfully, as they sipped their sherry, "I sometimes wonder whether my Uncle Henry and your uncle Charles Fengallon ever got their mutual misconceptions straightened out."

"You may be clever, my dear, but for once your memory fails you. Mr. James spent less and less time in Rye and finally moved back to London as his health failed. He and uncle not only patched up their misunderstandings, they became good friends and Uncle Charles assisted at Mr. James's funeral at Chelsea Old Church."

"Why, yes, I ought to have remembered that. But it seems so long ago and memory is a funny thing—who knows what I've never told you and you've never told me? You did tell me that your Uncle Charles had a gracious letter from Uncle Henry when Lambeth Palace reopened his case and cleared him of that trumped-up church scandal—and, to compensate, offered him a bishopric which he refused."

"A lot of high churchmen must have breathed a big sigh of relief. I'm not sure why Uncle Fengallon cared so passionately about those old liturgical issues. It went back to his under-graduate days and his love/hate relationship with Oxford. Maybe he should have tried psychoanalysis. It cured me."

"You know how Freud hated that word *cure*," Horace said. "He was afraid psychoanalysis would become a mere therapy. He reiterates it in that case history of Uncle Henry."

"Maybe I should stop using it, then."

"Why do you say that, Agnes?"

"Oh Horace, men can be so innocent. Don't you know that women never tell anyone all their secrets?" She softened the comment with one of her radiant smiles.

As he had done more than occasionally since Agnes had brightened his life, Horace caught an echo of unsounded depths. *What a funny old life it is,* he thought to himself—two people living in loving intimacy for decades, and yet never exhausting all their unmined mysteries. Somewhere in this woman he would gladly die for, there lingered that bright, pretty little girl from a troubled household in Kenya, suddenly sent away to an English parsonage and from there to a literary life in Baltimore, Maryland. And what did he really know about her? What unrevealed pains had all that turbulence cost her? But after all, what did the unknowns matter, anyway? The life they had made together was enough, and more.

THE END

AUTHOR'S NOTE AND ACKNOWLEDGMENTS

To judge by the book reviews, historical fiction is flourishing. But even its practitioners, among whom I must necessarily be numbered, concede that it can be problematical. Henry James, one of the two principal characters of my story, did so, although in contradictory moods. In his letter to Sarah Orne Jewett, he calls "historic fiction" "humbug." But as his haunting preface to "The Aspern Papers" shows, he was not of settled mind; he admittedly wrote about what he memorably called "the visitable past." It is hard to believe that he would have persisted in his harsh verdict in the face of such masterworks of his time as Tolstoy's *Hadji Murad*—or, in our day, Michael Shaara's *The Killer Angels* or Bill Styron's *Confessions of Nat Turner*, or Shelby Foote's *Shiloh*, to name only those. In fact, such novels of James's middle period as *The Princess Casamassima* and *The Bostonians* are "historical" in the usual sense. James aspired, in those Balzacian works, to pay the French master's *Comédie Humaine* the tribute of imitation. But neither book prospered; and perhaps it was these disappointed hopes that later darkened his view of historical fiction.

When I was teaching, I used to tell my students that there is fact in fiction and fiction in fact—in other words, that the usual sharp distinction can be misleading. What is commonly viewed as an impermeable barrier is often an osmotic membrane. The difficulty of establishing what is historically "true" (as in many notorious forgeries, benign and otherwise) is an intrinsic impediment of the human record.

Historical fiction often begins, as does *Lions at Lamb House*, with a "what if?" It imagines scenes and situations we would enjoy witnessing if they had actually happened, although good historical fiction is certainly no cousin to the bastard form known as "docudrama," which poses as truth while frequently mangling it beyond recognition or good sense. The writer of historical novels is not licensed to defy probability or to twist familiar historical characters into caricatures.

Both Sigmund Freud and Henry James were imposing figures of their age; and while there is no evidence that they met, they were certainly aware of one another, and it was Freud's visit to England in 1908 that planted the seed of my tale. In that same year, James was at work on the New York Edition, a definitive revision of the novels and tales he wished to preserve and for which he wrote "prefaces" that endure among the monuments of literary criticism. He had also adopted the remedy for his digestive ills touted by Dr. Fletcher; and the great psychologist Williams James, who was to meet Freud personally the next year, disliked his novelist brother's "late style" and mocked it in irritating letters, though not to the serious impairment of brotherly affection. My other characters, except for James's constant correspondant, Edith Wharton and his valet Burgess Noakes, his servants, his secretary Theodora Bosanquet and his eventual biographer, Ernest Jones, are imaginary. So far as I know, there is no "fragment of a case history of Mr. HJ" in the Freud archive. If only there were!

I owe special thanks to those who read and commented on this story at various stages: my wife and artistic adviser Jane Warwick Yoder, a psychotherapist and student of the performing arts who knows psychoanalytic literature and clinical practice, both Jungian and Freudian; my friend of many decades, Martha Noel Evans, accomplished scholar of Freud's formative studies of hysteria in Paris, and for a decade general editor of books for the Modern Language Association; my fellow James fan, distinguished author and commentator (as "Miss Manners"), Judith Martin; and my perceptive and adventurous publisher Kent Carroll, who proposed valuable elaborations.

Finally, this book is dedicated, with gratitude and affection, to three colleagues in the life of writing: My agent Theron Raines, astute counselor and himself a writer and editor of distinction. He and his partner Joan Raines took an early liking to the story and guided me to touches that made it saleable. Jonathan Yardley, close friend and associate for half a century in North Carolina and Washington, is, in my view as his constant reader, the most engaging literary journalist since Edmund Wilson.

My late friend Peter Taylor, a consummate storyteller, once did me the honor of suggesting that I try my hand at the kind of writing of which he was a master. I was too busy then in newspaper and magazine journalism to listen, but for better or worse his gentle nudge proved prophetic. Peter and I shared an affection for Henry James, whose works I began reading with delight—fortunately—before I heard them pronounced unreadable. Peter would often say, in his droll fashion, "Ed Yoder defended Henry James in the Greensboro *Daily News*"—as if the Master's works might have lapsed into obscurity but for my advocacy in a regional newspaper of limited circulation and even more limited critical influence. No doubt Peter, with his pristine perception, was amused by the comic discrepancy between the intent and the medium; but I value his tribute to this day.

This dedication repays, inadequately, the generous contribution of all three friends to my life in writing.

Edwin M. Yoder Jr. is a North Carolinian with deep roots in his native state and Georgia. He was educated at the University of North Carolina, where he studied English, and at Oxford, where he studied political history as a Rhodes Scholar and is now an honorary fellow of Jesus College. He was a newspaper editor in North Carolina and Washington, where he won a Pulitzer Prize and wrote a column for the *Washington Post* and its syndicate. His articles and reviews appear widely. He taught at Georgetown and Washington and Lee universities and holds honorary degrees from other colleges and universities, including his alma mater at Chapel Hill. His interests include sailing, running (four marathons), racquet sports and watercolor painting. He lives with his wife Jane, a clinical social worker and Jungian psychotherapist, and their Siamese cat Cranberry in Alexandria, Virginia. He and his wife are the parents of a son and daughter and have three grandsons.

The Days of Abandonment
Elena Ferrante
Fiction - 192 pp - $14.95 - isbn 978-1-933372-00-6

"Stunning . . . The raging, torrential voice of the author is something rare."—*The New York Times*

"I could not put this novel down. Elena Ferrante will blow you away."—ALICE SEBOLD, author of *The Lovely Bones*

This gripping story tells of a woman's descent into devastating emptiness after being abandoned by her husband with two young children to care for.

Troubling Love
Elena Ferrante
Fiction - 144 pp - $14.95 - isbn 978-1-933372-16-7

"In tactile, beautifully restrained prose, Ferrante makes the domestic violence that tore [the protagonist's] household apart evident."—*Publishers Weekly*

"Ferrante has written the 'Great Neapolitan Novel.'"
—*Corriere della Sera*

Delia's takes a voyage of discovery through the chaotic streets and claustrophobic sitting rooms of contemporary Naples in search of the truth about her mother's untimely death.

www.europaeditions.com

Cooking with Fernet Branca
James Hamilton-Paterson
Fiction - 288 pp - $14.95 - isbn 978-1-933372-01-3

"Provokes the sort of indecorous involuntary laughter that has more in common with sneezing than chuckling. Imagine a British John Waters crossed with David Sedaris."—*The New York Times*

Gerald Samper has his own private Tuscan hilltop, where he whiles away his time working as a ghostwriter for celebrities and inventing wholly original culinary concoctions. His idyll is shattered by the arrival of Marta. A series of hilarious misunderstandings brings this odd couple into ever-closer proximity.

Old Filth
Jane Gardam
Fiction - 256 pp - $14.95 - isbn 978-1-933372-13-6

"This remarkable novel [...] will bring immense pleasure to readers who treasure fiction that is intelligent, witty, sophisticated and—a quality encountered all too rarely in contemporary culture—adult."—*The Washington Post*

The engrossing and moving account of the life of Sir Edward Feathers; from birth in colonial Malaya to Wales, where he is sent as a "Raj orphan," to Oxford, his career and marriage parallels much of the twentieth century's dramatic history.

Total Chaos
Jean-Claude Izzo
Fiction/Noir - 256 pp - $14.95 - isbn 978-1-933372-04-4

"Rich, ambitious and passionate . . . his sad, loving portrait of his native city is amazing."—*The Washington Post*

"Full of fascinating characters, tersely brought to life in a prose style that is (thanks to Howard Curtis's shrewd translation) traditionally dark and completely original."—*The Chicago Tribune*

The first installment in the Marseilles Trilogy.

www.europaeditions.com

Chourmo
Jean-Claude Izzo
Fiction/Noir - 256 pp - $14.95 - isbn 978-1-933372-17-4

"Like the best noir writers—and he is among the best—Izzo not only has a keen eye for detail but also digs deep into what makes men weep."—*Time Out New York*

Fabio Montale is dragged back into the mean streets of a violent, crime-infested Marseilles after the disappearance of his long-lost cousin's teenage son.

The Goodbye Kiss
Massimo Carlotto
Fiction/Noir - 192 pp - $14.95 - isbn 978-1-933372-05-1

"A nasty, explosive little tome warmly recommended to fans of
James M. Cain for its casual amorality and truly astonishing
speed."—*Kirkus Reviews*

An unscrupulous womanizer, as devoid of morals now as he once
was full of idealistic fervor, returns to Italy, where he is wanted for a
series of crimes. To avoid prison he sells out his old friends, turns
his back on his former ideals and cuts deals with crooked cops. To
earn himself the guise of respectability he is willing to go even further, maybe even as far as murder.

Death's Dark Abyss
Massimo Carlotto
Fiction/Noir - 192 pp - $14.95 - isbn 978-1-933372-18-1

"A narrative voice that in Lawrence Venuti's translation is cold and heartless—but, in a creepy way, fascinating."—*The New York Times*

A riveting drama of guilt, revenge, and justice, Massimo Carlotto's *Death's Dark Abyss* tells the story of two men and the savage crime that binds them. During a robbery, Raffaello Beggiato takes a young woman and her child hostage and later murders them. Beggiato is arrested, tried, and sentenced to life. The victims' father and husband, Silvano, plunges into a deepening abyss until the day the murderer seeks his pardon and he begins to plot his revenge.

Hangover Square
Patrick Hamilton
Fiction/Noir - 280 pp - $14.95 - isbn 978-1-933372-06-8

"Hamilton is a sort of urban Thomas Hardy: always a pleasure to read, and as social historian he is unparalleled."—NICK HORNBY

Adrift in the grimy pubs of London at the outbreak of World War II, George Harvey Bone is hopelessly infatuated with Netta, a cold, contemptuous small-time actress. George also suffers from occasional blackouts. During these moments one thing is horribly clear: he must murder Netta.

www.europaeditions.com

Boot Tracks
Matthew F. Jones
Fiction/Noir - 208 pp - $14.95 - isbn 978-1-933372-11-2

"More than just a very good crime thriller, this dark but illuminating novel shows us the psychopathology of the criminal mind . . . A nightmare thriller with the power to haunt."
—*Kirkus Reviews* (starred)

A commanding, stylishly written novel that tells the harrowing story of an assassination gone terribly wrong and the man and woman who are taking their last chance to find a safe place in a hostile world.

Love Burns
Edna Mazya
Fiction/Noir - 192 pp - $14.95 - isbn 978-1-933372-08-2

"This book, which has Woody Allen overtones, should be of great interest to readers of black humor and psychological thrillers."
—*Library Journal* (starred)

Ilan, a middle-aged professor of astrophysics, discovers that his young wife is having an affair. Terrified of losing her, he decides to confront her lover instead. Their meeting ends in the latter's murder—the unlikely murder weapon being Ilan's pipe—and in desperation, Ilan disposes of the body in the fresh grave of his kindergarten teacher. But when the body is discovered, the mayhem begins.

Departure Lounge
Chad Taylor
Fiction/Noir - 176 pp - $14.95 - isbn 978-1-933372-09-9

"Smart, original, surprising and just about as cool as a novel can get . . . Taylor can flat out write."—*The Washington Post*

A young woman mysteriously disappears. The lives of those she has left behind—family, acquaintances, and strangers intrigued by her disappearance—intersect to form a captivating latticework of coincidences and surprising twists of fate. Urban noir at its stylish and intelligent best.

Carte Blanche
Carlo Lucarelli
Fiction/Noir - 120 pp - $14.95 - isbn 978-1-933372-15-0

"This is Alan Furst country, to be sure."—*Booklist*

The house of cards built by Mussolini in the last months of World War II is collapsing, and Commissario De Luca faces a world mired in sadistic sex, dirty money, drugs and murder.

Dog Day
Alicia Giménez-Bartlett
Fiction/Noir - 208 pp - $14.95 - isbn 978-1-933372-14-3

"In Nicholas Caistor's smooth translation from the Spanish, Giménez-Bartlett evokes pity, horror and laughter with equal adeptness. No wonder she won the Femenino Lumen prize in 1997 as the best female writer in Spain."—*The Washington Post*

Delicado and her maladroit sidekick, Garzón, investigate the murder of a tramp whose only friend is a mongrel dog named Freaky.

The Big Question
Wolf Erlbruch
Children's Illustrated Fiction - 52 pp - $14.95 - isbn 978-1-933372-03-7

Named Best Book at the 2004 Children's Book Fair in Bologna.

"[*The Big Question*] offers more open-ended answers than the likes of Shel Silverstein's *Giving Tree* (1964) and is certain to leave even younger readers in a reflective mood."—*Kirkus Reviews*

A stunningly beautiful and poetic illustrated book for children that poses the biggest of all big questions: Why am I here?

The Butterfly Workshop
Wolf Erlbruch
Children's Illustrated Fiction - 40 pp - $14.95 - isbn 978-1-933372-12-9

Illustrated by the winner of the 2006 Hans Christian Andersen Award.

For children and adults alike: Odair, one of the Designers of All Things and grandson of the esteemed inventor of the rainbow, has been banished to the insect laboratory as punishment for his over-active imagination. But he still dreams of one day creating a cross between a bird and a flower.